MORE RAVES
FOR WILLIAM F. NOLAN!

"An essential to all book shelves."

—*Mystery Scene*

William F. Nolan's stories are "skillful renderings of the twisted psyche that blur the boundary between psychological and supernatural horror."

—*Publishers Weekly*

"Bright and individual. Mr. Nolan has considerable skills."
—*The New York Times*

"Nolan writes with dazzling dexterity."

—*The Vancouver Express*

"Nolan is a master of horror fantasy."

—Charles L. Grant

Nolan's work is "frighteningly alive and compelling."
—*School Library Journal*

"This collection proves Nolan's talents are equal to Charles Beaumont, Richard Matheson and Ray Bradbury."
—*Hellnotes*

WILLIAM F. NOLAN

DARK UNIVERSE

LEISURE BOOKS NEW YORK CITY

LEISURE BOOKS ®

December 2003

Published by

Dorchester Publishing Co., Inc.
200 Madison Avenue
New York, NY 10016

To my good friends who inspired many of these stories:
Ray Bradbury
Richard Matheson
Charles Beaumont

DARK UNIVERSE

TABLE OF CONTENTS

" 'The Waiting, Windless Dark' ": William F. Nolan's Universe

by Christopher Conlon

> *One of the few things I know about writing is this:*
> *spend it all, shoot it, play it, lose it, all, right away,*
> *every time. Do not hoard what seems good for a*
> *later place in the book, or for another book; give*
> *it, give it all, give it now.*
>
> —Annie Dillard, The Writing Life

1.

Sometimes at night—even now, all these years later—I see their faces. My father: his eyes, orb-like, aqueous, glaring hugely down at me with a threat all the more frightening precisely because it is not merely physical. And my mother, her grin turned slippery with alcohol, at times affectionate, more often mocking, her eyebrows arched with suspicion and sarcasm. Both of them gigantic in my range of vision, the two of them together blotting out light, sound, the very idea of future.

I am twelve years old, and I live in my room with those I think of as my friends. These are not imaginary companions. No, they are starkly real: I can hold them in my hands. They comfort me in this emotional nether world I occupy, helping me navigate through regions for which I as yet have no names, but will later call sorrow, grief, rage.

The names of my friends? Bradbury. Matheson. Beaumont. Nolan.

My father will stumble into my room angrily.

"For God's sake, why don't you *do* anything?" he'll demand, gesturing wildly at the room of pictures and papers as if it is somehow an insult to him. I do things, I want to tell him; I write stories, poems, plays. But to him that is not, of course, *doing* anything at all. My father holds my friends in his hands with disgust, bewilderment, sifting through them quickly as if he might find an answer hidden somewhere on their garish, color-splashed covers. He wonders, I know, how he ever came to be saddled with a son like me.

My mother is different, but only superficially. She too wonders why I don't have friends, not knowing that I do. She reads—glitzy soft-core romances, by the dozen—but only to pass the time, to get her from the bitter glare of day to the soothing, lubricated dark of night. She does not understand why I stay in my room, or what I do there. Drinking earlier and earlier, she will eventually bring the night on herself.

I've wondered in the years since how many other children have been as I was, how many have used stories of mystery and horror and fantasy not just as an escape—mere entertainment—but for actual succor. How many have found warm comfort in such no-holds-barred, high-wire visions of alternate worlds—genuine comfort, not only that such worlds might be possible but that there were actual men who could create them on the page and make them live within a reader's mind as vividly as dreams?

How many other children adrift in unimaginative, uncomprehending families have come to revere the storyteller, the *writer*, as someone little different from God? How many have felt that their own favorite weavers of dark and weird tales were somehow friends, secret ones who understood them as no one else could? And how many have found in these writers a spirit-sustaining alternative to the pallid, sluggish offerings of their English classes at school?

How many have combed used book stores for twenty-five cent paperbacks which, discovered, were as thrilling as buried treasure brought dazzlingly to light?

How many literary careers began with exactly these emotions?

Mine did. And these writers—the Bradburys, the Mathesons, the Beaumonts, the Nolans—quite literally saved my life.

I would sun myself through long summer afternoons in a hammock stretched between two crab apple trees in our backyard, sipping lemonade, munching on fresh-picked peaches, and reading the time away: *Something Wicked This Way Comes, I Am Legend, The Magic Man, Logan's Run.* Those were good days, when the darkness that would eventually crumple the light still seemed endless hours distant.

These writers taught me what it was to be alive when all around me was illness, neurosis, dysfunction and, eventually, death. Their imaginations, untamed by notions of literary safety or propriety, dared suggest what the adults in my daily life never would: that it was good to ask questions, to speculate, to wonder; that being different was not, in itself, bad, could even be good; and, most exhilarating of all, that authority—speak this softly, now—was not always necessarily right.

These notions are dangerous. But for a child trapped in an abyssal travesty of a home, alienated, afraid, they represented freedom—survival itself.

I have since attempted to thank these writers, those who survive, but there are really no words. These men spent too many years inside my head, roaming the chambers of my mind and depositing whispered wisdom there, for any vocabulary to express.

Some think of such stories as mere pulp fiction, literary detritus, nonsense. All I can say is that they were not that for me. These dark universes galvanized me, electrified my imagination in ways that tepidly conventional stories never could. More than most so-called "literary" fiction, then, this is the kind of writing that does what Annie Dillard requires: plays it full-out, nothing held back, every time. Writers such as Bradbury, Matheson, Beaumont, and Nolan thus represented a lifeline, one which I still admire my younger self for knowing to grab onto and hold. I hold them now.

2.

In his essay *Supernatural Horror in Literature* (1924), H.P. Lovecraft defines the genuine fiction of "cosmic terror" as separate and distinct from "the literature of mere physical fear and the mundanely gruesome." The "true weird tale," he writes,

> has something more than secret murder, bloody bones, or a sheeted form clanking chains according to rule. A certain atmosphere of breathless and unexplainable dread of outer, unknown forces must be present; and there must be a hint, expressed with a seriousness and portentousness becoming its subject, of that most terrible conception of the human brain—a malign and particular suspension or defeat of those fixed laws of Nature which are our only safeguard against the assaults of chaos and the daemons of unplumbed space.

This comes closer than any definition I know to describing the fundamental nature of real horror fiction—a type of writing that has, at its best, little to do with garden-variety bogeymen in the night, instead focusing on the true, ultimate terrors: the failure of the senses to perceive; of logic to explain; the breakdown, finally, of what we understand as *meaning* in the universe. This is the kind of deep "cosmic" fear that informs the tales of Poe, Blackwood, Bierce, Lovecraft himself—all the great horror writers of the past whose work, by tapping into these ancient and universal anxieties, has stood the test of time. And it is a kind of fear that is richly represented in the marvelous short stories of one of horror's contemporary masters, William F. Nolan.

Consider the opening paragraph of the first story in this collection, "The Underdweller":

In the waiting, windless dark, Lewis Stillman pressed into the building-front shadows along Wilshire Boulevard. Breathing softly, the automatic poised and ready in his hand, he advanced with animal stealth toward Western Avenue, gliding over the night-cool concrete past ravaged clothing shops, drug and department stores, their windows shattered, their doors ajar and swinging. The city of Los Angeles, painted in cold moonlight, was an immense graveyard; the tall, white tombstone buildings thrust up from the silent pavement, shadow-carved and lonely. Overturned metal corpses of trucks, buses, and automobiles littered the streets.

In four brilliantly evocative sentences, Nolan creates a world as tensely packed with "breathless and unexplainable dread of outer, unknown forces" as it is possible to imagine. Stillman is in familiar Los Angeles, but it has inexplicably changed. Has a nuclear war occurred? If so, why are the buildings still standing? Where are all the people? If there is no one, who looted the businesses Stillman sees? Why does he need a weapon? What is he afraid of? Overhanging all these questions is the nearly palapable sense of *dread*, created in part by Nolan's perfect descriptive word choices: the city "painted in cold moonlight," the buildings "shadow-carved," the vehicles "overturned corpses." Indeed, in this world of tension and suspense, even the windless dark itself is "waiting"—for what, we do not know, though anyone encountering this classic gem for the first time should rest assured that the final stunning revelation is anything but "clanking chains according to rule."

Nolan's imagination is a wildly varied one, and the finest of his stories are unique contributions to the development of the horror tale. Still, numerous influences can be perceived through these shadowy pages, including Poe (the theme of Nolan's "Coincidence" recalling "William Wilson") and Lovecraft (the structure of "Ceremony" being reminiscent of

"The Shadow Over Innsmouth"). The occasional tough-guy narrator, as in "A Good Day," echoes Dashiell Hammett; and the fast-paced, cinematic quality of many of the tales can be traced to Nolan's self-avowed love for the movies, which expresses itself directly in such stories as "Saturday's Shadow," "Major Prevue Here Tonite," and "Heart's Blood." But the greatest influence on Nolan's fiction derives from his close relationship with the writers he knew and loved when he was just beginning his career in the 1950s, including Ray Bradbury, Richard Matheson, and Charles Beaumont—all key participants, along with Nolan himself and a few others, in what has since become known as the "Southern California Group."

This is not the place for a comprehensive history of this unique creative affiliation which is, as far as I know, virtually unprecedented in the annals of American letters (at any rate, such a history exists in the anthology *California Sorcery,* co-edited by Nolan and William Schafer). It is enough to say that these writers, all at the start of their careers, shared uncommonly close bonds in the 1950s. The core of the Group—Nolan and Beaumont, along with John Tomerlin and George Clayton Johnson—went to movies and amusement parks together, ate together in restaurants, socialized with each others' families, and collaborated on writing projects, with the more-established Bradbury serving as friendly mentor and Matheson as frequent host and steadying influence. Together these men essentially *created* the modern horror genre, and their influence remains significant in the work of virtually every writer in the field today. But their closeness—the *gestalt* they were each part of for a little more than a decade, from the early 1950s to around 1963—also had the effect of sometimes making one author's work strikingly like that of others in the Group. After all, more than anything else, these men *talked:* about movies, women, politics, the fate of the world—everything, including each others' stories and ideas. Indeed, Bradbury has recalled vividly in print how a simple germ of a story idea might be raised by one of the Group members, a germ which would be picked up by another and amplified, then altered a bit by a third, given a new spin by a fourth—until, by the end of the evening, no one really knew who the story even belonged to anymore, and so it would simply be assigned to the writer who wanted it the most fervently. Thus, a story from this era "by" Charles Beaumont or "by" George Clayton Johnson might in fact have the ideas and even language of several writers within it.

The effect of the Group on Nolan's writing career was profound—perhaps, in those early days, too much so. As excellent as many of his stories of this time are, his influences are often too easily discernible, leaving the impression of a writer with enormous imagination and technical facility who has not yet quite discovered his own voice. "The Underdweller," for example, is brilliantly written, but in setting it clearly owes something to Matheson's *I Am Legend*—published only two years before. Much the same might be said of "And Miles to Go Before I Sleep," a fine piece of writing marred only by its similarity to some works of Bradbury (especially "Marionettes Inc."). In terms of his fiction, the Group would provide a sterling launch pad for Nolan, but one whose pervasive influence would be difficult to overcome. Indeed, when it came time for his first novel, *Logan's Run* (1967), it would be written in collaboration with Group member Johnson.

It seems to me that William F. Nolan's fiction truly comes of age in the 1970s. While the influences are still visible at times, in stories such as "Violation," "Dead Call," and "The Partnership" his work takes on a depth and quality which begin to mark out a definite "Nolan Country." He writes of cities on occasion, but his most evocative setting is small-town America. His characters are either ordinary people caught in extraordinary circumstances or extraordinary people who only *appear* to be ordinary. Plot predominates, in a style which emphasizes focus, economy, and narrative velocity. But while some of this description might also be appropriate to the fiction of Bradbury, Nolan's world lacks the nostalgic haze of *Dandelion Wine* or *The Martian Chronicles*; it is a harsher place, closer in tone to the stark landscapes of Edward Hopper than the warm Americana of Norman Rockwell. Still, while the "daemons of unplumbed space" sometimes triumph in Nolan, more often than not the individual is victorious. Nolan is no sentimentalist, but neither is he a pessimist. He believes, finally, in the human potential.

In the 1980s and '90s Nolan expanded and solidified his reputation in the horror field, turning out story after story more vivid and energetic than those of many writers half his age. Two of these, "Lonely Train a' Comin' " and "The Cure," formed the basis of his only full-length horror novel, *Helltracks* (1991), which some consider the best book of his career. In any event, time has not slowed him down, and he writes as well today—and as prolifically—as he did thirty years ago. If his reputation in the genre does not loom quite as large as Bradbury's, Matheson's, or Robert Bloch's, I suspect it is because his work is simply too mercurial, too difficult to categorize. Nolan is one of our great literary ventriloquists; we always know when we are reading a

Bradbury story, but Nolan's style adjusts itself to each new plot and set of characters. (Try comparing "Lonely Train a' Comin' " to "The Giant Man" or "Boyfren": they seem the work of totally different writers.)

An instantly identifiable style is a wonderful asset for any author to possess, but it could be argued that, in literary terms, Nolan's less visible approach is just as large an accomplishment. It allows him total artistic freedom, unfettered as he is by a clearly defined image behind his work. Late in their careers, many writers of large reputation end up trapped by their own personas: Hemingway spent the last twenty years of his life creating labored imitations of himself. This can never be a problem for Nolan, for when we think of his work it is not a style or an author we remember: it is a *story*. As Annie Dillard advises, he holds nothing back. In every tale, every novel, Nolan gives it, gives it all, gives it now.

3.

A final note, on the man himself.

I have never met William F. Nolan. I have adored his work since the traumatic days of my youth; I have collected it and researched his career. (Present

Nolanologists should be aware, by the way, of two excellent sites on the Web: www.williamfnolan.com and www.nolansworld.com.) But he and I live on opposite ends of the country, and our relationship has been sustained entirely through the mail—the old-fashioned kind, without an "e-" as a prefix. And while some academic theorists maintain that the author and his intentions are irrelevant to judging an artistic work, I do not believe this to be the case— and I suspect Nolan doesn't either. In the works of Hemingway, for instance, we can see a breathtaking solipsism and vulgar sexism alongside an intermittently staggering genius—qualities clearly reflected in what we know of Hemingway as a man. In the case of Nolan, his dark universe may be cold, but his characters rarely are. If they survive, it is usually due to the most basic of human virtues: courage, comradeship, love. If a sadist or psychopath succeeds in a Nolan story, it is never cause for laughter or titillation (as with the work of some younger writers in the genre, to whom everything is "ironic"— including, apparently, pain and death). In Nolan it is, instead, literally *horrifying*.

And so when I came into contact with his personal generosity—which can be attested to by dozens, hundreds, not just me—it did not come as a surprise. On the basis of reading just one of my short stories, he volunteered to write an Introduction to any fiction collection I might put together—and he did. When I have needed help with any aspect of research on his career of those of other Group members, his responses have invariably been immediate and comprehensive. And Nolan was on the case immediately when a friend began constructing my own website (www.christopherconlon.com), providing a highly complimentary "blurb" for the home page.

He did not need to do any of these things. He did them because of the kind of person he is—the kind of person whose values vividly permeate the stories in this book. Through them, you too will get to know William F. Nolan.

Turn the page. The windless dark awaits.

Isaac Asimov called this story "a classic about the struggle to survive." Certainly survival is our strongest human instinct, and in these pages Lewis Stillman fights for his life against overwhelming odds. A shorter draft was written in the summer of 1956, just four-and-a-half months after I had quit my office job to become a full-time working writer. This early version appeared in August of 1957 as "Small World" in Fantastic Universe, a digest-sized pulp; it was my ninth professionally printed story.

I had originally intended to write an entire novel about a man who lived under Los Angeles (the below-streets storm drain system I describe is real), but I lacked the ability, at that time, to handle such an ambitious project. (Didn't write my first novel, Logan's Run, until 1965.) I did expand the manuscript for a revised version, doubling its length, into "The Small World of Lewis Stillman," and later yet, into "The Underdweller."

During the past forty-six years, since its initial appearance, this story has never been out of print—having been selected for hard and softcover editions of eleven anthologies (including Modern Masters of Horror), as well as being included in four of my earlier story collections, and in a school magazine (Read). It has also been collected *overseas, dramatized for radio, adapted for television, illustrated for comic-book format, and even pirated in* Vampirella!

Like his colleague, Logan the Sandman, Lewis Stillman just keeps on running.

THE UNDERDWELLER

(Written: August 1956)

In the waiting, windless dark, Lewis Stillman pressed into the building-front shadows along Wilshire Boulevard. Breathing softly, the automatic poised and ready in his hand, he advanced with animal stealth toward Western Avenue, gliding over the night-cool concrete past ravaged clothing shops, drug and department stores, their windows shattered, their doors ajar and swinging. The city of Los Angeles, painted in cold moonlight, was an immense graveyard; the tall, white tombstone buildings thrust up from the silent pavement, shadow-carved and lonely. Overturned metal corpses of trucks, buses, and automobiles littered the streets.

He paused under the wide marquee of the Fox

Wiltern. Above his head, rows of splintered display bulbs gaped—sharp glass teeth in wooden jaws. Lewis Stillman felt as though they might drop at any moment to pierce his body.

Four more blocks to cover. His destination: a small corner delicatessen four blocks south of Wilshire, on Western. Tonight he intended bypassing the larger stores like Safeway and Thriftimart, with their available supplies of exotic foods; a smaller grocery was far more likely to have what he needed. He was finding it more and more difficult to locate basic foodstuffs. In the big supermarkets, only the more exotic and highly spiced canned and bottled goods remained—and he was sick of bottled oysters!

Crossing Western, he had almost reached the far curb when he saw some of *them*. He dropped immediately to his knees behind the rusting bulk of an Oldsmobile. The rear door on his side was open, and he cautiously eased himself into the back seat of the deserted car. Releasing the safety catch on the automatic, he peered through the cracked window at six or seven of them as they moved toward him along the street. God! Had he been seen? He couldn't be sure. Perhaps they were aware of his position! He should have remained on the open street, where he'd have a running chance. Perhaps, if his aim were true, he could kill most of them; but, even with its silencer, the gun might be heard and more of them would come. He dared not fire until he was certain they had discovered him.

They came closer, their small dark bodies crowding the walk, six of them, chattering, leaping, cruel mouths open, eyes glittering under the moon. Closer. Their shrill pipings increased, rose in volume. Closer.

Now he could make out their sharp teeth and matted hair. Only a few feet from the car . . . His hand was moist on the handle of the automatic; his heart thundered against his chest. Seconds away . . .

Now!

Lewis Stillman fell heavily back against the dusty seat cushion, the gun loose in his trembling hand. They had passed by; they had missed him. Their thin pipings diminished, grew faint with distance.

The tomb silence of late night settled around him.

The delicatessen proved a real windfall. The shelves were relatively untouched and he had a wide choice of tinned goods. He found an empty cardboard box and hastily began to transfer the cans from the shelf nearest him.

A noise from behind—a padding, scraping sound.

Lewis Stillman whirled about, the automatic ready.

A huge mongrel dog faced him, growling deep in its throat, four legs braced for assault. The blunt ears were laid flat along the short-haired skull and a thin trickle of saliva seeped from the killing jaws. The beast's powerful chest muscles were bunched for the spring when Stillman acted.

His gun, he knew, was useless; the shots might be heard. Therefore, with the full strength of his left arm, he hurled a heavy can at the dog's head. The stunned animal staggered under the blow, legs buckling. Hurriedly, Stillman gathered his supplies and made his way back to the street.

How much longer can my luck hold? Lewis Stillman wondered, as he bolted the door. He placed the box of tinned goods on a wooden table and lit the tall lamp nearby. Its flickering orange glow illumined the narrow, low-ceilinged room.

Twice tonight, his mind told him, twice you've escaped them—and they could have seen you easily on both occasions if they had been watching for you. They don't know you're alive. But when they find out . . .

He forced his thoughts away from the scene in his mind, away from the horror; quickly he began to unload the box, placing the cans on a long shelf along the far side of the room.

He began to think of women, of a girl named Joan, and of how much he had loved her.

The world of Lewis Stillman was damp and lightless; it was narrow and its cold stone walls pressed in upon him as he moved. He had been walking for several hours; sometimes he would run, because he knew his leg muscles must be kept strong, but he was walking now, following the thin yellow beam of his hooded flash. He was searching.

Tonight, he thought, I might find another like myself. Surely, *someone* is down here; I'll find someone if I keep searching. I *must* find someone!

But he knew he would not. He knew he would find only chill emptiness ahead of him in the long tunnels.

For three years, he had been searching for another man or woman down here in this world under the city. For three years, he had prowled the seven hundred miles of storm drains which threaded their way under the skin of Los Angeles like the veins in a giant's body—and he had found nothing. *Nothing*.

Even now, after all the days and nights of search, he could not really accept the fact that he was alone, that he was the last man alive in a city of twelve million . . .

*   *   *

The beautiful woman stood silently above him. Her eyes burned softly in the darkness; her fine red lips were smiling. The foam-white gown she wore continually swirled and billowed around her motionless figure.

"Who are you?" he asked, his voice far off, unreal.

"Does it matter, Lewis?"

Her words, like four dropped stones in a quiet pool, stirred him, rippled down the length of his body.

"No," he said. "Nothing matters, now, except that we've found each other. God, after all these lonely months and years of waiting! I thought I was the last, that I'd never live to see—"

"Hush, my darling." She leaned to kiss him. Her lips were moist and yielding. "I'm here now."

He reached up to touch her cheek, but already she was fading, blending into darkness. Crying out, he clawed desperately for her extended hand. But she was gone, and his fingers rested on a rough wall of damp concrete.

A swirl of milk-fog drifted away down the tunnel.

Rain. Days of rain. The drains had been designed to handle floods, so Lewis Stillman was not particularly worried. He had built high, a good three feet above the tunnel floor, and the water had never yet risen to this level. But he didn't like the sound of the rain down here: an orchestrated thunder through the tunnels, a trap-drumming amplified and continuous. Since he had been unable to make his daily runs, he had been reading more than usual. Short stories by Oates, Gordimer, Aiken, Irwin Shaw, Hemingway; poems by Frost, Lorca, Sandburg, Millay, Dylan Thomas. Strange, how unreal the world seemed when he read their words. Unreality, however, was fleeting, and the moment he closed a book the loneliness and the fears pressed back. He hoped the rain would stop soon.

Dampness. Surrounding him, the cold walls and the chill and the dampness. The unending gurgle and drip of water, the hollow, tapping splash of the falling drops. Even in his cot, wrapped in thick blankets, the dampness seemed to permeate his body. Sounds . . . Thin screams, pipings, chitterings, reedy whisperings above his head. They were dragging something along the street, something they'd killed, no doubt. An animal—a cat or a dog, perhaps . . . Lewis Stillman shifted, pulling the blankets closer about his body. He kept his eyes tightly shut, listening to the sharp, scuffling sounds on the pavement, and swore bitterly.

"Damn you," he said. "Damn all of you!"

* * *

Lewis Stillman was running, running down the long tunnels. Behind him, a tide of midget shadows washed from wall to wall; high, keening cries, doubled and tripled by echoes, rang in his ears. Claws reached for him; he felt panting breath, like hot smoke, on the back of his neck. His lungs were bursting, his entire body aflame.

He looked down at his fast-pumping legs, doing their job with pistoned precision. He listened to the sharp slap of his heels against the floor of the tunnel, and he thought: I might die at any moment, but my *legs* will escape! They will run on, down the endless drains, and never be caught. They move so fast, while my heavy awkward upper body rocks and sways above them, slowing them down, tiring them—making them angry. How my legs must hate me! I must be clever and humor them, beg them to take me along to safety. How well they run, how sleek and fine!

Then he felt himself coming apart. His legs were detaching themselves from his upper body. He cried out in horror, flailing the air, beseeching them not to leave him behind. But the legs cruelly continued to unfasten themselves. In a cold surge of terror, Lewis Stillman felt himself tipping, falling toward the damp floor—while his legs raced on with a wild animal life of their own. He opened his mouth, high above those insane legs, and screamed, ending the nightmare.

He sat up stiffly in his cot, gasping, drenched in sweat. He drew in a long, shuddering breath and reached for a cigarette, lighting it with a trembling hand.

The nightmares were getting worse. He realized that his mind was rebelling as he slept, spilling forth the pent-up fears of the day during the night hours.

He thought once more about the beginning, six years ago—about why he was still alive. The alien ships had struck Earth suddenly, without warning. Their attack had been thorough and deadly. In a matter of hours, the aliens had accomplished their clever mission—and the men and women of Earth were destroyed. A few survived, he was certain. He had never seen any of them, but he was convinced they existed. Los Angeles was not the world, after all, and since he had escaped, so must have others around the globe. He'd been working alone in the drains when the aliens struck, finishing a special job for the construction company on K tunnel. He could still hear the sound of the mammoth ships and feel the intense heat of their passage.

Hunger had forced him out, and overnight he had become a curiosity.

The last man alive. For three years, he was not harmed. He worked with them, taught them many things, and tried to win their confidence. But, eventually, certain ones came to hate him, to be jealous of his relationship with the others. Luckily, he had been able to escape to the drains. That was three years ago, and now they had forgotten him.

His subsequent excursions to the upper level of the city had been made under cover of darkness— and he never ventured out unless his food supply dwindled. He had built his one-room structure directly to the side of an overhead grating not close enough to risk their seeing it, but close enough for light to seep in during the sunlight hours. He missed the warm feel of open sun on his body almost as much as he missed human companionship, but he dare not risk himself above the drains by day.

When the rain ceased, he crouched beneath the street gratings to absorb as much as possible of the filtered sunlight. But the rays were weak, and their small warmth only served to heighten his desire to feel direct sunlight upon his naked shoulders.

The dreams . . . always the dreams.

"Are you cold, Lewis?"

"Yes. Yes, cold."

"Then go out, dearest. Into the sun."

"I can't. Can't go out."

"But Los Angeles is your world, Lewis! You are the last man in it. The last man in the world."

"Yes, but they own it all. Every street belongs to them, every building. They wouldn't let me come out. I'd die. They'd kill me."

"Go out, Lewis." The liquid dream-voice faded, faded. "Out into the sun, my darling. Don't be afraid."

That night, he watched the moon through the street gratings for almost an hour. It was round and full, like a huge yellow floodlamp in the dark sky, and he thought, for the first time in years, of night baseball at Blues Stadium in Kansas City. He used to love watching the games with his father under the mammoth stadium lights when the field was like a pond, frosted with white illumination, and the players dream-spawned and unreal. Night baseball was always a magic game to him when he was a boy.

Sometimes he got insane thoughts. Sometimes, on a night like this, when the loneliness closed in like a crushing fist and he could no longer stand it, he would think of bringing one of them down with him, into the drains. One at a time, they might be handled. Then he'd remember their sharp, savage eyes, their animal ferocity, and he would realize that the idea was impossible. If one of their kind disappeared, suddenly and without trace, others would certainly become suspicious, begin to search—and it would all be over.

Lewis Stillman settled back into his pillow; he closed his eyes and tried not to listen to the distant screams, pipings, and reedy cries filtering down from the street above his head.

Finally, he slept.

He spent the afternoon with paper women. He lingered over the pages of some yellowed fashion magazines, looking at all the beautifully photographed models in their fine clothes. Slim and enchanting, these page-women, with their cool enticing eyes and perfect smiles, all grace and softness and glitter and swirled cloth. He touched their images with gentle fingers, stroking the tawny paper hair, as though, by some magic formula, he might imbue them with life. Yet, it was easy to imagine that these women had never *really* lived at all, that they were simply painted, in microscopic detail, by sly artists to give the illusion of photos.

He didn't like to think about these women and how they died.

*   *   *

"A toast to courage," smiled Lewis Stillman, raising his wine glass high. It sparkled deep crimson in the lamplit room. "To courage and to the man who truly possesses it!" He drained the glass and hastily refilled it from a tall bottle on the table beside his cot.

"Aren't you going to join me, Mr. H.?" he asked the seated figure slouched over the table. "Or must I drink alone?"

The figure did not reply.

"Well, then——" He emptied the glass, set it down. "Oh, I know all about what one man is supposed to be able to do. Win out alone. Whip the damn world single-handed. If a fish as big as a mountain and as mean as all sin is out there, then this one man is supposed to go get him, isn't that it? Well, Papa H., what if the world is *full* of killer fish? Can he win over them all? One man, alone? Of course he can't. Nosir. Damn well *right* he can't!"

Stillman moved unsteadily to a shelf in one corner of the small wooden room and took down a slim book.

"Here she is, Mr. H. Your greatest. The one you wrote cleanest and best—*The Old Man and the Sea.* You showed how one man could fight the whole damn ocean." He paused, voice strained and rising. "Well, by God, show me, *now*, how to fight this ocean! My ocean is full of killer fish, and I'm one man and I'm alone in it. I'm ready to listen."

The seated figure remained silent.

"Got you now, haven't I, Papa? No answer to this one, eh? Courage isn't enough. Man was not meant to live alone or fight alone—or drink alone. Even with courage, he can only do so much alone—and then it's useless. Well, I say it's useless. I say the hell with your book, and the hell with *you!*"

Lewis Stillman flung the book straight at the head of the motionless figure. The victim spilled back in the chair; his arms slipped off the table, hung swinging. They were lumpy and handless.

More and more, Lewis Stillman found his thoughts turning to the memory of his father and of long hikes through the moonlit Missouri countryside, of hunting trips and warm campfires, of the deep woods, rich and green in summer. He thought of his father's hopes for his future, and the words of that tall, gray-haired figure often came back to him.

"You'll be a fine doctor, Lewis. Study and work hard, and you'll succeed. I know you will."

He remembered the long winter evenings of study at his father's great mahogany desk, poring over medical books and journals, taking notes, sifting and resifting facts. He remembered one set of books in particular—Erickson's monumental three-volume text on surgery, richly bound and stamped in gold. He had always loved those books, above all others.

What had gone wrong along the way? Somehow, the dream had faded; the bright goal vanished and was lost. After a year of pre-med at the University of California, he had given up medicine; he had become discouraged and quit college to take a laborer's job with a construction company. How ironic that this move should have saved his life! He'd wanted to work with his hands, to sweat and labor with the muscles of his body. He'd wanted to earn enough to marry Joan and then, later perhaps, he would have returned to finish his courses. It seemed so far away now, his reason for quitting, for letting his father down.

Now, at this moment, an overwhelming desire gripped him, a desire to pore over Erickson's pages once again, to recreate, even for a brief moment, the comfort and happiness of his childhood.

He'd once seen a duplicate set on the second floor of Pickwick's bookstore in Hollywood, in their used books department, and now he knew he must go after it, bring the books back with him to the drains. It was a dangerous and foolish desire, but he knew he would obey it. Despite the risk of death, he would go after the books tonight. *Tonight.*

*   *   *

One corner of Lewis Stillman's room was reserved for weapons. His prize, a Thompson submachine gun, had been procured from the Los Angeles police arsenal. Supplementing the Thompson were two automatic rifles, a Luger, a Colt .45, and a .22 calibre Hornet pistol equipped with a silencer. He always kept the smallest gun in a spring-clip holster beneath his armpit, but it was not his habit to carry any of the larger weapons with him into the city. On this night, however, things were different.

The drains ended two miles short of Hollywood—which meant he would be forced to cover a long and particularly hazardous stretch of ground in order to reach the bookstore. He therefore decided to take along the .30 calibre Savage rifle in addition to the small hand weapon.

You're a fool, Lewis, he told himself as he slid the oiled Savage from its leather case, risking your life for a set of books. Are they *that* important? Yes, a part of him replied, they are that important. You want these books, then go *after* what you want. If fear keeps you from seeking that which you truly want, if fear holds you like a rat in the dark, then you are worse than a coward. You are a traitor, betraying yourself and the civilization you represent.

If a man wants a thing and the thing is good, he must go after it, no matter what the cost, or relinquish the right to be called a man. It is better to die with courage than to live with cowardice.

Ah, Papa Hemingway, breathed Stillman, smiling at his own thoughts. I see that you are back with me. I see that your words have rubbed off after all. Well, then, all right—let us go after our fish, let us seek him out. Perhaps the ocean will be calm.

Slinging the heavy rifle over one shoulder, Lewis Stillman set off down the tunnels.

Running in the chill night wind. Grass, now pavement, now grass beneath his feet. Ducking into shadows, moving stealthily past shops and theaters, rushing under the cold, high moon. Santa Monica Boulevard, then Highland, then Hollywood Boulevard, and finally—after an eternity of heartbeats—Pickwick's

Lewis Stillman, his rifle over one shoulder, the small automatic gleaming in his hand, edged silently into the store.

A paper battleground met his eyes.

In filtered moonlight, a white blanket of broken-backed volumes spilled across the entire lower floor. Stillman shuddered; he could envision them, shrieking, scrabbling at the shelves, throwing books wildly across the room at one another. Screaming, ripping, destroying.

What of the other floors? *What of the medical section?*

He crossed to the stairs, spilled pages crackling like a fall of dry autumn leaves under his step, and sprinted up to the second floor, stumbling, terribly afraid of what he might find. Reaching the top, heart thudding, he squinted into the dimness.

The books were undisturbed. Apparently they had tired of their game before reaching these.

He slipped the rifle from his shoulder and placed it near the stairs. Dust lay thick all around him, powdering up and swirling as he moved down the narrow aisles; a damp, leathery mustiness lived in the air, an odor of mold and neglect.

Lewis Stillman paused before a dim, hand-lettered sign: MEDICAL SECTION. It was just as he remembered it. Holstering the small automatic, he struck a match, shading the flame with a cupped hand as he moved it along the rows of faded titles. Carter . . . Davidson . . .

Enright . . . *Erickson.* He drew in his breath sharply. All three volumes, their gold stamping dust-dulled but legible, stood in tall and perfect order on the shelf.

In the darkness, Lewis Stillman carefully removed each volume, blowing it free of dust. At last, all three books were clean and solid in his hands.

Well, you've done it. You've reached the books and now they belong to you.

He smiled, thinking of the moment when he would be able to sit down at the table with his treasure and linger again over the wondrous pages.

He found an empty carton at the rear of the store and placed the books inside. Returning to the stairs, he shouldered the rifle and began his descent to the lower floor.

So far, he told himself, my luck is still holding.

But as Lewis Stillman's foot touched the final stair, his luck ran out.

The entire lower floor was alive with them!

Rustling like a mass of great insects, gliding toward him, eyes gleaming in the half-light, they converged upon the stairs. They'd been waiting for him.

Now, suddenly the books no longer mattered. Now only his life mattered and nothing else. He moved back against the hard wood of the stair-rail, the carton of books sliding from his hands. They had stopped at the foot of the stairs; they were silent, looking up at him with hate in their eyes.

If you can reach the street, Stillman told himself, then you've still got a chance. That means you've got to get through them to the door. All right then, *move*.

Lewis Stillman squeezed the trigger of the automatic. Two of them fell as Stillman charged into their midst.

He felt sharp nails claw at his shirt, heard the cloth ripping away in their grasp. He kept firing the small automatic into them, and three more dropped under his bullets, shrieking in pain and surprise. The others spilled back, screaming, from the door.

The pistol was empty. He tossed it away, swinging the heavy Savage free from his shoulder as he reached the street. The night air, crisp and cool in his lungs, gave him instant hope.

I can still make it, thought Stillman, as he leaped the curb and plunged across the pavement. If those shots weren't heard, then I've still got the edge. My legs are strong; I can outdistance them.

Luck, however, had failed him completely on this night. Near the intersection of Hollywood Boulevard and Highland, a fresh pack of them swarmed toward him.

He dropped to one knee and fired into their ranks, the Savage jerking in his hands. They scattered to either side.

He began to run steadily down the middle of Hollywood Boulevard, using the butt of the heavy rifle like a battering ram as they came at him. As he neared Highland, three of them darted directly into his path. Stillman fired. One doubled over, lurching crazily into a jagged plate glass store front. Another clawed at him as he swept around the corner to Highland, but he managed to shake free.

The street ahead of him was clear. Now his superior leg power would count heavily in his favor. Two miles. Could he make it before others cut him off?

Running, reloading, firing. Sweat soaking his shirt, rivering down his face, stinging his eyes. A mile covered. Halfway to the drains. They had fallen back behind his swift stride.

But more of them were coming, drawn by the rifle shots, pouring in from side streets, from stores and houses.

His heart jarred in his body, his breath was ragged. How many of them around him? A hundred? Two hundred? More coming. God!

He bit down on his lower lip until the salt taste of blood was on his tongue. You can't make it, a voice inside him shouted. They'll have you in another block and you know it!

He fitted the rifle to his shoulder, adjusted his aim, and fired. The long rolling crack of the big weapon filled the night. Again and again he fired, the butt jerking into the flesh of his shoulder, the bitter smell of burnt powder in his nostrils.

It was no use. Too many of them. He could not clear a path.

Lewis Stillman knew that he was going to die.

The rifle was empty at last; the final bullet had been fired. He had no place to run because they were all around him, in a slowly closing circle.

He looked at the ring of small cruel faces and thought, the aliens did their job perfectly; they stopped Earth before she could reach the age of the rocket, before she could threaten planets beyond her own moon. What an immensely clever plan it had been! To destroy every human being on Earth above the age of six—and then to leave as quickly as they had come, allowing our civilization to continue on a primitive level, knowing that Earth's back had been broken, that her survivors would revert to savagery as they grew into adulthood.

Lewis Stillman dropped the empty rifle at his feet and threw out his hands. "Listen," he pleaded, "I'm really one of you. You'll *all* be like me soon. Please, *listen* to me."

But the circle tightened relentlessly around him.

Lewis Stillman was screaming when the children closed in.

It is said that an author can never judge his or her own work, but I disagree. Who else knows it better——its strengths and weaknesses, flaws and merits? I rate "Saturday's Shadow" among my top stories. It has a layered texture that is both amusing and terrifying. Also, it deals with one of my prime passions, motion pictures, and with the legendary stars who have enhanced my dream life on the silver screen. Many of them are here. Errol Flynn, John Wayne, Marilyn Monroe, Alan Ladd, Marlon Brando, Judy Garland, Humphrey Bogart——even ole King Kong.

I was honored to have "Saturday's Shadow" voted one of the five best stories of 1979 by the World Fantasy Convention. It was read, with fervor and brilliance, by Roddy McDowell, another legendary actor, for Dove Books on Tape—— and I selected it to represent my best genre work in Dennis Etchison's anthology, Masters of Darkness.

I'll honestly admit that I'm quite proud of this one.

SATURDAY'S SHADOW

(Written: December 1977)

First, before I tell you about Laurie—about what happened to her (in blood) I must tell you about primary shadows. It is vitally important that I tell you about these shadows. Each day has one, and they have entirely different characteristics, variant personalities.

Sunday's shadow (the one Laurie liked; her friend) is fat and sleepy. Snoozes all day.

Monday's shadow is thin and pale at the edges. The sun eats it fast.

Tuesday's shadow is silly and random-headed. Lumpy in the middle. Never knows where it's been or where it's going. No sense of purpose to it.

Wednesday's shadow is pushy. Arrogant. Full of

bombast. All it's after is attention. Ignore it, don't humor it.

Thursday's shadow is weepy . . . lachrymose. Depressing to have it cover you, but no harm to it.

Friday's shadow is slick and swift. Jumps around a lot. Okay to run with it. Safe to follow it anywhere.

Now, the one I really want to warn you about is the last one.

Saturday's shadow.

It's dangerous. Very, very dangerous. The thing to do is keep it at a distance. The edges are sharp and serrated, like teeth in a shark's jaw. And it's damned quiet. Comes sliding and slipping toward you along the ground—widening out to form its full deathshape. Killshape.

I really *hate* that filthy thing! If I could—

Wait. No good. I'm getting all emotional again about it, and I must not *do* this. I must be cool and logical and precise—to render my full account of what happened to Laurie. I just *know* you'll be interested in what happened to her.

Okay?

I'll give it to you logically. I can be very logical because I work with figures and statistics at a bank here on Coronado Island.

No, that's not right. *She* works there, worked there, at a bank, and *I'm* not Laurie, am I? . . . I really honest-to-god don't think I'm Laurie. Me. She. Separate. She. Me.

Sheme.

Meshe.

Identity is a tricky business. We spend most of our lives trying to find out who we are. Who we *really* are. An endless pursuit.

I'm not going to be Laurie (in blood) when I tell you about all this. If I *am* then it ruins everything— so I ask you to believe that I was never Laurie.

Am never.

Am not.

Was not.

Can't be.

If I'm not Laurie, I can be very objective about her. No emotional ties. Separate and cool. That's how I'll tell it. (I could be Vivien. Vivien Leigh. She died, too. Ha! Call me Vivien.)

No use your worrying and fretting about who I am. Worry about who *you* are. That's the key to life, isn't it? Knowing your own identity.

Coronado is an island facing San Diego across an expanse of water with a long blue bridge over the water. That's all you *need* to know about it, but maybe you'll learn more as I tell you about Laurie. (Look it up in a California travel guide if you want square miles and length and history and all that boring kind of crap that does no good for anybody.)

It's a *place*. And Laurie lived at one end of it and worked at the other. Lived at the Sea Vista Arms. Four hundred and forty dollars a month. Studio apartment. No pets. No children. (Forbidden: the manager destroys them if he finds you with any.) Small bathroom. Off-white plasterboard walls. Sofa bed. Sliding closet door. Green leather reclining chair. Adjustable book shelves. (Laurie liked black-slave novels.) Two lamps, one standing. Green rug, Dun-colored pull drapes. You could see the bridge from her window. View of water and boats. Cramped little kitchen. With a chipped fridge.

She walked every day to work—to the business end of the island. Two- or three-mile walk every morning to the First National Bank of Coronado. Two- or three-mile walk home every afternoon. Late afternoon. (With the shadows very much alive.)

Ate her lunch in town, usually alone, sometimes with her brother, Ernest, who worked as a cop across the bay in San Diego. (Doesn't anymore, though. Ha!) He'd drive his patrol car across the long high blue bridge and meet her at the bank. For lunch down the street.

Laurie fixed her own dinner, alone, at her apartment. Worked all week. Stayed home nights and

Saturdays. Never left her apartment on Saturdays. (Wise girl. She *knew!*) On Sundays she'd walk to the park sometimes and tease Sunday's shadow. You know, joke with it, hassle it about being so fat and snoozing so much. It didn't mind. They were friends.

Laurie had no other friends. Just Sunday's shadow and her brother, Ernest. Parents both dead. No sisters. Nobody close to her at the bank or at the apartments. No boyfriends. Kept to herself mostly. Didn't say more than she had to. (Somebody once told her she talked like a Scotch telegram!) Mousey, I guess. That's what you'd call her. A quiet, small, logical, mousey, gray person living on this island in California.

One thing she was passionate about (strange word for Laurie—passion—but I'm trying to be precise about all this):

Movies.

Any kind of movies. On TV or in theaters. The first week she was able to toddle (as a kid in Los Angeles, where her parents raised her), she skittered away from Daddy and wobbled down the aisle of a movie palace. It was Grauman's Chinese, in Hollywood, and nobody saw her go in. She was just too damned tiny to notice. The picture was *Gone With the Wind*, and there was Gable on that huge screen (*really* huge to Laurie) kissing Vivien Leigh and telling her he didn't give a damn.

She never forgot it. Instant addiction. Sprocket-hole freak! Movies were all she lived for. Spent her weekly allowance on them . . . staying for hours and hours in those big churchlike theaters. Palaces with gilt-gold dreams inside.

Saturday's shadow had no strength in those days. It hadn't grown . . . amassed its killpower. Laurie would go to Saturday kiddie matinees and it wouldn't do a thing to her.

But it was growing. As she did. Getting bigger and stronger and gathering power each year. (It got a lot bigger than Laurie ever got.)

Ernest liked movies too. When she didn't go alone, he took her. It would have been more often, but Ernest wasn't always such a good boy and sometimes, on Saturdays, when he'd been bad that week (Ernest did things to birds), his parents made him stay home from the matinee and wash dishes. (Got so he hated the sight of a dish.) But when they *did* go to the movies together, Laurie and Ernest, they'd sit there, side by side in the flickered dark, not speaking or touching. Hardly breathing even. Eyes tight on the screen. On Tracy and Gable and Bogart and Cagney and Cooper and Flynn and Fonda and

Hepburn and Ladd and Garland and Brando and Wayne and Crawford and all the others. Thousands. A whole army of shadow giants up there on that big screen, all the people you'd ever need to know or love or fear.

Laurie had no reason to love or fear *real* people—because she had *them*. The shadow people.

Maybe you think that I'm rambling, avoiding the thing that happened to her. On the contrary. All this early material on Laurie is necessary if you're to fully appreciate what I'll be telling you. (Can't savor without knowing the flavor!)

So—she grew up, into the person she was destined to become. Her father divorced her mother and went away, and Laurie never saw him again after her eighteenth birthday. But that was all right with her, since she never understood him anyway.

Her mother she didn't give a damn about. (Ha!)

No playgirl she. Steady. Straight As in high school accounting. Sharp with statistics. Reliable. Orderly. Hard-working. A natural for banks.

Some years went by. Not sure how many. Laurie and Ernest went to college, I know. I'm sure of that. But their mother died before they got their degrees. (Did Laurie *kill* her? I doubt it. Really doubt anything like that. Ha!) Maybe Ernest killed her. (Secret!)

Afterward, Laurie moved from Los Angeles to

Coronado because she'd seen an ad in the paper saying they needed bank accountants on the island. (By then, she'd earned her degree by mail.)

Ernest moved down a year later. Drifted into aircraft work for a while, then got in with a police training program. Ernest is big and tough-fingered and square-backed. You don't mess around with Ernest. He'll break your frigging neck for you. How's *them* apples?

Shortly after, they heard that their daddy had suffered an attack (stroke, most likely) in Chicago in the middle of winter and froze out on some kind of iron bridge over Lake Michigan. A mean way to die—but it didn't bother Laurie. Or Ernest. They were both glad it never froze in San Diego. Weather is usually mild and pleasant there. Very pleasant. They really liked the weather.

Well, now you've got all the background, starting with Saturday's shadow—so we can get into *precisely* what happened to Laurie.

And how Ernest figures into it. With his big arms and shoulders and his big .38 Police Special. If he stops you for speeding, man, you *sign* that book! You don't smart mouth that cop or he puts one-two-three into you so fast you're spitting teeth before you can say Jack Robinson. (Old saying! Things stay with us, don't they? Memories.)

Laurie gets out of bed, eats her breakfast in the kitchen, gets dressed, and walks to work. (She'd never owned a car.)

It is Tuesday, this day, and Tuesday's shadow is silly and harmless. (No reason even to discuss it.) Laurie is "up." She saw a classic movie on the tube last night—*The Grapes of Wrath*—so she feels pretty chipper today, all things considered. She's seen *The Grapes of Wrath* (good title!) about six times. (The really solid ones never wear thin.)

But her mind was going. It's as simple as that, and I don't know how else to put it.

Who the hell knows why a person's *mind* goes? Drugs. Booze. Sadness. Pressures. Problems. A million reasons. Laurie wasn't a head; she didn't shoot up or even use grass. And I doubt that she had five drinks in her life.

Let me emphasize: she was *not* depressed on this particular Tuesday. So I'm not prepared to say what caused her to lose that rational precise cool logical mind.

She just didn't have it anymore. And reality was no longer entirely there for her. Some things were real and some things were not real. And she didn't know which was which.

Do *you*, for that matter, know what's real and what isn't?

(Digression: woke up from sleep once in middle of day. Window open. Everything bright and clear. And normal. Except that, a few inches away from me, resting half on my pillow and half off, was this young girl's severed head. I could see the ragged edges of skin where her neck ended. She was a blonde, hair in ringlets. Very fair skin. Fine-boned. Eyes closed. No blood. I couldn't swallow. I was blinking wildly. Told myself: not *real*. It'll go away soon. And I was right. Finally, I began to see through it. Could see the wall through the girl's cheeks. Thing faded right out as I watched. Then I went back to sleep.)

So what's real and what isn't? Dammit, baby, I don't even know what's real in this *story*, let alone in the life outside. Your life and my life and what used to be Laurie's life. Is a shadow real? You better believe it.

As Captain Queeg said, I kid you not. (Ha!)

So Laurie walks to work on Tuesday. Stepping on morning shadows, which are the same as afternoon shadows, except not as skinny, but all part of the same central day's primary shadowbody.

She gets to the bank and goes in and says a mousey good morning and hangs up her skinny sweater (like an afternoon shadow) and sits down at her always neat desk and picks up her account book and begins to do her day's work with figures. Cool. Logical. Precise. (But she's losing her senses!)

At lunchtime she goes out alone across the street to a small coffee shop (Andy's) and orders an egg salad sandwich on wheat and hot tea to drink (no sugar).

After lunch she goes back across the street to the bank and works until it closes, then puts on her sweater and walks home to her small apartment.

Once inside, she goes to the fridge for an apple and some milk.

Which is when Alan comes in. Bleeding. In white buckskins, with blood staining the shoulder area on the right side.

"He was fast," says Alan quietly. "Fast with a gun."

"But you *killed* him?" asks Laurie.

"Yes, I killed him," says Alan. And he gives her a tight, humorless smile.

"That shoulder will need tending," she said. (I'm changing this to past tense; says to said, does to did.) "It's beyond my capability. You need a doctor."

"A doc won't help," he said. "I'll just ride on through. I can make it."

"If you say so." No argument. Laurie never argued with anybody. Never in her life.

Alan staggered, fell to his knees in the middle of Laurie's small living room.

"Can I help . . . in *any* way at all?"

He shook his head. (The pain had him and he could no longer talk.)

"I'm going to the store for milk." she said. "I have apples here, but no milk."

He nodded at this. Blood was flecking his lower lip and he looked gray and gaunt. But he was still very handsome—and, for all Laurie knew, the whole thing could be an act.

She left him in the apartment and went out, taking the hall elevator down. (Laurie lived on floor three, or did I tell you that already? If I didn't, now you know.)

At the bottom ole Humphrey was there. Needed a shave. Wary of eye. Coat tight-buttoned, collar up. Cigarette burning in one corner of his mouth. (Probably a Chesterfield.) Ole Humph.

"What are you doing here?" Laurie asked.

"He's somewhere in this building," Humph told her. "I *know* he's in this building."

"You mean the Fat Man?"

"Yeah," he said around the cigarette. "He's on the island. I got the word. I'll find him."

"I'm not involved," Laurie said.

"No," Humph said, smoke curling past his glittery, intense eyes. "You're not involved."

"I'm going after milk," she said.

"Nobody's stopping you."

She walked out to the street and headed for the nearest grocer. Block and a half away. Convenient when you needed milk.

Fay was waiting near the grocer's in a taxi with the engine running. Coronado Cab Company. (I don't know what their rates are. You can find that out.)

"I'm just godawful scared!" Fay said, tears in her eyes. "I have to get across the bridge, but I can't do it alone."

"What do you mean?" Laurie was confused.

"He'll drive us," Fay said, nodding toward the cabbie, who was reading a racing form. (Bored.) "But I need someone *with* me. Another woman. To keep me from screaming."

"That's an odd thing to be concerned about," said Laurie. "I never scream in taxis."

"I didn't either—until this whole nightmare happened to me. But now . . ." Fay's eyes were wild, desperate-looking. "*Will* you ride across the bridge with me? I'm sure I'll be able to make it alone once we're across the bridge."

Fay looked beautiful, but her blonde hair was badly mussed and one shoulder strap of her lacy slip (all she wore!) was missing—revealing the lovely creamed upper slope of her breasts. (And they *were* lovely.)

"He'll be on the island soon," Fay told Laurie. "He's about halfway across. I need to double back to lose him." She smiled. Brave smile. "Believe me, I wouldn't ask you to be with me if I didn't *need* you."

"If I go, will you pay my fare back across, including the bridge toll?"

"I'll give you this ten-carat diamond I found in the jungle," said the distraught blonde, dropping the perfect stone into the palm of Laurie's right hand. "It's worth ten times the price of this cab!"

"How do I know it's real?"

"You'll just have to trust me."

Laurie held up the stone. It rayed light on her serious face. She nodded. "All right, I'll go."

And she climbed into the cab.

"Holiday Inn, San Diego," Fay said to the bored driver. "Quickly. Every second counts."

"They got speed limits, lady," the cabbie told her in a scratchy voice. "And I don't break speed limits. If that don't suit you, get out and walk."

Fay said nothing more to him. He grunted sourly and put the car in gear.

They'd reached the exact middle of the long blue

bridge when they saw him. Even the driver saw him. He stopped the cab. "Holy shit," he said quietly. "Will you look at *that*?"

Laurie gasped. She knew he'd be big, but the actual sight of him shocked and amazed her.

Fay ducked down, pressing close to the floor between seats. "Has he seen me?"

"I don't think so," said Laurie. "He's still heading toward the island."

"Then go *on*!" Fay agonized to the cabbie. "Keep driving!"

"Okay, lady," said the cabbie. "But if *he's* after you, I'd say you got no more chance than snow in a furnace."

Laurie could still see him when they reached the other side of the bridge. He was just coming out of the water on the island side. A little Coronado crowd had gathered to watch him, and he stepped on several of them getting ashore.

"You know how to find the Holiday Inn?" Fay asked the driver.

"Hell, lady, if I don't know where the Holiday is *I* should be in the back and you should be drivin' this lousy tub!"

So he took them straight there.

In front of the Holiday Inn, Fay scrambled out, said nothing, and ran inside.

"Who pays me?" asked the cabbie.

"I suppose I'm elected," said Laurie. She dropped the jungle diamond into his hand. He looked carefully at it.

"This'll do." He grinned for the first time (maybe in years). He juggled the stone in his hand. "It's the real McCoy."

"I'm glad," said Laurie.

"You want to go back across?"

Laurie looked pensive. "I *thought* I did. But now I've changed my mind. Screw the bank! Take me downtown."

And they headed for—wait a minute. I'm messing this up. I'm *sure* Laurie didn't say, "Screw the bank." She just wouldn't phrase it that way. Ernest would say, "Screw the bank," but not Laurie. And Ernest wasn't in the cab. I'm sure of that. Besides, she was finished at the bank for the day, wasn't she? So the whole—wait! I've got this part all wrong.

Let's just pick it up with her, with Laurie, at the curb in front of the U.S. Grant Hotel in downtown San Diego, buying a paper from a dwarf who sold them because he couldn't do anything else for a living.

Gary walked up to her as she fumbled in her purse for change. He waited until she'd paid the dwarf before asking, "Do you have a gun?"

"Not in my purse," she said.

"Where then?"

"My brother carries one. Ernest has a gun. He's a police officer here in the city."

"He with you?"

"No. He's on duty. Somewhere in the greater San Diego area. I wouldn't know how to contact him. And, frankly, I very much doubt that he'd hand his gun over to a stranger."

"I'm no stranger," said Gary. "You both know me."

She stared at him. "That's true," she said. "But still . . ."

"Forget it," he said, looking weary. "A policeman's handgun is no good. I need a machine gun. With a tripod and full belts. That's what I really need to hold them off with."

"There's an Army Surplus store farther down Broadway," she told him. "They might have what you need."

"Yep. Might."

"Who are you fighting?"

"Franco's troops. They're holding a position on the bridge."

"That's funny," she said. "I just came off the bridge and I didn't see any troops."

"Did you take the Downtown or the South 5 off-ramp?"

"Downtown."

"That explains it. They're on the South 5 side."

He looked tan and very lean, wearing his scuffed leather jacket and the down-brim felt hat. A tall man. Raw-boned. With a good honest American face. A lot of people loved him.

"Good luck," she said to him. "I hope you find what you're after."

"Thanks," he said, giving her a weary grin. Tired boy in a man's body.

"Maybe it's death you're *really* after," she said. "I think you ought to consider that as a subliminal motivation."

"Sure," he said. "Sure, I'll consider it." And he took off in a long, loping stride—leaving her with the dwarf who'd overheard their entire conversation but had no comments to make.

"Please, would you help me?" Little girl voice. A dazzle of blonde-white. Hair like white fire. White dress and white shoes. It was Norma Jean. Looking shattered. Broken. Eyes all red in the corners. Veined, exhausted eyes.

"But what can I do?" Laurie asked.

Norma Jean shook her blonde head slowly. Confused. Little girl lost. "They're honest-to-Christ trying to kill me," she said. "No one believes that."

"I believe it," said Laurie.

"Thanks." Wan smile. "They think I *know* stuff . . . ever since Jack and I . . . The sex thing, I mean."

"You went to bed with Jack Kennedy?"

"Yes, yes, yes! And that started them after me. Dumb, huh? Now they're very close and I need help. I don't know where to run anymore. *Can* you help me?"

"No," said Laurie. "If people are determined to kill you they will. They really will."

Norma Jean nodded. "Yeah. Sure. I guess they will okay. I mean, Jeez! Who can stop them?"

"Ever kick a man in the balls?" Laurie asked. (*Hell* of a thing to ask!)

"Not really. I sort of tried once."

"Well, just wait for them. And when they show up you kick 'em in the balls. All right?"

"Yes, yes, in the *balls!* I'll do it!" She was suddenly shiny-bright with blonde happiness. A white dazzle of dress and hair and teeth.

Laurie was glad, because you couldn't help liking Norma Jean. She thought about food. She was hungry. Time for din-din. She entered the coffee shop inside the lobby of the Grant (Carl's Quickbites), picked out a stool near the end of the counter, sat down with her paper.

She was reading about the ape when Clark came in, wearing a long frock coat and flowing tie. His vest was red velvet. He walked up to the counter, snatched her paper, riffled hastily through the pages.

"Nothing in here about the renegades," he growled. "Guess nobody *cares* how many boats get through. An outright shame, I say!"

"I'm sorry you're disturbed," she said. "May I have my paper back?"

"Sure." And he gave her a crooked smile of apology. Utterly charming. A rogue to the tips of his polished boots. Dashing. Full of vigor.

"What do you plan to do now?" she asked.

"Nothing," he said. "Frankly, I don't give a damn *who* wins the war! Blue or Gray. I just care about living through it." He scowled. "Still—when a bunch of scurvy renegades come gunrunning by night . . . well, I just get a little upset about it. Where are the patrol boats?"

She smiled faintly. "I don't know a thing about patrol boats."

"No, I guess you don't, pretty lady." And he kissed her cheek.

"Your mustache tickles," she said. "And you have bad breath."

This amused him. "So I've been told!"

After he left, the waitress came to take her order. "Is the sea bass fresh?"

"You bet."

Laurie ordered sea bass. "Dinner, or à la carte?" asked the waitress. She was chewing gum in a steady, circular rhythm.

"Dinner. Thousand on the salad. Baked potato. Chives, but no sour cream."

"We got just butter."

"Butter will be fine," said Laurie. "And iced tea to drink. *Without* lemon."

"Gotcha," said the waitress.

Laurie was reading the paper again when a man in forest green sat down on the stool directly next to her. His mustache was smaller than Clark's. Thinner and smaller, but it looked very correct on him.

"This seat taken?" he asked.

"No, I'm quite alone."

"King Richard's alone," he said bitterly. "In Leopold's bloody hands, somewhere in Austria. Chained to a castle wall like an animal! I could find him, but I don't have enough men to attempt a rescue. I'd give my sword arm to free him!"

"They call him the Lion-Hearted, don't they?"

The man in green nodded. He wore a feather in his cap, and had a longbow slung across his chest. "That's because he has the heart of a lion. There's not a man in the kingdom with half his courage."

"What about *you?*"

His smile dazzled. "Me? Why, mum, I'm just a poor archer. From the king's forest."

She looked pensive. "I'd say you were a bit more than that."

"Perhaps." His eyes twinkled merrily. "A *bit* more."

"Are you going to order?" she asked. "They have fresh sea bass."

"Red meat's what I need. Burger. Blood-rare."

The waitress, taking his order, frowned at him. "I'm sorry, mister, but you'll have to hang that thing over there." She pointed to a clothes rack. "We don't allow longbows at the counter."

He complied with the request, returning to wolf down his Carlburger while Laurie nibbled delicately at her fish. He finished long before she did, flipped a tip to the counter from a coinsack at his waist.

"I must away," he told Laurie. And he kissed her hand. Nice gesture. Very typical of him.

The waitress was pleased with the tip: a gold piece from the British Isles. "Some of these bums really stiff you," she said, pocketing the coin. "They come in, order half the menu, end up leaving me a lousy *dime!* Hell, I couldn't make it at this lousy job without decent tips. Couldn't make the rent. I'd have my rosy rear kicked out." She noticed that Laurie flushed at this.

On the street, which was Broadway, outside the U.S. Grant, Laurie thought she might as well take in a flick. They had a neat new cop-killer thing with Clint Eastwood playing half a block down. Violent, but done with lots of style. Eastwood directing himself. She could take a cab back to Coronado after seeing the flick.

It was dark now. Tuesday's shadow had retired for the week.

The movie cost five dollars for one adult. But Laurie didn't mind. She never regretted money spent on films. Never.

Marl was in the lobby, looking sullen when Laurie came in. He was wearing a frayed black turtleneck sweater, standing by the popcorn machine, with his hair thinning and his waist thick and swollen over his belt. He looked seedy.

"You should reduce," she told him.

"Let 'em use a double for the long shots," he said. "Just shoot my face in close-up."

"Even your face is puffy. You've developed jowls."

"What business is it of yours?"

"I admire your talent. Respect you. I hate to see you waste your natural resources."

"What do *you* know about natural resources?" he growled. "You're just a dumb broad."

"And you are crude," she said tightly.

"Nobody asked you to tell me I should reduce. Nobody."

"It's a plain fact. I'm stating the obvious."

"Did you ever work the docks?" he asked her.

"Hardly." She sniffed.

"Well, lady, crude is what you get twenty-four hours out of twenty-four when you're on the docks. And I been there. Or the police barracks. Ever been in the police barracks?"

"My brother has, but I have not."

"Piss on your brother!"

"Fine." She nodded. "*Be* crude. Be sullen. Be overweight. You'll simply lose your audience."

"My audience can go to hell," he said.

She wanted no more to do with him, and entered the theater. It was intermission. The overheads were on.

How many carpeted theater aisles had she walked down in her life? Thousands. Literally thousands. It was always a heady feeling, walking down the long aisle between rows, with the carpet soft and reassuring beneath her shoes. Toward a seat that promised adventure. It never failed to stir her soul, this magic moment of anticipation. Just before the lights dimmed and the curtains slipped whispering back from the big white screen.

Laurie took a seat on the aisle. No one next to her. Most of the row empty. She always sat on the aisle down close. Most people like being farther back. Close, she could be swept *into* the screen, actually be part of the gleaming, glowing action.

A really large man seated himself next to her. Weathered face under a wide Stetson. Wide jaw. Wide chest. He took off the Stetson and the corners of his eyes were sun-wrinkled. His voice was a rasp.

"I like to watch ole Clint," he said. "Ole Clint don't monkey around with a lot of fancy-antsy trick shots and up-your-nostril angles. Just does it straight and mean."

"I agree," she said. "But I call it art. A basic, primary art."

"Well, missy," said the big, wide-chested man, "I been in this game a lotta years, and *art* is a word I kinda like to avoid. Fairies use it a lot. When a man goes after *art* up there on the screen he usually comes up with horse shit." He grunted. "And I know a lot about horse shit."

"I'm sure you do."

"My Daddy had me on a bronc 'fore I could walk. Every time I fell off he just hauled me right back aboard. And I got the dents in my head to prove it."

The houselights were dimming slowly to black.

"Picture's beginning," she said. "I never talk during a film."

"Me neither," he said. "I may fart, but I never talk." And his laughter was a low rumble.

Laurie walked out halfway through the picture. This man disturbed her, and she just couldn't concentrate. Also, as I have told you (and you can see for yourself by now), she was losing her mind.

So Laurie left the theater.

Back in her apartment (in Coronado), Judy was there, looking for a slipper. Alan had gone, but Judy didn't know where; she hadn't seen him.

"What color is it?" asked Laurie.

"Red. Bright red. With spangles."

"Where's the *other* one?"

"In my bedroom. I just wore one, and it slipped off."

"What are you doing in this apartment?"

Judy stared at her. "That's obvious. I'm looking for my slipper."

"No, I mean—why did you come *here* to look for it? For what reason?"

"Is this U-210?"

"No, that's one floor below."

"Well, honey, I thought this was U-210 when I

came in. Door was open—and all these roach pits look just alike."

"I've never seen a roach anywhere in this complex," said Laurie. "I'm sure you—"

"Doesn't matter. All that matters is my slipper's gone."

"It can't be *gone*. Not if you were wearing it when you arrived."

"Then *you* find it, hotshot!" said Judy. She flopped loosely into the green reclining chair by the window. "You got a helluva view from here."

"Yes, it's nice. Especially at night."

"You can see all the lights shining on the water," said Judy. "Can't see doodly-poop from my window. You must pay plenty for this view. How much you pay?"

"Four-forty per month, including utilities," Laurie said.

Judy jumped to her stockinged feet. "That's twenty *less* than I'm paying! I'm being ripped off!"

"Well, you should complain to the manager. Maybe he'll give you a reduction."

"Nuts," sighed Judy. "I just want my slipper."

Laurie found it in the kitchen under the table. Judy could not, for the life of her, figure out how it got into the kitchen.

"I didn't even go *in* there. I hate sinks and dishes!"

"I'm glad I was able to find it for you."

"Yeah—you're Little Miss Findit, okay. Little Miss Hunt-and-Findit."

"You sound resentful."

"That's because I hate people who go around finding things other people lose."

"You can leave now," Laurie said flatly. She'd had enough of Judy.

"Can you lay some reds on me?"

"I have no idea what you mean." (And she really *didn't!*)

"Aw, forget it. You wouldn't know a red if one up and *bit* you. Honey, you're something for the books!"

And Judy limped out wearing her spangled slipper.

Laurie shut the door and locked it. Then she took a shower and went to bed.

And slept until Saturday.

I know, I know . . . what happened to Wednesday, Thursday, and Friday, *right*? Well, it's like that with crazy people; they sleep for days at a stretch. The brain's all fogged. Doesn't function. Normally, the brain is like an alarm clock—it wakes you when you sleep too long. But Laurie's clock was haywire; all the cogs and springs were missing.

So she woke up on Saturday.

In a panic.

She knew all about Saturday's shadow, and each Friday night, she carefully drew the drapes across the window, making sure it couldn't get in. She never left the place, dawn to dark, on a Saturday. Ate all her meals from the fridge, watched movies on TV, and read the papers. If the phone rang, she never answered it. Not that anyone but Ernest ever called her. And he knew enough not to call her on Saturday. (Shadows can slip into a room through an open telephone line.)

But now, here it was Saturday, and the windows were wide open, with the drapes pulled back like skin on a wound with the shadow in the middle.

Of the apartment.

In the middle of *her* apartment.

Not moving. Just lying there, dark and venomous and deadly. It had entered while she slept.

Laurie stared at it in horror. Nobody had to tell her it was Saturday's shadow; she recognized it instantly.

The catch was (Ha!) it was between her and the door. If she could reach the door before it touched her, tore at her, she could get into the hallway and stay there, huddled against the wall, until it left.

There were no windows in the hall. It couldn't follow her there.

Problem: how to reach the door? The shadow wasn't moving, but that didn't mean it *couldn't* move, fast as an owl blinks. It would cut off her retreat, and when its shark-sharp edges touched her skin she'd be slashed . . . and eaten alive.

Which was the really lousy part. You *knew* it was devouring you while it was doing it. Like a snake swallowing a mouse; the mouse always knows what's happening to it.

And Laurie was a mouse. All her life, hiding in the dark, dreaming cinema dreams, she'd been a mouse.

And now she was about to be devoured.

She knew she couldn't stay where she was—because it would come and get her if she stayed where she was. The sofa folded out to make a studio bed, and that's where she was.

With the shadow all around her. Black and silent and terrible.

Waiting.

Very slowly . . . very, very slowly, she got up.

It hadn't moved.

Not yet.

She wished, desperately, that ole Humph was here. Or Gary. Or Alan. Or Clark. Or Clint. Or even Big John. They could deal with shadows because they were shadow people. They moved in shadowy power across the screen. *They* could deal with Saturday's shadow. It couldn't hurt *them* . . . kill *them* . . . eat *them* alive . . .

I'll jump across, she (probably) told herself. It doesn't extend more than four feet in front of me— so I should be able to stand on the bed and *leap* over it, then be out the door before it can—Oh, God! It's *moving!* Widening. Coming toward the bed . . . flowing out to cover the gap between the rug and the door.

Look how *swiftly* it moves! Sliding . . . oiling across the rug . . . rippling like the skin of some dark sea-thing . . .

Laurie stood up, ready to jump.

There was only a thin strip of unshadowed wood left to land on near the door. If she missed it the shadow-teeth would sink deep into her flesh and she'd—

"Don't!" Ernest said from the doorway. He had his .38 Police Special in his right hand. "You'll never make it," he told Laurie.

"My God, Ernest—what are you doing with the gun?" Note of genuine hysteria in her voice. Understandable.

"I can save you," Ernest told her. "Only *I* can save you."

And I shot her. Full load.

The bullets banged and slapped her back against the wall, the way Alan's bullets had slapped Palance back into those wooden barrels at the saloon.

I was fast. Fast with a gun.

Laurie flopped down, gouting red from many places. But it didn't hurt. No pain for my sis. I'd seen to that. I'd saved her.

I left her there, angled against the wall (in blood), one arm bent under her, staring at me with round glassy dead eyes, the strap of her nightgown all slipped down, revealing the lovely creamed upper slope of her breasts.

Had *she* seen that in the cab near the grocer's, or had I seen that?

Was it Ernest who'd talked to Gary outside the U.S. Grant?

It's very difficult to keep it all cool and precise and logical. Which is vital. Because if everything isn't cool and precise and logical, nothing makes any sense. Not me. Not Laurie. Not Ernest. No part. Any sense.

Not even Saturday's shadow.

Now . . . let's see. Let's see now. *I'm* not Laurie. Not anymore. Can't be. She's all dead. I guess I was always Ernest—but police work can eat at you like a shadow (Ha!) and people yell at you, and suddenly you want to fire your .38 Police Special at something. You *need* to do this. It's very vital and important to discharge your weapon.

And you can't kill Saturday's shadow. Any fool knows that.

So you kill your sister instead.

To save her.

But now, right now, I'm not Ernest anymore either. I'm just *me*. Whoever or whatever's left inside after Laurie and Mama and Ernest have gone. That's who I am: what's left.

The residual me.

Oh, there's one final thing I should tell you.

Where I am now (Secret!) it can't ever reach me.

All the doors are locked.

And the windows are closed. With drawn curtains.

To keep it out.

You see, I took her away from it.

It really wanted her.

(Ha! Fooled it!)

It hates me. It really *hates* me.

But it can't *do* anything.

To get even.

For taking away Laurie.

Not if I just

stay

and stay and stay

```
                    here
I'm
                              safe
where
                    it can't
ever
find
me (Mama)
me (Laurie)
me (Ernest)
me!
```

This one has been printed in the regional anthology, A Treasury of American Horror Stories, with fiction chosen for each state. My story was selected to represent Montana.

"Lonely Train A'Comin'" has an unusual history. In the winter of 1980 I awoke from a dream with the image of a cowboy waiting at a small, abandoned rail depot on the flat Montana plains. A distant mountain range loomed in the background. The cowboy was waiting for a particular train; his sister had died on the train and he was determined to board it and avenge her death.

I had never been to Montana, but later I was cosmically drawn to go there. When I visited the state I was shocked to find a small, abandoned rail depot (Ross Fork) on the flat plains, with a mountain range (the Little Belt) in the background. What I found precisely matched my dream. An eerie feeling. Had I actually been here before—perhaps in another lifetime?

The story you are about to read is literally the stuff of dreams put to paper.

It may be the most frightening tale I've written to date.

LONELY TRAIN A'COMIN'

(Written: December 1980)

> *Lonely train a'comin'*
> *I can hear its cry*
> *Lonely train from nowhere*
> *Takin' me to die*
>   —folk ballad fragment, circa 1881

At Bitterroot, Ventry waited.

Bone-cold, huddled on the narrow wooden bench against the paint-blistered wall of the depot, the collar of his fleece-lined coat turned up against the chill Montana winds blowing in from the Plains, he waited for the train. Beneath the wide brim of a work-blackened Stetson, sweat-stained along the headband, his eyes were intense, the gunmetal color of blued steel. Hard lines etched into the mahogany of his face spoke of deep-snow winters and glare-sun summers; his hands, inside heavy leather work gloves, were calloused and blunt-fingered from punishing decades of ranch work.

Autumn was dying, and the sky over Bitterroot was gray with the promise of winter. This would be the train's last run before snow closed down the route. Ventry had calculated it with consummate patience and precision. He prided himself on his stubborn practicality, and he had earned a reputation among his fellow ranchers as a hard-headed realist.

Paul Ventry was never an emotional man. Even at his wife's death he had remained stolid, rock-like in his grief. If it was Sarah's time to die, then so be it. He had loved her, but she was gone and he was alone and that was fact. Ventry accepted. Sarah had wanted children, but things hadn't worked out that way. So they had each other, and the ranch, and the open Montana sky—and that had been enough.

Amy's death was not the same. Losing his sister had been wrong. He did *not* accept it. Which was why he was doing this, why he was here. In his view, he had no other choice.

* * *

He had been unable to pinpoint the train's exact arrival, but he was certain it would pass Bitterroot within a seven-day period. Thus, he had brought along enough food and water to last a week. His supplies were almost depleted now, but they could be stretched through two more days and nights if need be; Ventry was not worried.

The train *would* be here.

It was lonely at Bitterroot. The stationmaster's office was boarded over, and bars covered the windows. The route into Ross Fork had been dropped from the rail schedule six months ago, and mainline trains bound for Lewistown no longer made the stop. Now the only trains that rattled past were desolate freights, dragging their endless rusted flatcars.

Ventry shifted the holstered axe pressing against his thigh, and unzipping a side pocket on his coat, he took out the thumb-worn postcard. On the picture side, superimposed over a multicolored panoramic shot of a Plains sunset, was the standard Montana salutation:

GREETINGS FROM
THE BIG SKY COUNTRY!

And on the reverse, Amy's last words. How many times had he read her hastily scrawled message, mailed from this depot almost a year ago to the day?

> Dear Paulie,
>   I'll write a long letter, I promise, when I get to Lewistown, but the train came early so I just have time, dear brother, to send you my love. And don't you worry about your little kid sister because life for me is going to be super with my new job!
>
> Luv and XXXXXXX,
Amy

And she had added a quick P.S. at the bottom of the card:

> You should see this beautiful old train! Didn't know they still ran steam locomotives like this one! Gotta rush—'cuz it's waiting for me!

Ventry's mouth tightened, and he slipped the card back into his coat, thinking about Amy's smiling eyes, about how much a part of his life she'd been. Hell, she was a better sheep rancher than half the valley men on Big Moccasin! But, once grown, she'd wanted city life, a city job, a chance to meet city men.

"Just you watch me, Paulie," she had told him, her face shining with excitement. "This lil' ole job in Lewistown is only the beginning. The firm has a branch in Helena, and I'm sure I can get transferred there within a year. You're gonna be real proud of your sis. I'll *make* you proud!"

She'd never had the chance. She'd never reached Lewistown. Amy had stepped aboard the train . . . and vanished.

Yet people don't vanish. It was a word Paul refused to accept. He had driven each bleak mile of the rail line from Bitterroot to Lewistown, combing every inch of terrain for a sign, a clue, a scrap of clothing. He'd spent two months along that route. And had found nothing.

Ventry posted a public reward for information leading to Amy's whereabouts. Which is when Tom Hallendorf contacted him.

Hallendorf was a game warden stationed at King's Hill Pass in the Lewis and Clark National Forest. He phoned Ventry, telling him about what he'd found near an abandoned spur track in the Little Belt range.

Bones. *Human* bones.

And a ripped, badly stained red leather purse.

The empty purse had belonged to Amy. Forensic

evidence established the bones as part of her skeleton.

What had happened up there in those mountains?

The district sheriff, John Longbow, blamed it on a "weirdo." A roving tramp.

"Dirt-plain obvious, Mr. Ventry," the sheriff had said to him. "He killed her for what she had in the purse. You admit she was carryin' several hundred in cash. Which is, begging your pardon, a damn fool thing to do!"

But that didn't explain the picked bones.

"Lotta wild animals in the mountains," the lawman had declared. "After this weirdo done 'er in he just left her layin' there—and, well, probably a bear come onto 'er. It's happened before. We've found bones up in that area more than once. Lot of strange things in the Little Belt." And the sheriff had grinned. "As a boy, with the tribe, I heard me stories that'd curl your hair. It's wild country."

The railroad authorities were adamant about the mystery train. "No steamers in these parts," they told him. "Nobody runs 'em anymore."

But Ventry was gut-certain that such a train existed, and that Amy had died on it. Someone had cold-bloodedly murdered his sister and dumped her body in the mountains.

He closed down the ranch, sold his stock, and

devoted himself to finding out who that someone was.

He spent an entire month at the main library in Lewistown, poring through old newspaper files, copying names, dates, case details.

A pattern emerged. Ventry found that a sizable number of missing persons who had vanished in this area of the state over the past decade had been traveling by *rail*. And several of them had disappeared along the same basic route Amy had chosen.

Ventry confronted John Longbow with his research.

"An' just who is this killer?" the sheriff asked.

"Whoever owns the steamer. Some freak rail buff. Rich enough to run his own private train, and crazy enough to kill the passengers who get on board."

"Look, Mr. Ventry, how come nobody's *seen* this fancy steam train of yours?"

"Because the rail disappearances have happened at night, at remote stations off the main lines. He never runs the train by daylight. Probably keeps it up in the mountains. Maybe in one of the old mine shafts. Uses off-line spur tracks. Comes rolling into a small depot like Bitterroot *between* the regular passenger trains and picks up whoever's on the platform."

The sheriff had grunted at this, his eyes tight on Paul Ventry's face.

"And there's a definite *cycle* to these disappearances." Ventry continued. "According to what I've put together, the train makes its night runs at specific intervals. About a month apart, spring through fall. Then it's hidden away in the Little Belt each winter when the old spur tracks are snowed over. I've done a lot of calculation on this, and I'm certain that the train makes its final run during the first week of November—which means you've still got time to stop it."

The sheriff had studied Paul Ventry for a long, silent moment. Then he had sighed deeply. "That's an interesting theory, Mr. Ventry, *real* interesting. But . . . it's also about as wild and unproven as any I've heard—and I've heard me a few. Now, it's absolute natural that you're upset at your sister's death, but you've let things get way out of whack. I figger you'd best go on back to your ranch and try an' forget about poor little Amy. Put her out of your mind. She's gone. And there's nothing you can do about that."

"We'll see," Ventry had said, a cutting edge to his voice. "We'll see what I can do."

*   *   *

Ventry's plan was simple. Stop the train, board it, and kill the twisted son of a bitch who owned it. Put a .45 slug in his head. Blow his fucking brains out—and blow his train up with him!

I'll put an end to this if no one else will, Ventry promised himself. And I've got the tools to do it.

He slipped the carefully wrapped gun rig from his knapsack, unfolded its oiled covering, and withdrew his grandfather's long-barreled frontier Colt from its worn leather holster. The gun was a family treasure. Its bone handle was cracked and yellowed by the years, but the old Colt was still in perfect firing order. His granddaddy had worn this rig, had defended his mine on the Comstock against claim jumpers with this gun. It was fitting and proper that it be used on the man who'd killed Amy.

Night was settling over Bitterroot. The fiery orange disc of sun had dropped below the Little Belt Mountains, and the sky was gray slate along the horizon.

Time to strap on the gun. Time to get ready for the train.

It's coming tonight! Lord God, I can feel it out there in the gathering dark, thrumming the rails. I can feel it in my blood and bones.

Well, then, come ahead, god damn you, whoever you are.

I'm ready for you.

Ten P.M. Eleven. Midnight.

It came at midnight.

Rushing toward Bitterroot, clattering in fierce-wheeled thunder, its black bulk sliding over the track in the ash-dark Montana night like an immense, segmented snake—with a single yellow eye probing the terrain ahead.

Ventry heard it long before he saw it. The rails sang and vibrated around him as he stood tall and resolute in mid-track, a three-cell silver flashlight in his right hand, his heavy sheepskin coat buttoned over the gun at his belt.

Have to flag it down. With the depot closed it won't make a stop. No passengers. It's looking for live game, and it doesn't figure on finding any here at Bitterroot.

Surprise! *I'm* here. *I'm* alive. Like Amy. Like all the others. Man alone at night. Needs a ride. Climb aboard, partner. Make yourself to home. Drink? Somethin' to eat? What's your pleasure?

My pleasure is your death—and the death of your freak train, mister!

That's my pleasure.

* * *

It was in sight now, coming fast, slicing a bright round hole in the night—and its sweeping locomotive beam splashed Paul Ventry's body with a pale luminescence.

The rancher swung his flash up, then down, in a high arc. Again. And again.

Stop, you bastard! *Stop!*

The train began slowing.

Sparks showered from the massive driving wheels as the train reduced speed. Slowing . . . slower . . . steel shrieking against steel. An easing of primal force.

It was almost upon him.

Like a great shining insect, the locomotive towered high and black over Ventry, its tall stack shutting out the stars. The rusted tip of the train's thrusting metal cowcatcher gently nudged the toe of his right boot as the incredible night mammoth slid to a final grinding stop.

Now the train was utterly motionless, breathing its white steam into the cold dark, waiting for him as he had waited for it.

Ventry felt a surge of exultation fire his body. He'd been right! It was here—and he was prepared to destroy it, to avenge his sister. It was his destiny. He felt no fear, only a cool and certain confidence in his ability to kill.

A movement at the corner of his eye. Someone was waving to him from the far end of the train, from the last coach, the train's only source of light. All of the other passenger cars were dark and blind-windowed; only the last car glowed hazy yellow.

Ventry eased around the breathing locomotive, his boots crunching loudly in the cindered gravel as he moved over the roadbed.

He glanced up at the locomotive's high, double-windowed cabin, but the engineer was lost behind opaque, soot-colored glass. Ventry kept moving steadily forward, toward the distant figure, passing along the linked row of silent, lightless passenger cars. The train bore no markings; it was a uniform, unbroken black.

Ventry squinted at the beckoning figure. Was it the killer himself, surprised and delighted at finding another passenger at this deserted night station?

He slipped the flash into his shoulder knapsack, and eased a hand inside his coat, gripping the warm bone handle of the .45 at his waist. You've had one surprise tonight, mister. Get ready for another.

Then, abruptly, he stopped, heart pounding. Ventry recognized the beckoning figure. Impossible! An illusion. Just *couldn't* be. Yet there she was, smiling, waving to him.

"Amy!" Ventry rushed toward his sister in a stumbling run.

But she was no longer in sight when he reached the dimly illumined car. Anxiously, he peered into one of the smoke-yellowed windows. A figure moved hazily inside.

"Amy!" He shouted her name again, mounting the coach steps.

The moment Ventry's boot touched the car's upper platform the train jolted into life. Ventry was thrown to his knees as the coach lurched violently forward.

The locomotive's big driving wheels sparked against steel, gaining a solid grip on the rails as the train surged powerfully from Bitterroot Station.

As Paul Ventry entered the coach, the door snap-locked behind him. Remote-control device. To make sure I won't leave by the rear exit. No matter. He'd expected that. He could get out when he had to, when he was ready. He'd come prepared for whatever this madman had in mind.

But Ventry had *not* been prepared for the emotional shock of seeing Amy. Had he *really* seen her? *Was* it his sister?

No. Of course not. He'd been tricked by his subconscious mind. The fault was his. A lapse in concentration, in judgment.

But *someone* had waved to him—a young girl who looked, at first sight, amazingly like his sister.

Where was she now?

And just where was the human devil who ran this train?

Ventry was alone in the car. To either side of the aisle the rows of richly upholstered green velvet seats were empty. A pair of ornate, scrolled gas lamps, mounted above the arched doorway, cast flickering shadows over antique brass fittings and a hand-carved wood ceiling. Green brocade draped the windows.

He didn't know much about trains, but Ventry knew this one *had* to be pre-1900. And probably restored by the rich freak who owned it. Plush was the word.

Well, it was making its last run; Ventry would see to that.

He pulled the flash from his shoulder pack, snapping on the bright beam as he moved warily forward.

The flashlight proved unnecessary. As Ventry entered the second car (door unlocked; guess he doesn't mind my going *forward*) the overhead gas lamps sputtered to life, spreading their pale yellow illumination over the length of the coach.

Again, the plush velvet seats were empty. Except for one. The last seat at the far end of the car. A woman was sitting there, stiff and motionless in the dim light, her back to Ventry.

As he moved toward her, she turned slowly to face him.

By Christ, it *was* Amy!

Paul Ventry rushed to her, sudden tears stinging his eyes. Fiercely, he embraced his sister; she was warm and solid in his arms. "Oh, Sis, I'm so glad you're *alive!*"

But there was no sound from her lips. No words. No emotion. She was rigid in his embrace.

Ventry stepped away from her. "What's wrong? I don't understand why you—"

His words were choked off. Amy had leaped from the seat, cat-quick, to fasten long pale fingers around his throat. Her thumbs dug like sharp spikes into the flesh of Ventry's neck.

He reeled back, gasping for breath, clawing at the incredibly strong hands. He couldn't break her grip.

Amy's face was changing. The flesh was falling away in gummy wet ribbons, revealing raw white bone! In the deep sockets of Amy's grinning skull her eyes were hot red points of fire.

Ventry's right hand found the butt of the Colt, and he dragged the gun free of its holster. Swinging the barrel toward Amy, he fired directly into the melting horror of her face.

His bullets drilled round, charred holes in the grinning skull, but Amy's fingers—now all raw bone and slick gristle—maintained their death grip at his throat.

Axe! Use the axe!

In a swimming red haze, Ventry snapped the short-handled woodsman's axe free of his belt. And swung it sharply downward, neatly removing Amy's head at shoulder level. The cleanly severed skull rolled into the aisle at his feet.

Yet, horribly, the bony fingers increased their deadly pressure.

Ventry's sight blurred; the coach wavered. As the last of his oxygen was cut off, he was on the verge of blacking out.

Desperately, he swung the blade again, missing the Amy-thing entirely. The axe buried itself in thick green velvet.

The train thrashed; its whistle shrieked wildly in the rushing night, a cry of pain—and the seat rippled in agony. Oily black liquid squirted from the sliced velvet.

At Ventry's throat, the bony fingers dropped away.

In numbed shock, he watched his sister's rotting corpse flow down into the seat, melting and mixing with the central train body, bubbling wetly.

Oh, sweet Jesus! Everything's moving! The whole foul train is alive!

And Ventry accepted it. Sick with horror and revulsion, he accepted it. He was a realist, and this thing was real. No fantasy. No dream.

Real.

Which meant he had to kill it. Not the man who owned it, because such a man did not exist. Somehow, the train itself, ancient and rusting in the high mountains, had taken on a sentient life of its own. The molecular components of iron and wood and steel had, over a slow century, transformed themselves into living tissue—and this dark hell-thing had rolled out onto the Montana plains seeking food, seeking flesh to sustain it, sleeping, sated, through the frozen winters, hibernating, then stirring to hungry life again as the greening earth renewed itself.

Lot of strange things in the Little Belt.

Don't think about it, Ventry warned himself. Just do what you came to do: *kill it!* Kill the foul thing. Blow it out of existence!

He carried three explosive charges in his knap-sack, each equipped with a timing device. All right, make your plan! Set one here at the end of the train, another in the middle coach, and plant the final charge in the forward car.

No good. If the thing had the power to animate its dead victims it also had the power to fling off his explosive devices, to rid itself of them as a dog shakes leaves from its coat.

I'll have to go after it the way you go after a snake; to kill a snake, you cut off its head.

So go for the brain.

Go for the engine.

The train had left the main rail system now, and was on a rusted spur track, climbing steeply into the Lit-tle Belt range.

It was taking Ventry into the high mountains. One last meal of warm flesh, then the long winter's sleep.

The train was going home.

Three cars to go.

Axe in hand, Ventry was moving steadily toward the engine, through vacant, gas-lit coaches, won-dering how and when it would attack him again.

Did it know he meant to kill it? Possibly it had no fear of him. God knows it was strong. And no human had ever harmed it in the past. Does the snake fear the mouse?

Maybe it would leave him alone to do his work; maybe it didn't realize how lethal this mouse could be.

But Ventry was wrong.

Swaying in the clattering rush of the train, he was halfway down the aisle of the final coach when the tissue around him rippled into motion. Viscid black bubbles formed on the ceiling of the car, and in the seats. Growing. Quivering. Multiplying.

One by one, the loathsome globes swelled and burst—giving birth to a host of nightmare figures. Young and old. Man, woman, child. Eyes red and angry.

They closed on Ventry in the clicking interior of the hell coach, moving toward him in a rotting tide.

He had seen photos of many of them in the Lewistown library. Vanished passengers, like Amy, devoured and absorbed and now regenerated as fetid ectoplasmic horrors—literal extensions of the train itself.

Ventry knew that he was powerless to stop them. The Amy-thing had proven that.

But he still had the axe, and a few vital seconds before the train-things reached him.

Ventry swung the razored blade left and right,

slashing brutally at seat and floor, cutting deep with each swift blow. Fluid gushed from a dozen gaping wounds; a rubbery mass of coil-like innards, like spilled guts, erupted from the seat to Ventry's right, splashing him with gore.

The train screamed into the Montana night, howling like a wounded beast.

The passenger-things lost form, melting into the aisle.

Now Ventry was at the final door, leading to the coal car directly behind the engine.

It was locked against him.

The train had reached its destination at the top of the spur, was rolling down a side track leading to a deserted mine. Its home. Its cave. Its dark hiding place.

The train would feast now.

Paul Ventry used the last of his strength on the door. Hacking at it. Slashing wildly. Cutting his way through.

Free! In a freezing blast of night wind, Ventry scrambled across the coal tender toward the shining black locomotive.

And reached it.

A heavy, gelatinous membrane separated him

from the control cabin. The membrane pulsed with veined life.

Got to get inside . . . reach the brain of the thing . . .

Ventry drove the blade deep, splitting the veined skin. And burst through into the cabin.

Its interior was a shock to Ventry's senses; he was assailed by a stench so powerful that bile rushed into his throat. He fought back a rising nausea.

Brass and wood and iron had become throbbing flesh. Levers and controls and pressure gauges were coated with a thick, crawling slime. The roof and sides of the cabin were moving.

A huge, red, heart-like mass pulsed and shimmered wetly in the center of the cabin, its sickly crimson glow illuminating his face.

He did not hesitate.

Ventry reached into the knapsack, pulled out an explosive charge, and set the device for manual. All he needed to do was press a metal switch, toss the charge at the heart-thing, and jump from the cabin.

It was over. He'd won!

But before he could act, the entire chamber heaved up in a bubbled, convulsing pincer movement, trapping Ventry like a fly in a web.

He writhed in the jellied grip of the train-thing. The explosive device had been jarred from his grasp.

The axe, too, was lost in the mass of crushing slime-tissue.

Ventry felt sharp pain fire along his back. *Teeth!* The thing had sprouted rows of needled teeth and was starting to eat him alive!

The knapsack; he was still wearing it!

Gasping, dizzy with pain, Ventry plunged his right hand into the sack, closing bloodied fingers around the second explosive device. Pulled it loose, set it ticking.

Sixty seconds.

If he could not fight free in that space of time he'd go up with the train. A far better way to die than being ripped apart and devoured. Death would be a welcome release.

Incredibly, the train-thing seemed to *know* that its life was in jeopardy. Its shocked tissues drew back, cringing away from the ticking explosive charge.

Ventry fell to his knees on the slimed floor.

Thirty seconds.

He saw the sudden gleam of rails to his right, just below him, and he launched himself in a plunging dive through the severed membrane.

Struck ground. Searing pain. Right shoulder. Broken bone.

Hell with it! *Move, damn you, move!*

Ventry rolled over on his stomach, pain lacing his

body. Pushed himself up. Standing now.

Five seconds.

Ventry sprawled forward. *Legs won't support me!*

Then *crawl!*

Into heavy brush. Still crawling—dragging his lacerated, slime-smeared body toward a covering of rocks.

Faster! No more time . . . Too late!

The night became sudden day.

The explosion picked up Ventry and tossed him into the rocks like a boneless doll.

The train-thing screamed in a whistling death-agony as the concussion sundered it, scattering its parts like wet confetti over the terrain.

Gobbets of bleeding tissue rained down on Ventry as he lay in the rocks. But through the pain and the stench and the nausea his lips were curved into a thin smile.

He was unconscious when the Montana sun rose that morning, but when Sheriff John Longbow arrived on the scene he found Paul Ventry alive.

Alive and triumphant.

Every beginning writer is influenced by other writers he or she admires. In my case, the poetic, beautifully-textured works of Ray Bradbury made a deep impression on me early in my career. Bradbury's influence is clearly evident in this story, yet it retains an originality and emotional core of its own that has prompted it to be selected for school textbooks, for a magazine in Russia, for seven anthologies and collections, and for comic-book illustration. Very recently, in 2000, I adapted it for a new dramatic radio series and discovered, all over again, how much I liked it.

I hope you will, too. This one's from the heart.

AND MILES TO GO BEFORE I SLEEP

(Written: March 1957)

Alone within the humming ship, deep in its honey-combed chambers, Robert Murdock waited for death. While the rocket moved inexorably toward Earth—an immense silver needle threading the dark fabric of space—he waited calmly through the final hours, knowing that hope no longer existed.

After twenty years in space, Murdock was going home.

Home. Earth. Thayerville, a small town in Kansas. Clean air, a shaded street and a white two-story house near the end of the block. Home after two decades among the stars.

The rocket knifed through the black of space, its

atomics, like a great heartbeat, pulsing far below Robert Murdock as he sat quietly before a round port, seeing and not seeing the endless darkness surrounding him.

Murdock was remembering.

He remembered the worried face of his mother, her whispered prayers for his safety, the way she held him close for a long, long moment before he mounted the ship's ramp those twenty years ago. He remembered his father: a tall, weathered man, and that last crushing handshake before he said goodbye.

It was almost impossible to realize that they were now old and white-haired, that his father was forced to use a cane, that his mother was bowed and wasted by the years.

And what of himself?

He was now forty-one—and space had weathered him as the plains of Kansas had weathered his father. He, too, had fought storms in his job beyond Earth, terrible, alien storms; worse than any he had ever encountered on his own planet. And he, too, had labored on plains under burning suns far stronger than Sol. His face was square and hard-featured, his eyes dark and buried beneath thrusting ledges of bone.

Robert Murdock removed the stero-shots of his

parents from his uniform pocket and studied their
faces. Warm, smiling, *waiting* faces: waiting for their
son to come home to them. Carefully, he unfolded
his mother's last letter. She had always been stubborn about sending tapes, complaining that her
voice was unsteady, that she found it so difficult to
speak her thoughts into the metallic mouth of a cold,
impersonal machine. She insisted on using an old-
fashioned pen, forming the words slowly in an almost archaic script. He had received this last letter
just before his take-off for Earth, and it read:

Dearest,

We are so excited! Your father and I listened to your voice again and again, telling
us that you are coming home to us at last, and
we both thanked our good Lord that you were
safe. Oh, we are so eager to see you, son.
As you know, we have not been too well of
late. Your father's heart doesn't allow him to
get out much any more. Even the news that
you are coming back to us has over-excited
him. Then, of course, my own health seems
none too good as I suffered another fainting
spell last week. But there is no real cause for
alarm—and you are not to worry!—since Dr.
Thom says I am still quite strong, and that

these spells will pass. I am, however, resting as much as possible, so that I will be fine when you arrive. Please, Bob, come back to us safely. We pray to God you will come home safe and well. The thought of you fills our hearts each day. Our lives are suddenly rich again. Hurry, Bob. Hurry!

All our love,
Mother

Robert Murdock put the letter aside and clenched his fists. Only brief hours remained to him—and Earth was *days* away. The town of Thayerville was an impossible distance across space; he knew he could never reach it alive.

Once again, as they had so many times in the recent past, the closing lines of the ancient poem by Robert Frost came whispering through his mind:

But I have promises to keep,

And miles to go before I sleep . . .

He'd promised that he would come home, and he would keep that promise. Despite death itself, he would return to Earth.

"Out of the question!" the doctors had told him. *"You'll never reach Earth. You'll die out there. You'll die in space."*

Then they had shown him. They charted his death

almost to the final second; they told him when his heart would stop beating, when his breathing would cease. This disease—contracted on an alien world—was incurable. Death, for Robert Murdock, was a certainty.

But he told them he was going home nonetheless, that he was leaving for Earth. And they listened to his plan.

Now, with less than thirty minutes of life remaining, Murdock was walking down one of the ship's long corridors, his bootheels ringing on the metal walkway.

He was ready, at last, to keep his promise.

Pausing before a wall storage-locker, he twisted a small dial. The door slid back. Murdock looked up at the tall man standing motionless in the interior darkness. He reached forward, made a quick adjustment. The tall man spoke.

"Is it time?"

"Yes," replied Robert Murdock, "it is time."

The tall man stepped smoothly down into the corridor; the light flashed in the deep-set eyes, almost hidden under thrusting ledges of bone. The man's face was hard and square-featured. "You see," he smiled, "I *am* perfect."

"And so you are," said Murdock. But then, he reflected, everything *depends* on perfection. There must be no flaw, however small. None.

"My name is Robert Murdock," said the tall figure in the neat spaceman's uniform. "I am forty-one years of age, sound of mind and body. I have been in space for two decades—and now I am going home."

Murdock smiled, a tight smile of triumph which flickered briefly across his tired face.

"How much longer?" the tall figure asked.

"Ten minutes. Perhaps a few seconds beyond that," said Murdock slowly. "They told me it would be painless."

"Then . . ." The tall man paused, drew in a long breath. "I'm sorry."

Murdock smiled again. He knew that a machine, however perfect, could not experience the emotion of sorrow—but it eased him to hear the words.

He'll be fine, thought Murdock. He'll serve in my place and my parents will never suspect that I have not come home to them. A month, as arranged, and the machine would turn itself in to company officials on Earth. Yes, Murdock thought, he will be fine.

"Remember," said Murdock, "when you leave them, they *must* believe you are going back into space."

"Naturally," said the machine. And Murdock listened to his own voice explain: "When the month I am to stay with them has passed, they'll see me board a rocket. They'll see it fire away from Earth, outbound, and they'll know that I cannot return for two more decades. They will accept the fact that their son must return to space—that a healthy spaceman cannot leave the Service until he has reached sixty. Let me assure you, all will go exactly as you have planned."

It *will* work, Murdock told himself; every detail has been taken into consideration. The android possesses every memory that I possess; his voice is *my* voice, his small habits my own. And when he leaves them, when it appears that he has gone back to the stars, the pre-recorded tapes of mine will continue to reach them from space, exactly as they have in the past. Until their deaths. They will never know I'm gone, thought Robert Murdock.

"Are you ready now?" the tall figure asked softly.

"Yes," said Murdock, nodding. "I'm ready."

And they began to walk slowly down the long corridor.

Murdock remembered how proud his parents had been when he was accepted for Special Service. He had been the only boy in the entire town of Thayerville to be chosen. It had been a great day! The local band playing, the mayor—old Mr. Harkness with those little glasses tilted across his nose—making a speech, telling everyone how proud Thayerville was of its chosen son . . . and his mother crying because she was so happy.

But then, it was only right that he should have gone into space. The other boys, the ones who failed to make the grade, had not *lived* the dream as he had lived it. From the moment he had watched the first moon rocket land, he had known, beyond any possible doubt, that he would become a spaceman. He had stood there, in that cold December, a boy of twelve, watching the rocket fire down from space, watching it thaw and blacken the frozen earth. And he had known, in his heart, that he would one day follow it back to the stars. From that moment on, he had dreamed only of moving up and away from Earth, away to vast and alien horizons, to wondrous worlds beyond imagining.

And many of the others had been unwilling to give up *everything* for space. Even now, after two decades, he could still hear Julie's words: *"Oh, I'm sure you love me, Bob, but not enough. Not nearly enough to give up your dream."* And she had left him, gone out of his life because she knew there was no room in it for her. There was only space—deep space and the rockets and the burning stars. Nothing else.

He remembered his last night on Earth, twenty years ago, when he had felt the pressing immensity of the vast universe surrounding him as he lay in his bed. He remembered the sleepless hours before dawn—when he could feel the tension building within the small white house, within himself lying there in the heated stillness of the room. He remembered the rain, near morning, drumming the roof and the thunder roaring across the Kansas sky. And then, somehow, the thunder's roar blended into the atomic roar of a rocket, carrying him away from Earth, away to the far stars . . . away . . .

Away.

The tall figure in the neat spaceman's uniform closed the outer airlock and watched the body drift into blackness. The ship and the android were one; a pair of complex and perfect machines doing their job.

For Robert Murdock, the journey was over, the long miles had come to an end.

Now he would sleep forever in space.

When the rocket landed, on a bright morning in July, in Thayerville, Kansas, the crowds were there, waving and shouting out Robert Murdock's name. The city officials were all present to the last man, each with a carefully rehearsed speech in his mind;

the town band sent brassy music into the blue sky and children waved flags. Then a hush fell over the assembled throng. The atomic engines had stilled and the airlock was sliding back.

Robert Murdock appeared, tall and heroic in a splendid dress uniform which threw back the light of the sun in a thousand glittering patterns. He smiled and waved as the crowd burst into fresh shouting and applause.

And, at the far end of the ramp, two figures waited: an old man, bowed and trembling over a cane, and a seamed and wrinkled woman, her hair blowing white, her eyes shining.

When the tall man finally reached them, pushing his way through pressing lines of well-wishers, they embraced him feverishly. They clung tight to his arms as he walked between them; they looked up at him with tears in their eyes.

Robert Murdock, their beloved son, had come home to them at last.

"Well," said a man at the fringe of the crowd, "there they go."

His companion sighed and shook his head. "I *still* don't think it's right, somehow. It just doesn't seem right to me."

"It's what they wanted, isn't it?" asked the other.

"It's what they put in their wills. They vowed their son would never come home to death. In another month he'll be gone anyway. Back for twenty more years. Why spoil what little time he has, why ruin it all for him?" The man paused, indicating the two figures in the near distance. "They're *perfect*, aren't they? He'll never know."

"I guess you're right," agreed the second man. "He'll never know."

And he watched the old man and the old woman and the tall son until they were out of sight.

When I wrote the teleplay for Melvin Purvis: G-Man, I immersed myself in the 1930s, a truly violent decade in our nation's history. This was the era of Ma Barker, Machine-Gun Kelly, Bonnie and Clyde, Dillinger, and Pretty Boy Floyd. It was the dark time of the Great Depression and these ruthless outlaws were embraced as heroes by a large segment of the American public. Their bank-robbing exploits were supported by jobless men who were losing their homes to foreclosure. They cheered the robberies: the damn banks were merciless and corrupt and therefore deserved to be robbed.

This is a savage story about a young man of that era who sets out to emulate these notorious lawbreakers. He's violent, ruthless, and totally amoral—a product of his times.

He's on the prowl in "A Good Day."

And God help anyone who gets in his way.

A GOOD DAY

(Written: December 1996)

I shot him in the belly, twice. He spilled forward over the counter like a loose jellyfish. He owned the hash joint. Had . . . until I shot him in the belly. Now he didn't own anything.

I shot the cook when he came out from in back and then I shot the cashier. It was early and there were just two customers and they ran out yelling.

When I got back to the Chevy she was all excited with her eyes kind of marble shiny and she asked, "How much?"

"Nineteen," I said, driving fast. The Chevy stepped out real good. We cleared town fast.

"I thought you'd get more." Now she kind of looked like a slapped kid, all pouty.

"Nineteen is swell," I said. And it was. For 1933 it was swell.

A motor cop started following us and I shot him off his cycle. His hat rolled away into the grass and he had his mouth open, flat on his back, with the flies already at him.

It was July, and real hot. Even this early with the sun just up. I knew it would get a lot hotter.

"Where we goin'?" Hazel asked me.

That was her name. Hazel. She was pretty. Young and pretty. About sixteen. I never ask them how old they are, I just go by what appeals to me. But I'm young too so it figures I like them that way.

I felt real good, all kind of tingly inside, like after you drink champagne. I had it once in Kansas City for New Year's and remember the tingles. Shooting people always makes me feel like that.

"Here." I threw her the gun. "Reload it. There's a box of shells behind the seat."

She shrugged and put in fresh bullets. I took it back and put it away in my coat.

"Where we goin'?" she asked me again.

"To the farm," I said. "It's Ma's birthday. But first I got to find her a present."

Hazel made what sounded like a grunt.

"You got problems with us goin' to Ma's?"

"Naw," she said. "Except that I thought we'd keep

movin' after what you done back in that café. All the shooting."

"So what?" I kept my eyes on the road. Nothing to see on either side. Flat Kansas country. "So I shot up some mugs. What's it your business?"

"The cops could be waiting for us at your Ma's."

"Yeah, they could," I said, "except they won't be because they don't know who did the shooting and so that's just a lot of crap."

"Suit yourself." She kind of huddled against the seat with her arms crossed. She had on a tight yellow blouse that made her tits look good and a tight kid's skirt from school. But her hair was a mess.

"You oughta fix your hair," I told her. "Looks like a rat's been at it."

She put a hand up to her hair, running her fingers through. "The wind messes it," she said. "I'll comb it later."

The wind was pretty strong all right. Across the Kansas flat, blowing the wheat all which way.

"How far to your ma's? I gotta pee."

"So I'll stop and you can go outside."

I braked the Chevy. The highway was two lanes, quiet and open, with stubbled grass on each side. She could pee in the grass.

"Somebody'll see me," she said.

"Naw they won't," I said. "Just go do it."

She opened the door on her side and slipped out, hiking up her skirt. The wind made a whining sound and the sky was blue like Ma's eyes. Real intense blue. No clouds.

But it might rain by late tonight. That's what the radio said. Clouds could come up and it might rain.

I leaned across the seat. "You done yet?"

"Just hold your horses," she said. About a minute or so later she wiggled back in the seat and slammed the car door.

"I feel a lot better," she said.

We drove on till I found a general store. I pulled the Chevy to a stop in the gravel yard in front and went in.

"Help you, son?" asked this tall gink with squinty eyes and thick glasses. He wore green suspenders.

I picked up a shiny metal iron. Heavy. "Ma needs a new one," I said. "You got any ironing boards? Hers is wore out."

"Sure, you bet," said the squinty gink and he hauled out a long wooden ironing board for me.

"That'll be three fifty."

"Too much," I said and hit him with the iron. He went down bleeding and didn't say anything else.

I wiped off the iron with a new towel from a stack on the counter, took what he had in the cash register, and left with Ma's presents. She'd be real pleased to get them.

"Why'd you hit that guy?" Hazel wanted to know when I got back to the Chevy.

"Cuz I wanted to," I said. "Why don't you shut your yap."

"I didn't mean nothin'." And she looked pouty again.

"Quit askin' me dumb questions," I said, easing out to the highway.

"Sometimes I just wonder about stuff," she said.

"Well, keep your wonderin' to yourself. Just button it."

"You got a headache or something?"

"Naw, I'm feelin' good."

"Well, you're sure cranky. And when you got a headache you get cranky."

"I just don't like dumb questions is all."

We were almost to Ma's place when they came into sight around a long curve. Three cops in two patrol cars.

"Jeez, it's a roadblock," said Hazel. Her eyes were wide. "And they see us."

"So what?" I tromped hard on the gas and the Chevy jumped forward like a dog in the woods. "Not much of a damn roadblock with just three hick cops. I'll run it."

"They'll shoot! They got a rifle."

"Swell. Just duck down and you'll be okay."

I was moving fast when the bullets started. Most of them missed but one chipped the glass in my side vent and cut my cheek. Stung a little. Then I was on them, bang! Right through, and with me firing from the window.

Got one fat cop. Blew him away like a straw man. The other two ducked down inside their car.

The road curved again. Once we were out of their sight I swung off to a narrow dirt road with lots of trees for cover and heard them go by on the main highway, sirens blasting.

"They'll catch us," said Hazel. "You should not of shot that cop."

"They started it," I said. "Shooting at us. Trying to kill us. Hell, it was self-defense."

"Plus the motor cop you popped earlier," said Hazel. "They hate cop killers."

"So what? I hate cops. That makes us even."

Ma's place was good to see again. Just a plain weathered house with a black tar roof stuck in beside some big oaks with plowed ground behind and a rusty Dodge truck in the driveway. Used to be Pa's before the stroke took him. Ma used it to fetch back groceries from town.

She met us on the porch, smiling. "Well, goodness me, it's you, Hal! How are ya, son?"

"I'm swell, Ma," I said. "This here is Hazel. She's with me."

"Why, land sakes but you're a pretty little thing," Ma said, wiping her palms on her checked apron. Then she shook Hazel's hand.

"Thank you kindly, ma'am," said Hazel, looking sheepish. She didn't get told nice things much about her looks.

"Her hair's messed up," I said.

Hazel patted at it. "The wind," she told Ma. "It's blowin' fierce today."

"Sure is," said Ma. "Now you younguns step on inside. I got some coffee and pie in the kitchen."

That sounded swell. I was real hungry and Ma knew how to bake a pie.

"What kind?" I asked her, going inside. The house looked the same. The big picture of Jesus was still over the mantel.

"Blueberry. Your favorite."

I gave her a hug. "Happy birthday, Ma."

"Gracious!" She lit up like a searchlight. "You went and remembered!"

"Sure did." I gave her a smile. "Got some presents for ya out in the Chevy."

"Well, now, ain't that nice." She seemed real pleased. "Ain't that just the nicest thing!"

We ate Ma's blueberry pie and drank the coffee, and I asked for a second slice. It was like always. Tasted great. And filled me up good. Hazel liked it too.

I got out the iron and the ironing board and brought them inside to Ma. She about had a fit she was so glad to get the stuff. Gave me another hug.

"Ya know," Ma said to Hazel, "Hal here usta be a plain mischief to me. Cuttin' up all the time and gettin' into trouble." She shook her head. "But he always had the looks. Took after his pa."

She had the family scrapbook spread out on her lap and was showing Hazel some photos of me as a kid. I grabbed it away from her.

"Can it, Ma. Hazel don't wanna see all this crap." I shrugged. "So I was a lousy kid. All kids are lousy, and that's why I'll never have any."

Hazel started to protest about the scrapbook but I shot her a look and she kept shut.

"Look, Ma, we gotta push on," I said.

She seemed kind of pained. "Why the rush? Thought you kids could stay the night."

"Naw, we gotta push on," I said. "Want to make Railston before the weather goes bad. Radio said a storm is due."

"Hotels at Railston cost ya a bundle," Ma said. "You could stay here, go on to town come morning."

I shook my head and nudged Hazel through the pitted screen door ahead of me. "Sorry, but I gotta see a fella in Railston real early tomorrow. Big shot from K.C."

It was a lie, but it got us out with no more argument.

Ma walked us to the Chevy. "You drive careful now, Hal."

"Always, Ma," I said, giving her a final hug. Hazel gave her one too.

"Take care," Ma said, waving at us as we rolled out of the driveway.

We hit Railston by 2 P.M. The Farmers' Bank on the main street was still open.

"I'm gonna take it," I said. "You wait in the car. Keep the motor running. I'll be back in a jiffy."

"This is nuts with all the local law after us," Hazel complained. "It's like we're Bonnie and Clyde."

"Just shut up and keep the motor goin' that's all."

I went inside, walked up to the lady cashier and shot her in the head. Some people screamed and I told them to shut up. It was a hick bank with no guard. I got ninety-two dollars and ten cents. Hotcha! Almost a hundred smacks!

Outside I piled into the Chevy and took off fast. People were yelling behind us.

"You shot somebody else, didn't you?" asked Hazel. "I heard it."

"What I do is none of your goddamn business. If you don't like what I do then you can haul your butt outa this car."

We'd already cleared town and I braked hard, pulled over to the side of the highway and kicked open the passenger door.

"Go on . . . get outa here!"

"Then I will," she said, her face all tight and red. "I surely will."

When she was clear I reached across and yanked the door closed, hit the gas, and took off again.

I saw her in the rear-view mirror, standing there by the side of the road with her yellow blouse hanging out and her hair all messed.

She was nothing. There were plenty of others just like her in Topeka. I wouldn't have any trouble finding another one just as pretty.

I'd have to switch cars in Topeka. Cinch.

Everything was swell. I felt the tingles inside, like bubbles.

It was a good day.

The recent proliferation of school shootings, plus the uneasiness I've always felt about small towns (that they hide dark secrets behind their apple-pie façades), led me to write "Heart's Blood." It is yet another echo of my early life in the Midwest. My wife claims that in writing these regional terror tales I am "exorcising my Missouri demons." She may be right.

What actually goes on in the quiet little town of Caxton?

Why is the school closed?

Where are the children?

You'll find the answers in "Heart's Blood."

HEART'S BLOOD

(Written: June 1999)

Remember the shooting at that high school in Roanoke, Virginia, six years ago? The one where the 16-year-old student-body president mowed down a dozen of his classmates with an assault rifle? His name was Lucas Fraley, and when his friends were interviewed on TV they talked about how he was always so warm and cooperative and how popular he was with everyone. Lucas never touched drugs or alcohol, they said. Just an all-around great guy.

I recall the way his mother looked on the TV newscasts: no make-up, her hair severely pulled back in a bun, standing stiff-backed in front of the camera, chin up, defiant as a pit bull, as she declared that Lucas had never given her a single day's worry, that he was her "perfect child."

Then what had gone wrong?

During a televised prison interview, young Fraley provided the answer. He was a good-looking boy, tanned and fit, with the dark, probing eyes of a serious student, and he spoke in calm, measured tones.

"I've always been very religious," he stated. "My family has belonged to the Full Holiness Gospel Church my whole life, and for the last two years I've served as Junior Pastor in the Sunday School. Seems like I always knew that my life's calling was to the ministry."

During a ninth-grade course in World History, Farley developed what he admitted was a "total obsession" with Arthurian lore. "It was natural," he said, "once I discovered that King Arthur was my ancestor." Fraley explained that the celebrated King Arthur, who'd lived in Britain fourteen hundred years ago, was actually descended from the marriage of Jesus and Mary Magdalene. A thousand years after Arthur's death, the fabled monarch's descendants included England's King Charles II, who in his leisure hours had impregnated an unmarried palace servant girl named Elsbeth, then banished her and her unborn child to the New World colony of Virginia.

"Her son by King Charles, born right here in Virginia, was my direct ancestor," Fraley said.

He'd hesitated at this point, his dark eyes flashing with sudden anger. "One night my girlfriend and I were playing Truth or Dare. She asked me what my greatest secret was, the thing I didn't want *anyone* to know. I told her that I was the direct descendant of Jesus Christ, and that I carried his genes within mine. I thought she'd understand, but instead she laughed at me. Then she told our friends and *they* started laughing at me. That's why they had to die. People should never laugh at a son of Jesus."

The newspapers had a field day.

Self-styled Son of Jesus Confesses
Mentally Disturbed Youth Attempts
to Justify Killing Rampage

Fraley's father refused to be interviewed and wouldn't comment; his photo in the paper, with his dark eyes exuding religious zealotry, was chilling. A self-righteous, cold-hearted bastard if I ever saw one. After the shooting, the Fraleys separated, and later—despite the rigid precepts of the Full Holiness Gospel Church—Mrs. Fraley filed for divorce. Lucas had been their only child.

My parents had done the same thing . . . split up

when I was in high school. My father went away somewhere and I never heard from him again. And like Lucas, I didn't have any brothers or sisters. The court gave custody of me to my mother, of course, but I didn't like it. Mom would get drunk on the weekends. When she was smashed, she'd kind of paw at me and want me to hug her. Spooky. So I took off on my own when I was eighteen.

I don't have good memories of my parents. All my good memories center around my grandparents on Mom's side. Devin and Keara Carrick were their names, but I never called them anything but Gramps and Granny.

They lived in Caxton, Missouri, for all of their adult lives. Came over to the U.S. as Irish orphans after World War I, when they were both still kids. Gramps eventually became Caxton's postmaster; Granny won dozens of state and county fair ribbons for her cooking.

Gramps and Granny were the reason we ended up shooting *The Friday Massacre* in Caxton. I wrote the film script, basing my screenplay on the actual Lucas Fraley killings, and although I fictionalized the story, I kept it authentic.

I believe in authenticity. Whatever I write about I research thoroughly. For this project, I wanted to see what it was like to actually shoot a rapid-fire assault rifle. I *needed* this experience in order to do full justice to my script. I couldn't legally buy one in California so a writer friend of mine bought the weapon in Texas, no questions asked, and drove it and the ammo west so I wouldn't have to deal with all the legal red tape.

When I tried out the rifle at a shooting range in the mountains I used real bullets, even though the actor in our film would be firing blanks. As the weapon spewed out its deadly rounds I was able to project myself into the persona of Lucas Fraley on that fateful Friday morning when he'd fired on his helpless classmates. It was a sick, ugly feeling.

When I finally stowed the rifle away in the trunk of my Lexus, safely disarmed, I had no desire to fire it again. I now had what I'd been after.

Authenticity.

I was pleased with my final draft of the script. Because this was a fictional take on the actual story, I'd changed all of the real names and added a romantic sub-plot between two of the teachers. The woman teacher gets wounded in the shooting, but she survives. I thought about killing her off, but decided against it. American audiences like happy endings.

I have great memories of visiting Gramps and Granny in Caxton each summer when I was young.

Those were magical times and I've always considered Caxton to be my real home. Living with Mom in Kansas was a bummer.

Truthfully, Caxton is nothing much to look at. It's a sleepy little town nestled on the southern border of Missouri. Big shade trees on every street: maples, elms, oaks. Nice park, too, with a great playground for the kids. Gramps used to take me there and I'd spend hours riding the teeter-totter with him. I wore him out on those afternoons.

Granny spoiled me, for sure. At the beginning of each summer she'd always have a tall metal drum of her incredible ice cream waiting for me when I arrived. Butter brickle, my favorite. God, I can still taste it! She made it in her old-fashioned, hand-cranked freezer with triple-thick cream, farm-fresh egg yolks, and sugar which had been slowly infused with genuine vanilla beans.

Gramps liked to fish, and he'd take me out to Lake Louise, a few miles from town, and I'd row the boat across the dark green water, still as glass, until he told me to stop. Gramps knew the best places to catch fish. Down deep, near the rocks where they liked to hide. I hated baiting the hook with those wiggly gray worms, but I did it for Gramps because I loved him. You do a lot of things you don't want to do for the people you love.

They're both gone now, of course. Jan, my wife, never got to know them. Or Caxton, either. In fact, before we shot *The Friday Massacre* there, she'd never seen the town, but I'd told her about it, and I had photos of the place in Granny's faded yellow scrapbook that Jan always enjoyed leafing through. There was even a picture of Caxton's Main Street with some old cars parked at the curb in front of the post office, including "Bessy," Gramps' sun-faded '36 Dodge sedan that he would never part with. Granny was always after him to buy a new automobile, but he never budged. "Who needs a new car?" he'd say. "This is the one I used to drive you to high school in when you and I were sparkin'. Runs just dandy. Old things are better."

I always remembered him saying that. I guess it went in deep, because I collect antiques. Toys, furniture, old books. Actually, Jan and I spent a lot of our spare time hunting for antiques together. Just like me, she appreciated the past.

But the future can be just as fascinating as the past. Jan and I met because of the future, at a science-fiction preview in Hollywood. She'd always been as much a nut for sci-fi as I am. Strangers, we spent several hours sharing the same section of sidewalk down the block from the Egyptian Theatre, waiting in line, patiently, for the film to open. I'd asked her to hold my place while I went in search of a rest room and, when I returned, we began talking. We never stopped.

There was a twelve-year age gap between us, but never a generation gap. Women mature at a younger age than men do. Before the trip to Caxton we'd been married for a full decade, and we were just about to have our first baby. It had been a rough ten years for both of us because I'd been trying to get out of writing sitcoms for what had seemed like a century. Despite the excellent pay, I hated scripting those insipid episodes about skunks on a bus, broken toilets, and lost puppy dogs, writing for sour-faced producers who hadn't smiled since Abe Lincoln's second inauguration.

I was finally liberated when Lyle Samuels hired me to write *The Friday Massacre*. My first big-screen break. Jan and I celebrated at Musso & Frank's, giggling at each other, toasting the occasion with tall summer glasses of iced tea. We were sure that my days as a sitcom wage slave were over. I was free at last.

At my suggestion, Jerry Meins, our company location scout, flew from California to Missouri. To Caxton.

When he got back he told Lyle Samuels (our producer and director) that the town was definitely out as a location. Why? It seems that Caxton's only high school was closed, which meant that no students were available for crowd scenes. (We'd planned on using local talent to fill out the cast.)

"Not possible," I told Jerry. "When Gramps was alive, they had full enrollment. More than a hundred students."

Meins scowled. "How long since you were back there?"

"Thirty years," I admitted. "My last summer visit was just after I'd turned ten. The next winter, my grandparents both died in a traffic accident during an ice storm, so I never went back."

"A lot can happen in thirty years."

I shook my head. "Not in Caxton. It's always the same there. Gramps used to say that time stood still in Caxton."

"I'm tellin' ya, the town's like a graveyard," Jerry declared. "Even the elementary school's been shut down. Never saw a single kid on the street. And not many adults, either. Place gave me the creeps. Most of the stores are boarded over. Movie house is closed. So's the drugstore. Whole town's like an empty stage set."

I seized on that last sentence. "Makes it perfect for

us," I said, turning to Samuels. "No hassle with crowds the way you had in Chicago. We'll have the place all to ourselves."

"Well . . . I dunno," Lyle mused. "I'd have to bus in a bunch of extras for the school scenes. And we'd need to spruce the place up. Make it look active." He hesitated. "And how do we know we can get permission to use the school?"

"Leave it to me," I said. "I'll personally go to Caxton and contact whoever it takes to swing the permit."

And that's what I did. My very pregnant wife stayed in California with her sister while I flew to St. Louis, then drove a rental car south to Caxton.

When I arrived I discovered that Jerry had been right. About the place being like a graveyard. Maybe a dozen cars downtown. A few businesses still open, including Annie's Eats, the local cafe. (I remembered how good her apple pie had been, but the original Annie was long dead by now. She'd been at least eighty when I'd seen her last.)

I waved hello to an old guy on a bicycle who just glared at me. The park was deserted and no kids were on the weed-grown playground. The teeter-totter had fallen over and the swings hung silent, with cobwebs between the chains.

My grandparents' house on Forest Avenue was

boarded up, but the boards in three of the windows had been broken, along with the glass underneath. The empty spaces looked like missing teeth in a wooden skull. Wild grass claimed the yard. The house had been willed to Granny's maiden aunt, but just before she died she hadn't been able to pay the property taxes so the house was now owned by the town of Caxton.

But some things hadn't changed. The bronze statue of Robert E. Lee still dominated the courthouse square, reminding me that this part of Missouri had supported the Confederacy during the Civil War. And City Hall looked exactly the same with its graceful Ionic pillars fronting the entrance.

I was halfway across the square when a hand gripped my shoulder. I turned, startled, to face a tall, beefy man in a dark uniform whose flushed face and ample gut evidenced a lifetime of too much greasy food. A walking coronary. He wore a wide-brimmed Stetson, and his badge read SHERIFF.

"You got ID?" he asked.

I produced my wallet, removed my California driver's license, and handed it to him. He looked it over, then gave it back.

"New in town, are ya?" His tone was affable, but there was menace and suspicion in his eyes. He wore a holstered revolver, and rested a meaty, sun-freckled hand on the butt of his weapon.

"I arrived this morning."

"Got business in Caxton?"

"I hope to have."

"What's *that* mean?"

"It means I need to talk to your mayor."

" 'Bout what?"

I ignored his question. "Have I broken some law?"

"Nope." His eyes were fixed on me. Folds of heavy flesh turned them into dark slits.

"Then I'm free to go?"

He shrugged his thick shoulders. "We don't get many strangers to town . . . but I guess you're all right."

"That's nice to hear," I said, turning back toward City Hall. I felt his eyes on me all the way to the entrance.

I've never liked small town cops.

Inside the municipal building, in the middle of the hall on the second floor, I located a frosted glass door that read MAYOR STAFFORD in gilt leaf. When I stepped inside, a dull-faced male office worker glanced up at me.

"I need to see the mayor," I told him.

His jaw tightened. "Mayor's busy. What business you got with him?"

"I came here from Los Angeles. Name's Cahill. I'm with a motion picture production company. We want to make a film in Caxton and we need a permit to use the high school."

"School's closed," he said tartly.

"I know. We'll open it again."

He stared at me. "We don't much appreciate strangers poking around."

"We won't be poking, we'll be filming," I said. "Besides; I'm no stranger. My grandparents lived right here in Caxton for most of their lives. Gramps was Devin Carrick, the town postmaster. He and Granny lived in the big white Victorian house at 33rd and Forest."

That didn't faze him. "We don't want you film people, an' that's final."

His stony attitude was beginning to annoy me. "Are you speaking for the mayor?"

"I'm speaking for all the folks in Caxton." His tone was strident.

The inner door opened and a tall, white-haired man peered out, like a bear from his cave. "What's the problem, Carl?"

"No problem," he said. "Except that this fella is from California and he wants to make a movie here in town. I told him no."

The mayor aimed a politician's smile in my direction. "I'm Byron Stafford. Named after the poet. You ever read Lord Byron?"

"Yes, I've read him," I said, returning his smile. "Happy to meet you, Mayor Stafford. I'm David Cahill."

We shook hands. His palm was sweaty.

"Come into my office, Mr. Cahill. Let's have us a little talk."

Stafford's office was crowded and stuffy, with gray walls, a glass-topped desk, two dark wooden file cabinets, three black-leather wing chairs, and several ashtrays that should have been emptied weeks ago. A framed portrait of Harry Truman loomed over the desk. The mayor offered me a cigar, but I told him no thanks, I didn't smoke.

"That's to your credit," he said. "My late wife was a chain smoker. She got me started."

On cigars? I wondered. I sat down in a leather chair as he lit a thick brown stogie.

When I reminded him, Stafford remembered the school shooting in Virginia. "Dreadful business," he said darkly. "Dreadful. The boy was obviously deranged."

I told him about my screenplay, how I hoped it would exert a helpful influence and maybe keep some other kid from doing what Lucas Fraley had done. "This film will carry a strong, positive message for young people everywhere." I figured this was just corny enough to impress him.

"What do you want from me, Mr. Cahill?" he asked, puffing thoughtfully on his cigar.

"A permit to shoot at Caxton High School. We'll be happy to pay any fee you require. Shouldn't need it for more than two . . . maybe three weeks at the outside."

"I'm afraid the answer is no," he said, rolling the cigar in his fingers. "We're a quiet little town. Folks wouldn't take kindly to you Hollywood people comin' in and stirring up a ruckus. I'm sorry to tell you that strangers are not welcome here."

"Yeah, your sheriff made that clear. He treated me like a leper."

Stafford shrugged. "Oh, doncha mind Pete. He just enjoys bein' ornery. Pete's all right, once you get to know him."

"Uh-huh," I said.

"He just don't take to strangers."

"As I told your man here in the office, I'm no stranger. Used to visit my grandparents here in Caxton every summer. I want my wife to see the town. She's heard me talk so much about it."

"Any children?"

"Not yet, but Jan's about to have a baby."

Stafford pursed his lips. "Ah . . . the miracle of birth. How far along is she?"

"Eight months. She's due next month. That's one of the reasons I want Jan here on location with me. So that I'll be with her when she has our child."

The mayor stubbed out his cigar, got up, walked to the window. He stood there, gazing out for a full minute, hands clasped behind his back. Then he turned to me.

"Maybe I'm being unreasonable," he said. "I suppose there's no real harm in letting you make your film here." He smiled. "I'm sure we can work something out."

So that's how we got our permit. My talking about Jan seemed to soften the mayor's attitude. Probably had children of his own. Obviously, I'd said just the right thing.

It was early June, already hot and humid, but ideal for the film. School had been just about to end for the summer when Lucas Fraley went on his killing rampage, so we would be able to match the weather perfectly, giving us the precise look we were after.

Jan was excited about seeing Caxton, although I warned her that the town had changed a lot. She didn't care; she wanted to have our baby in the place I'd loved as a boy. A bond with my past. She repeated what Granny had said to me at the birth of a neighbor's child: "A new baby is the heart's blood of any marriage."

All indications were that Jan was going to have a trouble-free birth, but when she informed her obstetrician, Dr. Malloy, of our plans for the cross-country drive to Caxton, he was not pleased. Eventually Malloy reluctantly agreed to the trip, as long as we met his conditions:

1. Jan must have a sonogram to insure that the baby was healthy. (She did, which is when we found out that we'd be having a son. We named him Devin Michael, after Gramps.)

2. The medical facilities in Caxton must be approved by Malloy. (He had the Missouri hospital fax him their operating license, and he also talked to the doctor who would deliver Devin. In return, Malloy faxed Jan's medical records to the Caxton doctor.)

3. We had to carry a cell phone with us on the trip and make certain that each night's stopover was close to a major hospital in case Jan went into early labor. (She didn't, and we arrived in Caxton without a hitch. The trip had been great.)

I was optimistic about the future: my first produced screenplay, and our first child.

I had no way of knowing, back then, about the dark time that was coming.

*   *   *

Things began beautifully.

I'd taken a lot of photos before I left town. When Lyle Samuels saw them, he agreed with me that it was worth the cost of busing in the extras in order to shoot in town. Caxton had everything my script called for: a small, backwater Midwestern town, dozing under a hot summer sun, suddenly becoming the stage for an eruption of blood and violence. The match between locale and drama was seamless.

The production crew opened Caxton High and dressed it for the camera, closely followed by the cast and film crew who moved in so they could begin the shoot in mid-week. Time is money, and Lyle was determined to bring in *Massacre* under budget.

I've been to my fair share of locations and there's one thing you can always count on: an excited local audience crowding in to catch the action. Only this time, in Caxton, it was different. Nobody in town seemed to give a hoot about watching us. Oh, sure, a few of the townspeople wandered by, looking hostile. Sometimes a car or truck would drive slowly past. The odd thing was, we didn't see a single woman or child during the entire shoot.

Strange. Damned strange.

Mayor Stafford showed up during the second week, while we were still shooting at the high school, to find out how the film was going. Earlier, he'd arranged for the house on Forest to be partially renovated for Jan and me so we could stay there while we were in town. Which I thought was very generous of him.

When the mayor arrived Lyle was busy directing a scene, so we met at the steps of the school. I told him we were right on schedule.

"Well, now . . . that's good to hear. Means your people will be moving out by the end of next week for sure."

"Right," I said. "After we're finished here, we'll be doing some pickup shots downtown. Local color. You're welcome to stand in as an extra. I might even write a speech for you."

The mayor chortled, shaking his head. "No-siree, Mr. Cahill, I'm no movie actor an' that's a flat fact."

"What about some of the others here in town?" I asked. "They could fill in for the crowd scenes."

"Afraid not," he said firmly. "Folks in Caxton like to keep to themselves. Our local theater shut down a few years ago, so nobody goes to the pictures anymore. We're not interested. We're not like you Hollywood people."

"There's one thing I've been really curious about," I said.

"What would that be?"

"Where are all the women and children? Usually, on a location shoot like this—"

"They keep to home," cut in Stafford. "An' speakin' of women, I was hoping to meet your wife. I'd consider it an honor."

"Of course," I said. "Jan's been taking it easy since we arrived. She's resting in the office trailer."

"Wouldn't like to disturb her."

"No, she's been wanting to meet you. C'mon, it's this way."

I led him across a snake-tangle of black electric cables toward our location office.

As we walked he told me how impressed he was with the way we'd fixed up Caxton High.

"Looks real smart . . . all spic-an'-span," he declared. "Like it was when it was open."

"Why did it close?" I asked. "It's the only high school in town. It would seem—"

He cut me off again. "A losing proposition. Not enough new students. Lotta folks started movin' to the big cities and took their kids along. Quiet little town like ours wasn't exciting enough for 'em . . . or maybe it's those big-city dollars they wanted. So we lost our students. Had to shut down. No choice, really."

I tapped lightly on the trailer door. "Company, Jan. It's Mayor Stafford."

Jan appeared in the doorway, smiling out at us. I never tired of seeing her smile. Radiant. That's the word for it. Jan was naturally pretty, but when she smiled, she was radiant.

The mayor offered her his hand. "Mighty happy to meet you, ma'am."

She nodded. "David's told me about your cooperation," my wife said. "Without you, we wouldn't be here. Without the permit, I mean. And your opening David's grandparents' house to us . . . we really appreciate it!"

"Pleased to be of service, Mrs. Cahill."

We stepped inside and Jan awkwardly shifted her weight, then sat down gingerly on the couch, folding her hands across her distended stomach. "I must look a sight," she said to Stafford, who sat down in the armchair across from her. "I'm almost due."

"Now, don't you go talking that way," the mayor chided. "In the Lord's eyes, all pregnant women are beautiful. Human birth is a miracle and a blessing."

Jan took my hand. "That's exactly what this baby is going to be," she said. "A blessing."

"Amen," nodded Stafford.

"Can I offer you anything?" I asked him. "There's some cold beer in the fridge."

"Tempting," he said. "But I'm due back to the office. Got a town to run."

"Caxton is a wonderful place," said Jan. "I don't know why anyone would ever want to leave it."

The mayor agreed, thanked us for our hospitality, and exited the trailer.

"He seems like a really nice man," Jan said.

Our key sequence at Caxton High was underway.

Billy Pitts, who was playing "Alex Staley," the student killer, pulled an assault rifle from his hallway locker, then ran down the stairs, camera following, to the school cafeteria.

Our set designer had done his job and the scene looked totally real. Teenaged extras jostled one another in the food line as they filled their trays with sandwiches, milk, and cookies, while others were at the cafeteria tables, talking and laughing and generally showing off for each other. A typical teenaged din.

Then Pitts burst in with his rifle and began firing, setting off instant panic. Bodies fell everywhere. The cafeteria turned into a slaughter house.

"Cut!" shouted Lyle Samuels. From the floor, several "dead" students sat up as the action ceased.

Lyle walked over to Pitts. "You're supposed to be nuts, Billy . . . over the edge, freaked out. Where's the madness, the rage? I want to see it in your face.

You're *killing* people, for Christ's sake! You're not at some church picnic."

"Sorry," muttered Pitts, head down. "Guess I lost focus."

Lyle sighed heavily. "All right . . . we'll take it again from you coming through the door. Just keep telling yourself, 'I'm a nutcase . . . I'm a nutcase.' Got it?"

"I got it," Pitts responded.

The next take was perfect.

We used up three bottles of ketchup in this sequence. That's one thing about the film business which has remained constant in the wake of a multitude of technical advances: on most movie sets, blood is still ketchup.

What I couldn't know then was how much real blood would be spilled before this trip was over.

After three weeks of shooting we were done. Our school scenes had been filmed and our love story told. Cast and crew had performed at top level and Lyle had directed with force and precision. My script had attained vivid life. And despite the fact that we had been virtually ignored by the local citizens, we had all the location shots we needed. Lyle would do a few interiors and some pickup crowd stuff back in L.A. to fill in the gaps, but the basic work was finished.

The Friday Massacre was a wrap.

Jan and I said good-bye to everyone that weekend as they boarded the charter bus for the trip north to the airport in St. Louis. We'd be seeing them back in California within the next thirty days.

"You sure you want your kid born in a spooky town like this?" Lyle asked Jan.

"Absolutely," she said. "Besides, I'm so far along now, I'd probably give birth on the plane if I tried to go back with you."

"Well, it's your baby," said Lyle. "Me, I'm damned glad to be getting out of here. Jerry Meins had it right: this place gives me the creeps."

"That's silly," Jan declared. "Caxton is a lovely little town. No wonder David's grandparents lived here for so many years."

"To each his own," shrugged Lyle. He kissed Jan on the cheek, then shook my hand. "See you both in L.A."

"Right," I said. "Have a good trip back."

And we were left alone in Caxton.

Anxiously, we awaited the birth of our son. Once Devin was born and Jan had recovered, our newly-formed family would drive back to California.

Everything was in order. I'd checked with the local hospital when we'd arrived in Caxton and they had assured me they were ready to take Jan in on a moment's notice. Once she went into labor they would send an ambulance for her.

I visited the maternity ward. It was clean and modern, but I was shocked to find that all of the bassinets were empty. No babies. When I questioned a male nurse (all the nurses were male!), he told me that births were rare in Caxton these days, then hurried away before I could question him further.

The house on Forest had unleashed a flood of memories for me and I kept expecting my grandparents to step through the door, their faces shining with happiness, their arms outstretched to hug me. But of course, that didn't happen. They were gone, and no ghosts had been left behind. Unless you counted their heavy Victorian furniture. At night, with the full midsummer moon casting an ivory glow on chairs and sofas and tables, the furniture *did* seem to take on a ghostly aura.

Jan adored the house. Her fascination for antiques found full expression here. "Isn't it simply wonderful?" she'd exclaim at a new discovery, and I'd agree.

But somehow I failed to share her joy. Without

the warm presence of Gramps and Granny, the house on Forest seemed cold, almost . . . sinister. Crazy word for the beloved old Victorian mansion I'd so loved as a kid, but I couldn't shake a mounting sense of unease. And things about Caxton I'd never particularly noticed when I was a kid—the too-lush greenery, humidity so bad I was never really dry, and the nearly deafening sound of millions of noisy insects—now seemed oppressive.

In truth, I was looking forward to the day we could leave.

A week later, near midnight, Jan went into labor. The contractions were steady and evenly spaced when I phoned the hospital. They would send an ambulance immediately, I was told.

It rolled up to the house in less than ten minutes, siren blaring and red lights flashing, with a crew of two rushing attendants.

"The ambulance is here," I told Jan. "Everything's going to be fine."

She gave me a pained smile. "Men should have babies. Then they'd know what women go through."

The attendants quickly placed Jan on a gurney, covered her with a blanket, and transferred her to the back of the ambulance. I started to climb in beside her when one of the attendants, a burly fellow with football shoulders, put a restraining hand against my chest.

"Sorry, but we're not allowed to transport unauthorized individuals."

"What do you mean, 'unauthorized'?! She's my *wife*. I belong with her."

"Not permitted," snapped the second attendant. He looked equally tough.

I grabbed his jacket collar and thrust my face close to his. "To hell with your authority, I'm going along!"

He wrenched free and punched me in the stomach. Hard. As I doubled over, gasping for breath, the ambulance sped away, its siren wailing.

"Can't let them do this," I muttered, heading for my car. I jumped behind the wheel of the Lexus, fired the engine, and gunned after them.

The house on Forest was less than two miles from the hospital, straight down Troost Avenue, and I expected to see the ambulance pull off Troost for the hospital's emergency entrance, but it didn't. It passed the hospital and kept right on going.

I was shocked and angry. What was happening here? Where were they taking Jan? She was in labor! The situation was insane and I could make no rational sense of it.

The ambulance raced ahead of me like a white

phantom through the night, increasing speed as it cleared the outskirts of town.

Helpless and frustrated, I continued the pursuit, but when the vehicle abruptly swung sharp-left, onto a rutted dirt road leading into the hills, I cut my lights before I followed. Let them think they'd lost me.

In the midnight blackness, without being able to see the road surface, I drove blindly, following the dim glow of their taillights. At the top of the hill the ambulance slowed and stopped. I pulled the Lexus into an area of heavy brush and cut the engine.

The hill had been bulldozed to form a wide, flat plateau, surrounded by thick trees which looked ancient. A low-roofed brick building sat at one edge of the clearing, while in the center, there was a structure of some kind. I moved closer through the obscuring wall of wild undergrowth.

A group of white-robed figures, each bearing a flaming torch, emerged from the building, led by a tall man whose bright crimson robe was trimmed in ermine. They moved to the center, to what I could now see was a stone edifice. It reminded me of those archaic altars archaeologists excavate at prehistoric sites. My attention was also drawn to a thick book, bound in rich leather and ribbed in gold, which had been placed on the top stone by two of the group.

The figure in red turned to face the others and I drew in a sharp breath: Mayor Stafford! Face flushed and eyes flashing, he raised his hand. "Let the women come forth to share in this miracle," he intoned.

From the building at the edge of the clearing came the women of Caxton. They walked single file, like zombies, heads down, trancelike, as they moved to surround the altar.

Stafford kept talking in the measured tone of a tent-show preacher at a Sunday revival: "We are blessed on this auspicious occasion with one who is new among us and who will deliver a child unto us." He gestured. "Bring her forth."

Jan, groaning and writhing in pain and on the verge of delivering, was carried from the ambulance to the altar.

Christ! She was going to give birth here and now. And there was nothing I could do about it.

They spread a red cloth covering across the altar and placed her upon it. Two of the tranced women moved in to assist with the birth. Jan was struggling and crying out: "No! No . . . leave me alone!"

Stafford poured thick liquid from a gold urn into a tall, jeweled chalice. He elevated the vessel and spoke some words I couldn't hear, then brought it to Jan's lips. He forced her to swallow the liquid, and Jan's struggles ceased. Obviously, it was some kind of sedative.

Then, as I watched helplessly, my child was born. Jan cried out once in pain, and I saw a glistening round head emerge from between her legs. Then the rest of the small body followed. The umbilical cord was severed and the tiny infant was lifted into the air for all to see. Our son!

The baby began to cry in the cool night air and a soft murmur swept through the robed figures. Jan's head fell back against the blanket as she lapsed into unconsciousness.

My throat was dry and my heart was pounding like a flesh drum inside my chest. The scene was surreal, nightmarish, beyond anything I could have believed possible.

And then the true horror began.

Our baby was placed on the highest point of the altar, directly in front of Stafford. He reached into the folds of his crimson robe and brought forth a short-bladed knife, set with flashing jewels along the ornate handle. The blade glittered wickedly in the torchlight as he raised it above his head.

"This woman has delivered unto us the fruit of her womb so that we may all partake of it. As warriors in ancient times devoured the heart of the slain beast to attain fresh life, so will we benefit in sharing together the heart's blood of this newborn child. I shall now read from the *Sacred Book of Brotherhood* . . ."

The robed figures clasped hands as Stafford opened the thick, leatherbound book.

"And ye shall drink of the newborn and devour its heart so that its radiant energy may flow into thee. This life force, pure and uncorrupted, shall renew and sustain thee. So it has ever been. So shall it ever be."

He bowed his head, as did all of his unholy cult. The group began rhythmically chanting.

I was already running desperately for the Lexus, knowing that I had only bare seconds.

At the car, I keyed open the trunk and snatched up the assault rifle, quickly loading it. Then I plunged back through the thick green overgrowth, bursting wildly from the high grass to confront the robed figures.

Now we'd see whose blood was spilled!

I squeezed the trigger as the robed figures broke away from the altar.

Die, you bastards. Die!

Like rows of scythed wheat, they fell under the relentless rain of bullets from my weapon.

When I reached Jan and our baby, Mayor Stafford—wounded in one shoulder and his face convulsed with rage—rushed at me, the jeweled knife raised.

"You sick son of a bitch!" I shouted as I cut him down with a short, savage burst from my rifle.

Somehow, in a numbed haze, I managed to get Jan and our baby into the Lexus, then drove away rapidly from the blood-soaked plateau, heading straight for Bridge Road and the Interstate. And I'd grabbed the *Sacred Book*. I'd need it to prove that all this was real.

Jan was weak, but she insisted on clutching our child close to her chest. Bonding with our newborn seemed to give her strength. But she didn't speak and her eyes were glazed with shock and exhaustion.

"Everything's all right now," I said. "We'll soon be clear of this hellhole. It's over."

But it wasn't.

We were about to crest the hill on Bridge Road when I saw them. Pete the sheriff and three of his uniformed deputies.

They'd angled their two patrol cars in the middle of the bridge, forming a barrier. Pete brandished a shotgun, and the deputies had unholstered their revolvers.

I rolled the Lexus to a stop a few hundred feet short of the bridge.

"I can smash through them," I told Jan. "Just make sure you and the baby are secure because it's going to be rough."

"They want my baby," she said numbly.

"Sure they do! The whole town's in on this. But don't worry, honey. They'll never—"

I suddenly felt cold steel pressing against the skin of my neck.

Stafford's knife! Jan must have taken it from his body at the altar. She was holding the razored blade at my throat, and the glaze in her eyes took on new meaning for me. She had the same trance-like expression I'd seen on the faces of the Caxton women.

"Whatever was in that chalice," I said slowly. "It *changed* you."

"I don't want to kill you, David. Give up the baby and let us have the *Sacred Book*."

She kept the blade at my throat as she eased open the passenger door and gestured to the sheriff and his men.

They advanced toward us, moving cautiously. For all they knew, I might be armed. But I wasn't. I'd discarded the empty assault rifle back on the hill.

I looked at the innocent pink face of our baby.

No, dammit. No! I twisted away from Jan and knocked the knife from her hand. It skittered to the floor of the car. I dived for it, came up with the knife in my grasp. Jan lunged for it, then gasped. The sudden thrust had driven the blade into her heart. She slumped back and fell from the car, onto the roadway, as blood coursed from the mortal wound.

I was devastated. My beautiful Jan, the dearest thing in my existence, lost to me forever! A huge part of my life had suddenly been chopped away, and I looked into a black void. How could I live without her?

The baby, a voice deep within me responded. *You must live for the baby.*

I slammed the passenger door and locked it. Little Devin was crying, but safe. As the engine of the Lexus roared to life, Pete smashed the butt of his shotgun against the driver's window. Another blow would shatter it.

I jammed my foot against the accelerator pedal and the Lexus surged forward, spinning Pete into the road. His deputies were firing at me as I gained speed, aiming for the center of the bridge.

"It's all here, I tell you! Right in these pages! Their history . . . rituals . . . everything!"

I was at the F.B.I. office in St. Louis, talking to a trio of hard-faced federal agents. On the way, I'd examined the *Sacred Book* and had been stunned by its contents.

"They call themselves the Brotherhood," I said. "And they've taken over Caxton."

"So everybody in town is really a *snake*, eh?" asked the first agent, a lean six-footer. He was perched on the edge of a straight-back chair, the sleeves of his sweat-soaked shirt rolled up. The other two stood behind him. I was at a table in the small, summer-hot room, the book opened in front of me.

"Not snakes, *reptilians*," I said. "Physically, they look like ordinary human beings."

"How'd they get to be . . . reptilians?" asked the second agent. He was shorter, and balding prematurely for his age.

"It took millions of years of genetic evolution," I explained. "These creatures go all the way back to the dinosaur. Dinosaurs didn't disappear from the Earth . . . they *evolved*."

"Uh-huh," nodded the third agent, a young guy who looked like he was fresh out of college. "How come they eat babies? Part of their diet?"

"Without a periodic intake of the blood of a newborn child, the reptilians can't maintain human form in this dimension."

The first agent grunted. "So now you're saying these reptilians are from another *dimension*?"

"No. They originated right here on Earth, but they'll be forced *into* another dimension if they don't continue to drink the blood of newborns."

"Where do all these 'newborns' come from?" asked the college guy.

"Mostly from their own females. They use women as breeders, to produce babies. Probably from human semen. Artificial insemination."

The tall agent: "These women . . . they don't mind having their kids served up as snake meat?"

"The females are kept in a trance state. Mental slaves under mind control. They're probably forced to drink the same stuff my wife did."

"So what, exactly, was in that drink she had?" asked the second agent. "Snake blood?"

"I don't know," I said, "but I *do* know it altered Jan's mind. She wanted to give them our baby, wanted me to hand him over to the sheriff."

The young agent's brows went up. "You mean ole Pete Adams? You're saying Pete's actually a reptile? A *snake*-sheriff?" The other two were grinning.

"The whole town's involved, and he's one of them."

The first agent was now pacing the room. "You tell us that your wife tried to kill you with a 'ritual knife,' but ended up stabbing herself. Right?"

"Right," I nodded.

"Where's the knife now?"

"I left it in Jan's body on Bridge Road . . . it's buried in her chest."

"You've got some problems, Mr. Cahill. If we do find your wife's body, you'll likely be facing a murder count. And if the rest of what you've said is true—about your shooting all those folks on the hill—you'll be charged with mass murder."

"I had no choice. They were going to sacrifice my child! Read this book! It's all in here."

They ignored the book and stared at me.

"Check out the wreckage on Bridge Road," I demanded. My voice was shrill. "Check that hill outside of Caxton. The bodies are *there*."

They checked Bridge Road. No Jan. No wreckage. The hill had been raked clean of blood and there were no bodies. The altar? Simply an old stone well.

There was nothing in Caxton to back up my incredible story.

Nothing.

What happened on that hot summer night in Missouri completely changed my life.

When I'd begun my screenplay, Lucas Fraley had seemed remote, the stuff of TV and news headlines, far removed from my world of reality. Yet now I, too, had used an assault rifle to deadly effect. We had, each of us, killed living creatures. Of course the circumstances were entirely different, but there was a dark parallel, proof that any of us can resort to overt violence when the brain commands it.

I gave up Hollywood, got out of the entertainment industry. No more scripts. No more location shoots. No more small towns. I moved to New York, the biggest city in North America, to raise my son. With Jan's and my savings I began investing in commercial real estate and the stock market. That's how I've been able to make a living for Devin and me.

I've never gotten over Jan's death. Her sweet smile still haunts my mind.

And what of the reptilians in Caxton?

I'd killed most of their breeders, so there weren't enough newborns to sustain them. Unable to maintain human form, the reptilians were forced from Earth into another dimension.

No more blood. No more human sacrifices.

By now, they're gone forever.

At least that's what I believe. Pray God it's true.

This tart little tale from the pages of Twilight Zone Magazine *was selected for* Dark Crimes: Great Noir Fiction. *Once again the story takes its source material from a real-life experience.*

Years ago I spent a rainy San Francisco afternoon in a deserted wax museum near the Bay, moving slowly past the parade of frozen figures. I felt alone in a dead world, oddly detached from the living world beyond the doors. What could a place like this do to a deranged individual? You know, one of those "walking crazies" (as Hemingway called them) you see on the street, gesturing expansively and talking loudly to themselves. You avoid eye contact and make sure that you move quickly past them. They inhabit their own crazed space and it's nothing you want any part of.

But what if you were one of them?

What if you were Stoner?

STONER

(Written: March 1988)

The thing is, thought Stoner, I shouldn't have gone into this lousy wax museum, that's for damsure. Plenty to see here in Frisco without me buying a ticket and going into this frigging museum of corpses.

I mean, said Stoner to Stoner, that's what they *look* like, right? Like dead people standing there staring at you with those glassy dead eyes of theirs.

It was a rainy Tuesday, late in the afternoon, and Stoner was alone in the place. The heavy-lidded ticket-taker hardly blinked when he took Stoner's money. Looked like a big fat frog to Stoner. Ought to be put on some pond sitting on a lily pod or whatever the hell frogs sat on in ponds.

Stoner was crazy and it bothered him, being crazy, but then a lot of things about Stoner bothered Stoner. Always had, ever since he'd been a kid. Fought with himself a lot.

When he was walking along the street Stoner would argue violently with himself in a loud voice. Some people would turn and look at him but most people ignored Stoner. Most of his life, except when he did really crazy things, Stoner had been ignored. Stoner was used to people moving away from him when he walked toward them while he was scowling and swearing at Stoner.

Stoner didn't like dead people. They reminded him he'd maybe be dead someday and Stoner hated the whole idea of being dead. He swore to himself he wouldn't be. "I'll never be dead," said Stoner, "and that's for damsure."

The museum entrance was at the bottom of a long flight of stairs and Stoner smelled the rubber matting on the stairs. It smelled like ether in a hospital. Or in a morgue.

The guard who was supposed to watch people in the museum was snoozing on his high wooden stool, tipped back against the puke-colored wall at the foot of the stairs. Maybe he was dead, too. Frigging dead guard!

"How are things?" a voice asked him as Stoner

walked into the museum. It was Stoner's voice.

"Not so damn good," said Stoner.

"You should maybe have killed that guy today, the one who gave you the ride up from San Diego," said Stoner. "He probably had some cash on him and a watch or a ring you could've hocked."

"I don't kill people," said Stoner. "You're nuts."

"Hey, we're both nuts," said Stoner. "So what else is new?"

"Why don't you just shut yer gob?" asked Stoner. "Give me some frigging peace."

"Smoke?" And a dark hand, very tan with a lot of hair at the wrist, held out a cigarette. The hand looked like Stoner's. Sometimes, though, it was hard to tell.

"Obliged," said Stoner, taking the cigarette. The hand lit it. Stoner inhaled deeply.

"Sign says no smoking in here," said Stoner.

"Frig the sign."

Stoner was walking along a kind of aisle with ropes at both sides. Old velvet ropes smelling of wet rats. Behind the ropes were the wax people, staring out at Stoner.

He walked up to a buxom young woman. Redhead. She had on one of those long, flouncy *Gone With the Wind* kind of dresses, with a low-cut front. He put his hand inside the dress.

"Sign says don't touch them," said Stoner.

"So what? So who's to see what I do in here? We're all alone, right?"

"Yeah, I guess so."

Stoner kept walking. He stopped in front of a bearded guy in a tall stovepipe hat who was standing with his hand on the shoulder of a little black kid in tattered overalls and a checkered shirt. He was Abe Lincoln, the guy with the beard.

Stoner reached across the rope and knocked his hat off.

"Why'd you do that?" asked Stoner.

" 'Cuz I think it's a friggin' dumb hat is all," said Stoner.

"I wouldn't have done it," said Stoner. "You got no respect for the president."

"I got no respect for nobody," said Stoner.

Stoner kept going and turned a corner into another room. This one spooked Stoner. It was a room where the French Revolution cut people's heads off. There was a young girl with her hands tied behind her kneeling at the guillotine with her head already off and in a basket.

Stoner reached in and picked up the head.

"I wouldn't do that," said Stoner.

Stoner didn't answer. He tossed the girl's severed head into the air and caught it by its long golden hair. Then he put the head inside his shirt. It made him look pregnant.

"They'll never let you take that out of the museum," said Stoner.

"Frig what they won't let me do."

And he walked into a room full of pirates who were in the middle of a big fight on the deck of a ship. There was a painted ocean around the deck with the paint peeling off the waves.

Stoner stepped over the rope and went up to one of the fighting pirates with a patch over his eye and took the guy's sword.

"It's probably fake," said Stoner.

It wasn't.

It was real. And it was sharp. He cut the pirate's head off with it.

"Fake, my ass," said Stoner.

"You're acting crazy again."

"That's what crazy people do, right? Act crazy?"

And Stoner snorted out a laugh. Sometimes he got a laugh out of things.

He walked through the museum, cutting off heads. Every wax figure he came to he cut the head off. Zip-zap. Zip-zap. Zip-zap.

Stoner was having fun. Maybe coming here into this museum wasn't such a lousy idea after all.

Which was when the guard showed up. The one

who'd been snoozing at the bottom of the stairs.

"What the hell's going on?" he yelled at Stoner.

"I'm cutting off heads," said Stoner.

"You're under arrest, man," said the guard, reaching for the bright gun at his belt.

"Frig you!" said Stoner. And cut off his head. Zip-zap.

"I thought you said you don't kill people," said Stoner.

"Up to now, I didn't," Stoner replied. "But he was going to arrest me and put me in a cell and you *know* how much we hate being put in cells."

"Yeah," nodded Stoner.

"Boy, oh, boy," said Stoner, sitting on the floor. "I probably made a big mistake cutting off this guy's head." He put down the sword and lit another cigarette. The smoke made his mother's face in the air. He didn't like that.

"What you gonna do now?" asked Stoner.

"I have to think. To plan and figure and work things out."

"Hey, you!" It was the froggy ticket-taker and he was walking down the aisle toward Stoner. "Closin' time," he said. "We're closin' up."

When he got to Stoner he stopped and looked down at the dead guard and then he looked at Stoner.

"Jeez," the ticket-taker said softly. And he began to back away, his face all green. Stoner had to laugh, because now he really *did* look like a frog.

"Where you going off to?" asked Stoner.

But the froggy little man didn't answer. He turned to run.

Stoner finished him.

Zip-zap.

"Okay, boy, you've had it now," said Stoner. "The cops will come and put you in the gas chamber or hang you or put you in the electric chair or inject you with some kind of killer drug."

"I don't think so," said Stoner.

"You gonna plead self-defense?" And Stoner chuckled.

"I'm insane, right? Just like you are. Insane people do insane things. That's logic."

Stoner shook his head. "You never should of bought a ticket to a place like this," he said.

"I won't argue with you on that one," nodded Stoner. "I guess I really screwed up, buying a ticket to this lousy place."

He took the girl's head out of his shirt and looked at it. She was very pretty. He smoothed the long blonde hair and put the head down, gently, next to the dead guard's head.

Then he walked back to the French Revolution

room and stopped in front of the guillotine. He looked up at the suspended blade. A release cord was hanging down from it.

Stoner pushed aside the body of the girl with her hands tied and took her place, kneeling down to put his neck into the wooden groove underneath the blade. Then he jerked the cord.

"It's probably fake," said Stoner.

It wasn't.

This was written as the centerpiece story for a special "Nolan Issue" of The Horror Show, *a late-lamented, small-press magazine that represented the strongest quality elements of the genre. I was pleased to have this special issue devoted to my work, and equally pleased to have "The Cure" included in* Definitive Best of The Horror Show. *(I love having my work selected for these "Best" anthologies; they validate my efforts to write, always, at the highest level of which I am capable. I would never shortchange my readers—or myself.)*

The protagonist in this story conducts his life in a healthy, carefully-regulated manner. He's a polite, affable fellow who avoids destructive habits and strives for self-improvement.

He has only one problem.

He kills people.

THE CURE

(Written: January 1988)

The minute I opened my eyes in bed this morning I promised myself that I wouldn't kill anybody else for a month.

Made me feel great! Kind of re-born. All charged up with good intentions, you know. It's a vow, so I can't break it. Sacred and all. Going to be tough on me though—like when I first gave up smoking Camels for a month. (I'd never smoked another brand. Guess you could say I was loyal to Camels.) It was hell, with me a chain smoker and wanting a cigarette every day, sometimes every hour. I'm proud to say I don't smoke at all now and I think the start of my cure, of being able to quit the way I did, was the sacred vow I made about no cigs for a month. That helped me have the strength of character to do it. (My pop used to say that strength of character is all that really counts in life.) Smoking is just a habit.

Same with murder. With some people (like me!) it just gets to be a habit. After the first couple of them, if you've really enjoyed them like I did, it gets easy. Then, later, you find you're addicted to doing it. Sort of sneaks up on you. You get to like it, and then, you get to need it.

And right now I *need* to kill.

Which is why I'm writing in this notebook, to keep track of how I do on my vow and also just to put down some of what I think about on paper. I do a lot of thinking and I'm not married or anything so usually there's nobody to talk to. This is going to help, being able to write things in a notebook.

I don't know if anybody will ever see it. Maybe after I'm dead somebody will find this notebook and read what I say and if they do I guess they'll judge me as some kind of crazy man who goes around killing innocent people.

Well, first of all, nobody is innocent. (Except maybe babies, and I don't kill babies or children. Never have. Never will.) We are born many times, live many lives like Shirley MacLaine (spelling ??) says we do—and we carry our old sins around with us from all these other lives. So no man or woman is innocent in this world today.

And we *all* have to die, right? So when I strangle somebody it's not so terrible because that person is going to be dead anyway and maybe I've saved them from getting cancer or AIDS or having a whole series of painful heart attacks. Or from having a stroke. (Did you ever see pictures of people in iron lungs where only their eyes move? How would you like to be stuck there in some iron lung with only your eyes moving? That happens sometimes after a stroke.)

Now, I am not a violent person. I've never fired a gun in my life, not even a target pistol, and I'm almost thirty years old. (I will be in five months and two days.) And I *hate* knives. They give me the shivers. I'd never use one. I use my hands because it's pure to do it that way, and you are making direct personal contact with the one you're killing. Like an act of communion between me and the one I strangle. A pure act is the way I think of it.

Another thing, I don't just go around killing everybody I meet or go on some kind of blood rampage like that Speck guy that killed all those nurses, or the nut in Texas who climbed up on a tower and shot all those students. Or Charlie Manson, having his "family" go into Sharon Tate's home and butcher whoever they could find in there like hogs in a slaughterhouse. Boy, I think that's *sick!* I would never do any of these things. When you strangle a person there's no blood or any mess to clean up. (Except for the dead body and undertakers get paid for taking care of dead bodies, right?)

There was one weirdo I read about, I think Garcia was his last name—no, it was Corona, who chopped up maybe fifty or more fruit pickers in an orchard with his machete. Ugh! And you take those guys who butchered the Clutter family in Kansas—

I didn't mean to get started on all this today but I do want to tell whoever reads this about meeting Truman Capote. (You pronounce it Ka-pote-tey.) He was the funny-looking little guy who wrote that book about those two sicko punks who killed the Clutters. *In Cold Blood* it was called. He went to Kansas and lived there for maybe three years or so and talked to everybody and finally met the two punks after the cops grabbed them and fell in love with the one named Perry. Capote was a homosexual by nature, and he just ended up in love with this weirdo Perry. Cried like a baby when they executed him. Claimed it was the worst day of his life. You'd think it was his mother!

Anyhow, I met Truman Capote the same year he died, 1984, out in California where I'm going next again. (I mean, I plan to hitch there next week. It's getting onto winter here in the Midwest where I've been for the last six months and I need me a dose of California sunshine!)

What I wrote above about the year he died is meant to be the year *Capote* died, not the Perry guy. I keep getting sidetracked because I'm not used to writing in a notebook and the words kind of run off by themselves down the page. Like a cat named Milhouse I used to have (named after Nixon, who was terrific in foreign policy). Always running off.

So anyhow I was in San Francisco in 1984 and read about Truman Capote giving a lecture over in Berkeley for five dollars so I went to it and met him after. (Frankly, to be honest, I don't know why anybody would pay him to talk because he had this little high squeaky kind of voice like Mickey Mouse, but that's not my business, hiring people to talk and I guess if you're famous, like he was, they don't care *how* you sound.)

I walked up to him when he was signing his books at a table and said I'd read his *Cold Blood* book in a library and I don't read a whole lot of books by anybody but I read his about the Clutter killings. He asked me if I liked it and I laughed and said it made me kind of sick but it was all good except about his falling for that Perry creep. Well, he got all upset when I said this and used the "f" word on me. "F you," he said. I don't use words like the "f" word (you won't find any in this notebook) so I was shocked, but I just shrugged my shoulders and walked out of there. I held my temper, but I don't like anybody using the "f" word on me and that's a fact.

So that's how I met Truman Capote.

It is a week later. I'm really disgusted with myself. Only one week passes and I've broken my vow already. Here is what happened—

I met this biker. A heavy-set character with long stringy blond hair with curls in it and fancy boots made out of dead snakes with caked mud on the soles. Had on dirty brown Army pants and lots of Nazi crosses on his jacket and a big chain around his waist. On the back of the jacket it said *Hail, the Hellriders!* With a skull and crossed swords under it. His hands were covered with matted red hair and looked like a couple of tarantulas. (I guess he was a natural redhead and dyed his hair blond.)

I was chowing down a burger and fries in a fast food joint in Topeka, Kansas, when he came in looking steamed for some girlfriend of his. She was across the room on the other side of the counter from where I sat and she saw him coming and split for the back door but he grabbed her and slammed

her against the Coke machine, yelling and cursing like a madman. Then he dragged her outside and nobody tried to stop him. Me, I just sat there chewing my burger (well-done, I hate them rare like you're eating raw animal flesh) and watching him through the greasy plate-glass window.

Outside, in the parking lot, he gave her a whack or two and she climbed on his bike behind him and he took off. He had an unmuffled exhaust because it sounded like firecrackers going off when he peeled out of the gravel parking lot.

She was a good-looking young lady in a kind of a cheap way. I didn't personally find her all that attractive, but I keep telling myself I'm too particular when it comes to young ladies which is maybe why I don't have any.

Two days later I saw him again, the biker. I'd hitched a ride into Lawton, a little teeny runt of a town about 100 miles west of Topeka and I had just taken a piss at the local gas station, an Exxon, when I heard his cycle pulling in. (No mistaking the sound of that exhaust!) He was alone and was drinking from a wine bottle in a wrinkled paper sack. He passed me on the way to the Men's, swigging from the bottle. (I don't know what happened to the girl, but that doesn't matter.)

I followed him inside—the place stank of urine

and feces—and hit him from behind with a tire iron I'd picked up outside in the garage part of the station.

Then I strangled him.

It was all very fast and nobody was around to see anything. The Exxon guy was out by the pumps around the other side gassing an orange Ford so I just climbed on this creep's motorcycle and buzzed off. Ditched it in a field later than night.

I was in a rotten mood after that. Breaking a sacred vow to myself is a terrible thing. But when that biker walked past me I felt this compulsion kind of wash over me. And once the compulsion hits things always seem to end up with me killing somebody and the biker was the one in Lawton. It could have been the guy who ran the station because the old compulsion just hits me and, bam, that's all she wrote!

So that's why I'm so disgusted with myself. I guess when a habit has a hold on you the way this one has on me there's no easy way to break free of it. Vows don't help much. (Easier to quit smoking Camels, take my word.)

Well, that's enough this time for the notebook. I really am feeling low. Just don't feel like putting down any more words right now. Okay?

*   *   *

I killed another one today.

A bald-headed businessman with pink jowls and a big gold ring I'm wearing now. Flashy. (I also have a thousand dollars cash from his wallet and nobody with any sense in his head should carry that much cash with him on the road. Just not a wise policy.)

He picked me up when I was hitching out of Jefferson City. That wasn't very smart of him to begin with since I read somewhere that 80% of all hitchhikers have served time in jail. (I never have, by the way. What I do is considered wrong by society rules I know, but no policeman has ever arrested me for anything not even for an unpaid parking ticket or jaywalking. My record is spotless and that's nothing to be ashamed of.)

So what I'm saying is it's dangerous to pick up some guy you've never met who's got his thumb stuck out for a ride. But he stopped for me, this bald gentleman in his big chromed white Buick. It was one of the older models, long and roomy, and in perfect shape. I don't know the year, even though I'm something of a nut for cars. (I don't want to diverge from my topic here but I was driving the family car when I was 12 and I owned my first car—a used Chevy—when I was 16 and I ended up racing it in a stock car event in my town and came in third. At 16. So you know I like cars.)

The minute I got into the Buick old Baldy started talking a blue streak, about how he was coming home from some kind of farm equipment convention and how he'd had this buxom prostitute up to his hotel room and how she did all these kinky sexual things to satisfy him.

I didn't enjoy his dirty mouth. I don't happen to believe in pornography in any form, whether it's in a book or coming out of somebody's dirty mouth, so I just sat there not saying anything back to him. (Pop drank a lot but he never talked dirty. Never once.) Then he got around to asking me how far I was going. I said far enough. He kind of smiled but I could tell he didn't like my short answer. I was not feeling very friendly at the moment, although I'm generally a good-natured sort of person. I just don't like having to sit and listen to filth.

About an hour later, when the road was deserted, I asked him to stop the car. I'll get out here, I said, and he said fine and pulled over on the shoulder of the highway which is where I strangled him.

He had a beefy neck and his eyes popped and I have to laugh when I think about it because he looked like a circus clown. He thrashed around in the seat quite a bit but I didn't have any real problem with him because I'm a very strong individual. I don't think I've written about that before—about how strong an individual I am. I used to work out with weights and I still do push-ups every night before I go to sleep to maintain muscle tone. It's a real shame the way most people let their muscles go to slack as they get older. Fact is, I could be a gym instructor if I wanted to work at a steady job. But jobs hedge you in and I like to stay loose and go where the wind blows. I still remember that old Western with Greg Peck, *The Big Country* was the title, and it's sure true this is a mighty big country and I don't fancy living with a fence around me. (Ever hear that ole song, "Don't Fence Me In"? Looks like I'm full of nostalgia, huh? And me not yet thirty!)

Anyway, after I did in this businessman, I stuffed him into the trunk of the Buick. There was plenty of room for him and I think it's great the way those old Buick trunks were so roomy. Trunks are a lot smaller these days, even on Caddies, and I just think it's all part of the erosion of our culture, but I don't want to get into that right now.

I drove the car into some woods and got rid of the body. Dug a shallow grave so he wouldn't be found right away. I wanted to borrow his car for awhile.

It drove really well. The seats were soft, but with plenty of back support, and it had a nice heater.

That was about six days ago. I drove the Buick all the way to California after switching plates in New Mexico just to be on the safe side. Had a kind of funny thing happen on the freeway. (An expressway is called a freeway in California because you don't have to pay a toll to use them which I think is very fair.)

I was driving along feeling a little tired and I saw this cloud formation that looked exactly like a giant eagle. It got me to use my imagination and I thought, hey, what if a giant eagle swooped down from the sky and just picked up my car off the freeway in its claws and flew away with me up to a really high mountain. He drops the car into a huge nest he's got up there full of unhatched eagle eggs. Then he flies off to take a crap or whatever. (By the way, I don't think crap and piss are like the "f" word and I feel justified in using them without an apology as modern examples of our slang and not words of filth. Crap is okay, but s—t is not. I will never write the word s—t in this notebook.)

With the eagle gone I open the door of the Buick and jump out. Then I start to climb down the mountain, being careful not to slip, and feeling very worried about the eagle coming back before I can reach the bottom. And, sure enough, here he comes swooping down at me and he just sinks those big

claws into my flesh and carries me back to the nest
for food. Which is when I decided to quit imagining
about the huge eagle because it was making me nervous and affecting my driving. For one thing, I didn't
want to think about being eaten alive.

So I just quit thinking about the eagle.

Hey, I'm glad to be back in sunny California! I
ditched the white Buick in the underground parking
area of one of those big shopping malls they have
so many of here in L.A. Just left it there, threw away
the key, and walked out into some glorious sunshine.

If I ever do decide to settle down somewhere it'll
probably be right here in the City of Angels. Smog
doesn't bother me as much as cold and snow and
little icicles inside your nose where the hairs get frozen. (In Chicago, it's that way, cold enough to freeze
the tail off a brass monkey!)

This afternoon, at another shopping mall, I
bought a paperback from a Crown Books (discount
prices) about the Boston Strangler. And wow, but
he was one twisted dude. See, each time he strangled
a woman he was *really* strangling his own crippled
daughter whose name was Judy DeSalvo. He was
Albert. Also, he had sex with all of these women,
something I've never done and which frankly turns

my stomach. Then he used silk stockings to do the killing with, instead of his bare hands and that's an impure way to do it and I have no respect for someone who would use such a method. I just cannot identify with DeSalvo at all, despite what you might think we have in common. For one thing, I would say he was most likely insane and, despite my habit, I'm a very rational person with a higher-than-average I.Q. (I know, because I took the test they gave once in *Cosmopolitan*, the magazine, and I really scored high. Surprised myself. Before this test, and it was long—two full pages in the issue—I had considered myself as having an average mind, but the results showed I was far above what is called "the norm." An awful lot of people in this country today are not even literate let alone above average, so I guess I've got a lot to be proud of in the brains department.)

But that Al DeSalvo was a prime nutcase if you ask me.

For most of last night I had a real good restful sleep at a Traveler's Delight motel but near morning, just before it got light outside, I had some bad dreams about killing my father, and I blame that Boston Strangler book on them. Because in that book it told about DeSalvo's father beating up his mother and knocking all her teeth out when he was seven. Now, my pop belted Mom around some (I guess that's normal in any marriage, right?) but he never knocked a single one of her teeth out, but DeSalvo hated him for doing that to his mom and wanted to kill him. So that's how I figure I had this dream about killing Pop when the truth is he died a natural death. I mean, what kind of a son would I be if I did a thing like killing my own father? He drank too much (I never touch alcohol myself) and he was a little rough with me and Sis but I never hated him, really, and never wanted to kill him. Oh, well, I wish I'd never read that dumb book about Albert DeSalvo because books like that put crazy things in your head at night. Today I ripped that book into shreds and threw it in the trash.

People have to be careful about what they read.

This afternoon, at one of those Multi-Plex Movie places where they have five or six movies all going at once, I saw a Steve Martin comedy just to get that bad dream about Pop out of my head. Steve was his usual funny self. He played a trans-sexual (does it have a hyphen in it?), a guy who was once a cheerleader in high school with ample breasts and a nice little behind on her in those tight satin pants they wear when they jump around at the games. Steve had this sex change into a taxi driver who smoked cigars and here the cheerleader's old boyfriend from high school shows up to marry her except now she's Steve Martin with a cigar and it was all pretty funny. Still, I have to admit I didn't think it was in very good taste. Why is everything you see in movies and TV these days all sex, sex, and more sex? I'm no prude and I'm sure not a Jesus freak or anything like that but dirt can get into your soul. It eats at your moral fiber. So who needs it? Frankly, I wish they'd do more Westerns like *The Big Country*. Big, clean outdoor stories—but you just can't find Westerns on the screen hardly ever anymore. A good Western is like a tonic. I always feel great after seeing a good Western.

I killed a woman today. (You know, people often call a woman a girl but when a girl is out of her teens you should call her a woman out of basic respect, or common courtesy, and this one I'll tell you about had to be 25 at least.)

She worked at one of those all-night 7–11s (or however you spell them) and when she got off work I followed her to where she lived in this big apartment complex where there were a lot of dark paths and trees. I think it's on VanAlden or some such street. Kind of a spooky place at night. Made me nervous following her in there because I don't like being trapped in the dark.

When I knocked on her door I said I was Sergeant Hooker of the L.A.P.D. (got the name from Bill Shatner's TV series which I don't think is still on). I've noticed that people always open up fast for the police. They don't question you, they just open the door. Inside, they expect you to flash some I.D. but I didn't show any I.D. to this woman I just buried my thumbs in her neck and choked all the life right out. She made some funny gargling sounds, like a lot of them do, and peed her pants, then just went limp as an old dishrag and I knew she was dead.

It wasn't difficult. It never is for me and I've got to tell you, in all honesty, that there's something funny (humorous, that is) about how loose and floppy they get after I've done it.

Well, I took the money she had in her purse and whatever cash I could find around her place. She had a few twenty-dollar bills stuck in a desk drawer. Then I turned out the light (no use wasting electricity because *somebody* will have to pay the bill) and left her there lying on her back in the middle of the living room on a quite attractive little throw rug. (Her apartment was, for the most part, very tastefully decorated. Not overdone. I appreciate things like that. It was probably a talent she had.)

I felt all light and airy going back to my motel. I always feel that way after I get rid of the compulsion.

As if I'm just sort of floating along the street.

It's a good feeling.

I just read over what I wrote in the notebook last night and it sickens me. How can I feel *good* about giving in to this lousy habit of mine? Does an overweight person feel good about pigging out on a box of fudge bars? Does an alcoholic feel good about putting away six martinis at lunch? Well, if they do there's something *wrong* with them. They need to fight their compulsions not give in to them and then end up feeling great about what is basically a self-destructive act.

At least I know my own weakness, and owning up to what's wrong in your personality means you're halfway home in finding a cure. I never want to delude myself. I believe in being totally honest about whatever failings I may or may not have. I know I am far from perfect. But keep trying to improve myself and I don't give in to self-deception. That's the only true path to a healthy life.

Today I decided to take a bus to Palm Springs which is about 120 miles from L.A. out in the low desert. I have a real passion about dry, clean desert country and I just got this sudden yearning to stand under a wide blue desert sky and let the sun bake out the poisons in my system. (We all have these poisons which clog our bloodstream and only hot, raw sun can leech them out. It's personal therapy and we owe it to ourselves to allow our systems to undergo such a cleansing process. And the temple of the body shall be cleansed. I think that's from the Bible, but I'm not sure. It might be from a self-health book I read once that was worth ten times what I paid for it.)

I'd been to Palm Springs before—the same year I met Truman Capote—and I liked the town. (Fact is, I'm told Capote used to own a house there.) Everything is neat and cheerful in Palm Springs. All the buildings look fresh-scoured and the sidewalks are spotless.

It took me longer to get there on the bus than I'd figured, and it was almost dark when I stepped out onto the main drag and took in a deep lungful of smogless desert air. It smelled crisp and new-minted. (They should bottle it for Easterners!)

I needed a place for the night and already had one picked out. It was a house owned by a newspaper columnist for the *L.A. Times*. His name was Ray Spaulding. He lived all week in an apartment in L.A. and came out here on Saturdays and Sundays. (Today's Friday.) A bachelor, and I counted on his coming out alone.

I'd read a profile on him they had in the *Times* (in

the "Who's Behind the Desk" feature on Sundays) but it naturally didn't give the address of his house. I got that from finding out his license number and going to the Department of Motor Vehicles.

Anyhow, tonight I went out there to this columnist's house and figured out how his alarm system worked and put it out of action. Then I forced a back patio door and got inside with no trouble. I'm pretty clever when it comes to getting into places. Should be by now, since I've had so much practice.

The house was kind of small, just a one-story job, but it was neatly kept up. The yard was trimmed and he had some lovely flowers along the front walk. Inside, it was all pink and blue with dozens of bookcases, but I didn't feel like reading. When I do read I mostly enjoy true crime mags, but I was just tired and not in the mood at Ray Spaulding's house, even if he had any true crime mags there. I didn't bother to look. I just flopped down on his bed for some heavy sacktime. Knowing the guy would show up the next morning. Which he did.

And he was alone. He came in the front door, whistling some tune I didn't know (I'm not much for popular tunes and I never whistle) not knowing I was in there waiting for him, all refreshed after a good night's shuteye. (And no bad dreams!) I grabbed him by the throat and it went fast, like always. Well, not *that* fast because he was a big guy and he tried to put up a fight so it took a little extra effort on my part to kill him. No real problem though.

I got an expensive gold watch off his left wrist (always nice to come up with a bonus!) and a fair amount of cash. (He didn't keep any in the house.) I found a big panama hat in his front closet to shade me from the desert sun and before I left I took a swim in his heated pool outside the patio. It was quite relaxing. I just let the water rock me like a babe. There's an art in knowing how to release tension from your body. You just shut your mind down like turning off the engine of a car—and you kind of drift out of yourself. So it was a really nice swim.

Then I walked out to the highway and took a bus to Indio.

There's a lot of untamed desert between Palm Springs and Indio. Off the main highway, I mean. Walk out away from the road for a mile or two and you might as well be on the moon. It's okay by day—I don't mind the dry heat—but it's kind of creepy at night with the cactus looking like people standing there watching you. (I used to dream about people standing around my bed in a row, just staring at me back when I was a kid. They never *did* anything, just stared. But it was creepy.)

I wouldn't want to live out here all alone like McGrath does. Let me tell you, in detail, about McGrath because he is worth writing about, believe me.

First, I was off the bus before it got to Indio. I just decided what the hay let's do some walking. I get urges like that sometimes—so I just left the bus at the next stop and put on Ray Spaulding's big panama hat and walked away from the highway into the sand. (I'd been looking at the back of a young man's neck on the bus, at the way the sunlight lit up the little gold fuzz on his skin, and thinking I might want to kill him later if the chance afforded itself but after I got off the bus I forgot about him.)

I didn't have any goal in mind, walking. I just wanted to enjoy the pure air and the clean scrubbed smell of the sand. Somebody told me that all this sand was once glass that got ground up by the sea but that's hard to accept and I told this person, look, I'll have to check this out with a scientist. But I never did that.

I scooped up some sand and let it run through my fingers. I have big hands, strong fingers and thumbs, and I'd be awfully good at hand wrestling if I ever went for that sport. (I didn't see that Stallone film, *Over the Top*, but I heard it stinks so I guess I didn't miss much. It was about hand wrestling.)

I wore high-sided Army shoes since you've got to be careful of snakes out here. Rattlers. I also wore some good-fitting designer jeans I took off a guy just my size that I killed outside a bar in St. Louis and a nice sports shirt with one of those classy little alligators sewed on the pocket. And my panama hat with sunglasses. I looked sharp and felt pretty contented, all things considered.

None of my old buddies live in California and I don't have a girlfriend right now but that's okay, they get to thinking they own you and start ordering you around and I don't let anybody to that. Even as a schoolkid back in Ohio I used to just get up from my desk and split when some teacher tried to manipulate my mind and free will. That's all any of us have, our free will, and nobody's got the right to mess with your free will. It's in the Constitution for every citizen.

Anyhow, I don't mind being on my own but it gets a little lonesome sometimes, with nobody to talk to. So guess you could say this notebook was my only friend.

Until I met McGrath.

He lives out here in the middle of the desert, in a

tin-and-tarpaper shack he built himself. Understand me, he built it solid. Has to be, because the winds whip through here with terrific force. He's got wooden cross-bracing on it and it's a pretty snug little shack, a lot stronger than you'd think just by looking at it.

I'd been walking for about an hour by then and was getting thirsty when I saw McGrath's place and decided to stop and ask for some water. McGrath was inside and when I knocked on the door he yelled come in and I did. He was sitting in there watching one of those big green Gila monsters crawl over his leg like it was a pet kitty. Geez! I don't like scaly green lizards and this sucker was one of the biggest I've ever seen.

McGrath looked up at me and brushed the thing off his leg and I said hi, I need some water. Oh sure, says McGrath. This here is Barney, he said, pointing to the lizard and I just nodded. He went over to a homemade sink and got me some water. It tasted great going down. Revived my spirits.

I thanked him and started out but he invited me to sit "and jabber some." That was how he put it. He said it gets dead boring out here in the middle of the sand and he always enjoys seeing a stranger. Right away, I don't know how, but I sensed we were going to become friends. Destiny.

McGrath had on worn strap sandals and I could see where one of his big toes (left foot) was missing. Just a stub, real short. He told me he got it snakebit and when it got infected he just severed it and cauterized it. He also had this one eye, on the right. Wore a black leather patch over the left one like a pirate would. He was thick bearded like a pirate, too, and his mouth had three teeth missing in the front. He said he lost the eye in World War Two fighting the "yella Japs" in the Philippines. That was his term for the Japanese and I don't happen to appreciate racial slurs. But I didn't say anything as he was the host.

McGrath also told me that he had a steel plate in his right leg from the war (a land mine exploded) which replaced most of his kneecap. So he had a lot of parts missing, beginning with the toe.

His voice was soft as a woman's, which surprised me since it didn't go with the rest of him. And, another surprise, he smelled like fresh soap. You'd think otherwise, with him out here alone in the wild, but he was obviously a very clean individual, which pleased me. I hate body odors on people.

I asked him how he made enough to live on and he said it didn't take much, living like he did, and besides he had his war pension and a little money from his daughter who lived in another part of the state. She'd send checks from time to time.

How long had he lived out here, I asked, and he said about 15 or 20 years, he'd lost count. He didn't have any calendars or buy newspapers and he'd never owned a TV set in his life. He said the past has no meaning, only the present counts, and that's a pretty sound attitude. He'd once been a doctor in a small village in Rhode Island but gave up doctoring after the war. And he didn't know how old he was, or care.

We talked about vitamins. I guess *argued* is a better term. Me, I take a packet of vitamins every day, seven in all, which you get in health stores and is called a Varsity Pack. Has everything you need to maintain a proper body balance. Then, once in a while, I take some organic zinc and bee pollen—and, after a meal, I chew a couple of Super Papaya Enzyme tablets which aid the digestion. McGrath snorted like a horse at all this, said he prefers jackrabbit stew and that you get all the vitamins you need in a good jackrabbit stew.

It was getting late by then. The sun drops away fast in the desert and the dark can take you by surprise. Light one minute, dark the next. I was a long way from the main road and didn't know if I could find my way back at night. McGrath said he'd be pleased to have me stay over and I said great, I'd appreciate the courtesy.

When I woke up McGrath was standing in the doorway with a rifle in his hand. Scared me. I don't like firearms but he smiled and said he'd just shot our breakfast. And he held up a dead jackrabbit.

I'd never had jackrabbit for breakfast, but McGrath was a good cook and it tasted a lot better than I thought it would. (Better than awful is the way I'd describe it.)

I trusted McGrath. Don't know why, but I had this real calm deep feeling of basic trust regarding him. Which is rare for me. I don't usually trust people, but somehow McGrath was different.

I found myself telling him about my habit and how I wished to God I could find a cure for it. I just want to stop killing people, I told him. The way I stopped smoking. Only it's a lot harder to do. Good intentions don't seem to mean much. I told him about the biker in Lawton, and the bald businessman, and the girl from 7–11, and Ray Spaulding. I even told him about looking at that kid's neck on the bus. Not a kid, actually, but younger than any of the others.

He seemed very interested in what I had to say

about the compulsion and how it just swept over me and how I'd killed these various individuals in various cities over the last decade. It took me a long time to tell it all and I felt exhausted and wrung out after I'd finished. It was as if I'd emptied myself of all emotion.

McGrath sat there for about a full minute without a word when I was done, and then he stood up and slapped his hands together (big, meaty hands) and said he could cure me of the habit. For good and forever. He told me that if I cooperated with his cure he plain guaranteed me I'd never strangle another man or woman.

What you gonna do, shoot me, I asked, only half kidding. Maybe I'd said too much. Maybe he thought I was some kind of a monster with no more right to live than those desert Jacks he went after.

He smiled and said to trust him and I'd be fine. Well, let me tell you, I was excited. I felt like the Cosmos had something vital to do with all this, that I'd been Cosmically directed to get off that Indio bus when I did and walk out here to meet McGrath and get cured forever. I'm not a bad fellow, really, and I think the Universe was giving me some personal help when I needed it most. That's my theory about McGrath.

I felt kind of feverish, floaty and light-headed and I could feel my heart thumping. I'll do it, I told McGrath, I'll do whatever it takes to kick the habit.

So we shook hands on it.

The cure has been going on now for weeks. And it's rough. Rougher than I'd ever imagined—but I'm going to continue to the end because it's the only way I'll ever stop what I've been doing.

I'm not writing these words. McGrath is taking them down for me. I feel kind of sick, and couldn't write even if I wanted to. He's doing a lot of other things for me, too, like Mom used to do back in Ohio. Sometimes McGrath makes me feel like a baby but he says I'll get over that feeling once the cure is done. He's terribly kind and caring and I've never met anyone like him.

McGrath has become the best friend I've ever had. Goodness just radiates out of him like sunshine spilling from a wall crack. You know the halos they paint on those robed Saints in the art gallery. Well, he's got one.

This is the last entry for the notebook. There's no need for more. I'm going to have a fine life from now on, out here under this clean desert sky.

McGrath and me, we're not alone anymore. We have each other, like two brothers from the same womb.

The cure is almost complete. He took the last one yesterday and it's fine. He's an expert and I don't have any worries. I'll never kill again, just like McGrath promised, no matter if I get the compulsion or not because you can't strangle anybody without fingers and thumbs.

And I don't have any more of those.

As a youngster, I used to collect Big-Little Books. They were fat, undersized volumes, measuring 3½" by 4½", with stiff cardboard covers. Half large-type text, half illustrations on facing pages. Designed for kids. One of my favorites was Tiny Tim and the Mechanical Men, about a little boy who was able to climb inside the head of a giant robot.

Giants have always intrigued me, from Jack and the Beanstalk to the Jolly Green Giant (Ho, Ho, Ho!), but I'd never written about one. Not until the summer of 1991, when I got the idea for "The Giant Man."

Let's face it. He may not really exist in my story. He's probably a metaphor for New York, a huge city that can easily devour you. I didn't write about him with this in mind, but when I'd finished I was quick to recognize the symbolism.

However you wish to interpret it, "The Giant Man" was a lot of fun to write. And, I hope, to read.

THE GIANT MAN

(Written: July 1991)

The roof door was jammed.

The super always unlocked it in the mornings for her. She enjoyed sitting out there on the roof with a cup of hot breakfast coffee looking over the vast New York skyline. This had become a fixed morning habit, a moment of calm before the rush of work each day. Besides, it was Indian summer, and the weather was really very nice for sitting.

So she knew the door wasn't locked; something on the roof was blocking it.

She put a shoulder against the door and pushed, using her full strength, but it wouldn't open more than an inch or two. Not far enough for her to see what was out there.

Pulling the door closed, she went down the inside steps and crossed to the other side of the building. There was a dirt-smudged skylight that opened onto the roof. She found a ladder, climbed up, and peered out through the clouded glass.

What she saw greatly surprised her.

"There's a giant man on the roof," she told the building manager. "He appears to be sleeping, but he *could* be dead. No way of knowing."

"I'll go up and have a look," said the manager. "Is he a tenant?"

"No, no. He's much too large to fit into any of these apartments."

"How big is he?"

"Huge. He takes up the whole roof. He's lying in a fetal position."

The manager blinked at her.

"You'll have to go up by way of the fire escape," she told him. "The roof door is blocked. He's resting his upper thigh against it."

"Okay," said the manager.

She waited patiently in the hall until he returned.

"Did you see him?"

The manager shook his head. "Nobody up there. And the roof door opens just fine. Used it myself."

"Thank you for checking," she said.

*   *   *

At her desk in the office she couldn't stop thinking about the giant man. It affected her work. She kept getting her file numbers mixed up.

She always ate lunch in Central Park which was only six blocks from her office building. And she always sat in the same place, on a green wooden bench deep inside the park, away from the crowds. She didn't mind the long walk in order to gain the solitude she required for her lunch. And she always ate alone.

She had just bitten into her chicken sandwich when she saw him. The giant man. Stretched out comfortably behind a large stand of trees and rocks. Seeing him there in the park took away her appetite.

She discarded her uneaten lunch in a trash bin and walked to the top of the rocks for a better look at him.

He was definitely sleeping. Not dead, sleeping. She watched his immense chest rise and fall with his steady breathing. She stared at him, fascinated, for several minutes. Amazing!

Then she sought out one of the park's mounted police. It took her a while to find him, and she was out of breath.

"Just behind those rocks over there," she said, pointing. "There's a giant man. You'd better go see."

"He try to molest you?" the policeman asked,

looking down calmly from his dappled horse.

"Oh, no. Nothing like that." She smiled. "It's just that he doesn't *belong* here."

"It's a public park," the policeman said. "What's he doing?"

"Sleeping," she said.

The officer chuckled. "Then why should I go over there and wake the guy?"

"Because he's a *giant*," she said earnestly. "He could harm someone, a man that size."

"Just how big is he?"

"I'm not sure," she admitted. "I'm not very good at estimating height, but he must be at least a hundred feet tall. Maybe twice that."

"I see what you mean," the officer said with a grin on his face. "That's big, all right."

"Please, if you doubt my word, go over and see for yourself."

"You stay here and I'll be back in a jiffy," he said, riding off toward the rocks.

She waited on another wooden green bench, one she'd never sat on before, until the officer trotted back to her on his horse.

"Well?"

"Nobody there," he said. "Checked the whole area. No giants."

"He was on the roof of my apartment building

early this morning," she said. "I'm sure it was the same man. And now he shows up here in the park."

"Maybe he's following you."

"Perhaps," she said. Then she smiled up at the officer. "Thank you for checking on him."

"Hey," he shrugged. "That's my job, ma'am."

She left Central Park and returned to work.

After dark, when the pace of the city had slowed, she enjoyed sitting beside the Hudson River, watching the reflections of all the lights on the water. Often, as she did on this night, she would bring along a thermos of hot chocolate and a small sack of vanilla cookies, sipping contentedly from the thermos cup while she nibbled a cookie.

New York was a magic city. Anything could happen here. That's what her mother used to say back in Iowa, but she'd given it a negative connotation: "You be real careful, honey. *Anything* can happen to you in New York."

But her mother's warning meant nothing to her and she never worried about living in New York. She felt that the things that happened here weren't threatening, just magical.

Like the giant man.

She'd been thinking about him all afternoon. Imagine! A man of that size in her life. It was difficult

to think of anything else. His unexpected appearance that morning on the roof had altered all her
habits, making every hour fresh and new.

Then she saw him again.

In the water. Floating on his back—only this time
in tight white swim trunks. (He'd worn pressed navy
slacks and a pale blue open-neck knitted shirt earlier.) He had his arms extended out into the water
and she could see that his eyes were closed. Asleep
again? Or just floating out there in the Hudson, resting his eyes, relaxed and easy?

She capped the thermos of hot chocolate, dusted
cookie crumbs from her skirt, and walked two
blocks to Tony's Place, a small Italian restaurant
where she sometimes ate dinner.

"There's a giant man floating in the Hudson
River," she told the owner. (The original owner,
Tony, was long gone.)

"Dead body, call the cops," said the owner. He
was running a total from a stack of checks at the
cash register, one of the old-fashioned kind. The
whole restaurant was old-fashioned and charming.

"He's not dead," she told the owner. "I'm certain
of that."

"A giant you say?"

"Hundred fifty, two hundred feet tall."

The owner signed. "Right out of a fairy tale, *he* is."
He swung toward her. "So what you want me to do?"

"Call the river patrol. Have them check on him. He could be a hazard to small boats out there."

"Lady, can't you see I'm busy. You do it."

She picked up the phone and dialed 911.

Within five minutes, a patrol car pulled to the curb in front of Tony's. She explained about the giant.

"Just get in the car, ma'am," the officer who was driving said. "Show us where this guy is."

When they reached the river, he was gone.

The water was quiet, reflecting the city lights.

She went to a movie to get her mind off the giant man. The film was an action-detective thriller with an incredible amount of violence in it.

She left before the end, walking home. The weather was superb.

When she turned the corner into the block she found the giant man sitting in the street directly in front of her apartment building.

He was fully dressed in a nicely-cut charcoal gray business suit.

And he was wide awake, taking up most of the street, curb-to-curb.

"I waited for you," he said. "Hope you don't mind." Naturally, he had a booming voice.

She looked up at him. His eyes were blue and serene. Immense, intelligent eyes.

"You . . . you've been following me," she said. "All day. In the park . . . at the river . . . now here."

"That's true," he said.

"I don't believe in *giants*," she told him. "They don't exist."

"I exist," he said simply.

"Where do you come from?"

"Does it matter? I'm here." He smiled. His massive white teeth were slabs of gleaming marble.

She sat down on the curb next to him. Like a mouse beside an elephant. She felt numb, dizzy. She looked up at him. The halo from the street lights made his face glow.

Then he said, his voice a soft rumble: "I love you . . . and I know that *you* love me."

She blinked, feeling weak. Her heart beat rapidly. "Do I?" she said.

She reached out to touch his right thumb. The flesh was warm, yielding.

"You're all alone here in New York," he told her. "This is a big, cold city. You need me."

"It's impossible," she said, shaking her head. "Even if I am . . . attracted to you . . . our *sizes* . . . we can never get together."

"Sure we can," he said, popping her into his mouth and swallowing her. "There," he said, patting his stomach. "Now we're together."

When John Betancourt put together his anthology, Best of Weird Tales, he told me he'd be including one of mine. Dandy. As stated earlier, I'm always happy to be in these "Best" volumes.

In his Introduction, discussing various stories in the book, he cited my "substantial achievements in science fiction, fantasy, and horror" and declared "At Diamond Lake" to be "a ghost story as ghost stories ought to be written."

Which was nice to hear.

I've driven the mountainous, twisting highway into the Big Bear/Lake Arrowhead area of Southern California and it is always an adventure. But never, on any of these trips, have I encountered a ghost.

Get ready to meet one.

AT DIAMOND LAKE

(Written: December 1991)

"I don't understand why you won't go," his wife said. "I just don't understand it."

"We'll go to Disney World," Steve told her. "They say it's a real kick."

"To hell with Disney World!" she said sharply. "I want to go up to the lake."

"No, Ellen."

"Why no?"

"It's too damn cold up there in the fall."

"And this summer, when I wanted us to go up for the Fourth of July, you said it would be too damn hot."

He shrugged. "I'm going to sell it. I've got it listed with a realtor."

"Your father dies and leaves you a beautiful redwood house on Diamond Lake and you won't even let me *see* it!"

"What's to see? A lake. Some woods. An ugly little cabin."

"It looks charming in the scrapbook photos. As a boy you seemed so *happy* there."

"I wasn't. Not really." His eyes darkened. "And I'm not going back."

"Okay, Steve," she said. "You can spend *your* vacation at Disney World. I'm going to spend *mine* at Diamond Lake."

Ellen worked as an artist in a design studio; Steve was vice president of a local grocery chain.

For the past five years, since their marriage, they had arranged to share their two-week vacations together.

"You're being damned unreasonable," he said.

"Not at all," she told him. "What I want to do seems perfectly reasonable to me. We have a cabin on Diamond Lake and I intend to spend my vacation there. With or without you."

"All right, you win," he said. "As long as you're so set on it, I'll go with you."

"Good," she said. "I'll start packing. We can drive up in the morning."

*   *   *

It took them most of the day to get there. Once they left the Interstate the climb into the mountains was rapid and smooth; the highway had been widened considerably since Steve was a boy. When his father had bought property on the lake and built a cabin there, the two-lane road had been winding and treacherous; in those early days the long grade to Crestline, five thousand feet up, had seemed endless. Now, their new Chrysler Imperial swept them effortlessly to the summit.

"We need something special to celebrate with," Ellen said as they headed into the heavily wooded area. "I want to get some champagne. Isn't there a shopping center near the lake?"

"The village," Steve said, his hands nervously gripping the wheel. He'd been fine on the trip up, but now that they were here . . . "There's a general store at the village."

"Are you okay?" she asked him. "You look sick. Maybe I'd better drive."

"I'm all right," he said.

But he wasn't.

Coming back was wrong. All wrong.

A darkness waited at Diamond Lake.

The village hadn't changed much. A boxy multiplex cinema had been added, along with a sports clothing

store and a new gift shop. All in the same quaint
European motif, built to resemble a rustic village in
the Swiss Alps.

Ellen bought a bottle of Mumm's at Wade's General Store. Old man Wade was long dead, but his
son—who'd been a tow-headed youngster the last
time Steve had seen him—was running the place.
Looked a lot like his father; even had the same type
of little wire glasses perched on his nose, just the
way old Ben Wade used to wear them.

"Been a long time," he said to Steve.

"Yeah . . . long time."

Afterward, as Steve drove them to the cabin, Ellen
told him he'd been rude to young Wade.

"What was I supposed to do, kiss his hand?"

"You could have smiled at him. He was trying to
be nice."

"I didn't feel like smiling."

"Can't you just relax and enjoy being up here?"
she asked him. "God, it's *beautiful!*"

Thick pine woods surrounded them, broken by
grassy meadows bearing outcroppings of raw granite, like dark scars in a sea of dazzling fall colors.

"Do you know what kind of flowers they have up
here?"

"Dad knew all that stuff," he said. "There's lupine,

iris, bugle flowers, columbine . . . he liked to hike through the woods with his camera. Took color pictures of the wild life. Especially birds. Dad loved scarlet-topped woodpeckers."

"Did you walk with him?"

"Sometimes. Mostly, Mom went, just the two of them, while I'd swim at the lake. Dad was really at his best in the woods, but we only came up here twice after Mom died. When I turned fourteen we stopped coming altogether. I tried to get him to sell the place, but he wouldn't."

"I'm glad. Otherwise, I'd never have seen it."

"I'll be relieved when it's sold," he said darkly.

"Why?" she turned to him in the seat. "What makes you hate it so much?"

He didn't answer. They were passing Larson's old millwheel and Steve had his first view of Diamond Lake in fifteen years—a glitter of sun-bronzed steel flickering through the trees. A chill iced his skin. He blinked rapidly, feeling his heart accelerate.

He should never have returned.

The cabin was exactly as he remembered it—long and low-roofed, its redwood siding in dark contrast to the white, crushed-gravel driveway his father had so carefully laid out from the dirt road.

"It looks practically *new!*" enthused Ellen. "I

thought it would be all weathered and worn."

"Dad made sure it was kept up. He had people come out and do whatever was needed."

He unlocked the front door and they stepped inside.

"It's lovely," said Ellen.

Steve grunted. "Damp in here. There's an oil stove in the bedroom. Helps at night. Once the sun's down, it gets real cold this time of year."

The cabin's interior was lined in dark oak, with sturdy matching oak furniture and a fieldstone hearth. A large plate-glass window faced the lake.

On the far shore, rows of tall pines marched up the mountainside. A spectacular panorama.

"I feel like I'm inside a picture book," said Ellen. She turned to him, taking both of his hands in hers. "Can't we try and be happy here, Steve—for just these two weeks? *Can't we?*"

"Sure," he said, "we can try."

By nightfall, he'd conjured a steady blaze from the fireplace while Ellen prepared dinner: mixed leaf salad, angel hair pasta with stir-fried fresh vegetables and garlic, and apple tart with vanilla ice cream for dessert.

She ended the meal with a champagne toast, her

fire-reflecting glass raised in salute. "Here's to life at Diamond Lake."

Steve joined her; they clinked glasses. He drank in silence, his back to the dark water.

"I'll bet you had a lot of friends here as a boy," she said.

He shook his head. "No . . . I was mostly a loner."

"Didn't you have a girlfriend?"

His face tightened. "I was only thirteen."

"So? Thirteen-year-old boys get crushes on girls. Happens all the time. Wasn't there anyone special?"

"I *told* you I wasn't happy here. Do we have to go on and on about this?"

She stood up and began clearing the dishes. "All right. We won't talk about it."

"Look," he said tightly. "I didn't want to, but I *did* come up here with you. Isn't that enough?"

"No, it isn't enough." She hesitated, turning to face him. "You've been acting like a miserable grouch."

He walked over, kissed her cheek, and ran his right hand lightly along her neck and shoulder. "Sorry, El," he said. "I'm letting this place get to me and I promised myself I wouldn't. It's just all this talk about the past."

She looked at him intently. "Something bad happened to you up here, didn't it?"

"I don't know, . . ." he said slowly. "I don't really know *what* happened . . ."

He turned to stare out of the window at the flat, oily-dark expanse of lake. A night bird cried out across the black water.

A cry of pain.

The next morning was windy and overcast but Ellen insisted on a lake excursion ("I have to see what the place is like.") and Steve agreed. There was an outboard on his father's rowboat and the sound of the boat's engine kicked echoes back from the empty cabins along the shore.

They were alone on the wide lake.

"Where is everybody?" Ellen wanted to know.

"With the summer people gone, it's pretty quiet. Too cold for boating or swimming up here in October."

As if to confirm his words, the wind increased, carrying a sharp chill down from the mountains.

"We'd better head back," said Ellen. "This sweater's too thin. I should have taken a jacket. At least *you* were smart enough to wear one."

Steve had turned away from her in the boat, his eyes fixed on the rocky shoreline. He pointed.

"There's someone out there," he said, his tone intense, strained. "On that dark pile of boulders."

"I don't see anyone."

"Just *sitting* there," Steve said, "watching us. Not moving."

His words suddenly seemed ominous, disturbing her. "I don't *see* anyone," she repeated.

"Christ!" He leaned toward her. "Are you blind? *There* . . . on the rocks." He was staring at the distant shore.

"I see the rocks, but . . . Maybe the wind blew something over them that looked like—"

"Gone," he said, not listening to her. "Nothing there now."

He pushed the throttle forward on the outboard and the boat sliced through the lake surface, heading for shore.

A hawk flew low over the wind-scalloped water, seeking prey.

The sun was buried in a coffin of dark gray sky.

It would be a cold night.

At one A.M. under a full moon, with Ellen sleeping soundly back at the cabin, Steve had crossed the lake to the boulders. He felt the cold knifing his skin through the fleece-lined hunting jacket; the wind had a seeking life of its own. He was able to ignore the surface cold; it was the *inner* cold that gripped him, viselike. A coldness of the soul.

Because he knew.

The motionless figure he'd seen sitting here on these humped granite rocks was directly linked with his dread of Diamond Lake.

And, just as he had expected, the figure reappeared—standing at the dark fringe of pine wood. A woman. Somewhere in her twenties, tall, long-haired, with pale, predatory features and eyes as darkly luminous as the lake water itself. She wore a long gown that shimmered silver as she moved toward him.

They met at the water's edge.

"I knew you'd be back someday," she said, smiling at him. Her tone was measured, the smile calculating, without warmth.

He stared at her. "Who are you?"

"Part of your past." She opened the slim moon-fleshed fingers of her right hand to reveal a miniature pearl at the end of a looped bronze chain. "I was wearing this around my neck the last time you saw me. You gave it to me for my twelfth birthday. We were both very young."

"Vanette." He whispered her name, lost in the darkness of her eyes, confused and suddenly very afraid. He didn't know why, but she terrified him.

"You kissed me, Stevie," she said. "I was a shy little girl and you were the first boy I'd ever kissed."

"I remember," he said.

"What else do you remember," she asked, "about the night you kissed me, here at the rocks? It was deep summer, a warm, clear evening with the sky full of stars. The lake was calm and beautiful. Remember, Stevie?"

"I . . . I can't . . ." His tone faltered.

"You've blocked the memory," she said. "Your mind dropped a curtain over that night. To protect you. To keep you from the pain."

"After I gave you the necklace," he said slowly, feeling for the words, trying to force himself to remember, "I . . . I *touched* you . . . you didn't want me to, but I—"

"You raped me," she said, and her voice was like chilled silk. "I was crying, begging you to stop, but you wouldn't. You ripped my dress, you hurt me. You hurt me a lot."

The night scene was coming back to him across the years, assuming a sharp focus in his mind. He remembered the struggle, how Vanette had screamed and kept on screaming after he'd entered her virginal young body . . . but then the scene ended for him. He could not remember anything beyond her screams.

"I wouldn't be quiet and it made you angry," she told him. "Very angry. I kept screaming and you punched me with your fists to make me stop."

"I'm sorry," he said. "So sorry. I . . . I guess I was crazy that night."

"Do you remember what happened next?"

He shook his head. "It's . . . all a blank."

"Shall I tell you what happened?"

"Yes," he said, his tone muted, dreading what she would say. But he *had* to know.

"You picked up a rock, a large one," Vanette told him, "and you crushed my head with it. *I* was unconscious when you put me in your father's boat . . . *that* one." She pointed to the rowboat that Steve had used to cross the water. "You rowed out to the deep end of the lake. There was a rusted anchor and some rope in the boat. You tied me, so I wouldn't be able to swim, and then you—"

"No!" He was breathing fast, eyes wide with shock. "I didn't. Goddamn it, I *didn't*!"

Her voice was relentless: "You pushed me over the side of the boat into the water, with the anchor tied to me. I sank to the bottom and didn't come up. I died that night in the lake."

"It's a lie! You're alive. You're standing here now, in front of me, alive!"

"I'm here, but I'm not alive. I'm here as I would have been if I'd been able to grow up and become a woman."

"This is all—" His voice trembled. "You can't really expect me to believe that I'd ever—"

"—murder a twelve-year-old girl? But that's exactly what you did. Do you want to see what I was like when they took me from the lake . . . after the rope loosened and I'd floated to the surface?"

She advanced. Closer, very close.

"Get away from me!" Steve shouted, taking a quick step back. "Get the hell away!"

A little girl stood in front of him now, smiling. The left side of her head was crushed bone, stark white under the moon, and her small body was horribly swollen, blackened. One eye was gone, eaten away, and the dress she wore was rotted and badly ripped.

"Hi, Stevie," she said.

Steve whirled away from the death *figure* and began to run. Wildly. In panic. Using the full strength of his legs. Running swiftly through the dark woods, rushing away from the lake shore and the thing he'd left there. Running until his breath was fire in his throat, until his leg muscles failed. He stumbled to a panting halt, one hand braced against the trunk of a pine. Drained and exhausted, he slid to his knees, his labored breathing the only sound in the suddenly wind-hushed, moonlit woods. Then, gradually, as his beating heart slowed, he raised his head and . . . oh, God, oh Christ . . .

She was there!

Vanette's ravaged, lake-bloated face was *inches* from his—and her rotted hand, half mottled flesh, half raw gristle and bone, reached out, delicately, to touch his cheek . . .

Two years later, after Ellen had sold the lakefront property and moved to Florida, she fell in love with a man who asked her what had become of her first husband.

Her reply was crisply delivered, without emotion. "He drowned," she said, "at Diamond Lake."

Another experiment with fiction. I determined to write a story composed entirely of dialogue between two men in a prison setting. No interior thoughts. No description. The dialogue itself would delineate character, motivation, and background.

Dennis Etchison needed truly offbeat material for his important, trail-blazing anthology, Meta-horror. He rejected two of my earlier stories. They had struck out.

"The Visit" was a home run.

THE VISIT

(Written: May 1991)

"So . . ." he said. "You've been wanting to talk to me. I'm here. Let's talk."

"You're willing to be entirely open and frank?" I asked him.

"Sure."

"You'll tell it to me straight? No evasions. No bullshit."

"You got it."

"You'll answer any question I ask?"

"I said so, didn't I. But keep your face close to the screen. That way the guard can't hear us."

"I'll be taking notes. For the book I'm doing."

"Shit, you're not going to use my real name, are

you? I don't want my real name in some goddamn crime book."

"No, don't worry about that. I'll call you Dave. And I won't be using a last name. You'll be . . . a statistic."

"Great. I had a cousin named Dave. Real asshole."

"Shall we begin?"

"That's what I'm here for. Start your questions."

"How old were you when you killed for the first time?"

"Twelve. Like Billy the Kid. He knifed a guy when he was twelve, back in the Old West. I always felt close to the Kid. Wish I could have known him."

"Was it a man or a woman . . . the first one at twelve?"

"Neither. I snuffed a kid, same age as me. It was after he smart-mouthed me in class. I waited till he was walking home across the ravine, between the school and his house, and that's where I killed him, right there in the ravine."

"How?"

"With a stone. Crushed his skull. It broke open like an egg."

"Then what did you do?"

"Buried him. Ravine's a good place to bury people."

"Body ever found?"

"Nope. He just went to bone. His name was Bobby something. Big red-haired Irish kid. Had a real smart mouth on him."

"When was the next one?"

"When I was fifteen. After I ran away from home . . . that same summer."

"Man or woman?"

"Man. A bum. Railroad tramp. I was going West in this boxcar and he was in the same car, just the two of us. Had some food he didn't want to share so I wrung his skinny neck to get it. He was an old guy, so I had no trouble with him. But he *did* squawk like a chicken does when you twist its head off. Just like a damn chicken."

"Anyone find out? About the bum, I mean?"

"Christ, no. I pitched him out of the car when the train was crossing a river. Neat and easy. And the food made me sleepy. Had me a nice snooze."

"After these killings—the boy and the old man—did you have any remorse?"

"Me? Remorse? Hell, no. When you do somebody, it's like a high. You come down, but then you want another. Like with drugs."

"Ever use any?"

"Sure, I experimented some, but my real high was

doing people. So I quit the drugs. To keep my head clear so I could enjoy myself. Didn't want anything getting in the way."

"You're what . . . how old now . . . thirty?"

"Thirty-two."

"So how many have you done since the first one at twelve?"

"I'm not like you. I don't make notes. Don't write things down on paper. That's why I don't have any exact figure to give you."

"Take a guess."

"Well . . . fifty or more. Maybe sixty. I just never kept count. But it's under a hundred for sure. I'd know if I did a hundred. That'd be something to celebrate."

"What about mass killings? Ever been into those . . . or was it one at a time?"

"Hey, I've been into whatever comes up. Sure, I did some numbers once. In Frisco. In a big house near the Barbary Coast area. Big Victorian house."

"Tell me about it."

"It was at night, and this family came home before I expected them to. I was on the second floor, picking up whatever I could find, when the door slams downstairs and this guy and his wife and their two teenage daughters get home early from a play."

"Then you didn't go to the house planning to kill them?"

"No, it's like I said. I went there to pick up some money, jewels, whatever. Guy's gotta earn a living. I'd been staking out the place and earlier that evening I'd heard them through the screen, talking about going to this play, so I figured I'd have plenty of time to do a job on the place. But they left after the first act. Guess the play was lousy."

"So what happened after they came in?"

"I decided to do all four of them, just for the high. I'd never done four at once up to then."

"What were you carrying? What kind of weapon?"

"I had me a big belt knife and a sawed-off."

"Shotgun?"

"Yeah. It was a custom job. I'd trimmed the barrels. Turned it into a mean sonuvabitch."

"Shotguns make noise."

"I know—but I was careful about that. I've always been a real careful guy."

"Who'd you kill first?"

"The wife. She came upstairs to change her dress and I used the belt knife on her. Got excited and near cut her head off. I was using one of those big bowie type knives and I got a little carried away."

"Then what did you do?"

"Waited till the next one came upstairs. One of the daughters. She was about seventeen. Tall, with a nice ripe figure on her. I used one of her mother's stockings to do her."

"In my research, I've found that most killers use the same method in all of their kills. You've been . . . unusual in this respect."

"Yeah, well, I'm an unusual type of guy. As to how I did them, I like to improvise. Switch around, you know. Knife. Hammer. Rope. Stocking. Whatever. I get a different high each time. I get bored with the same routine, so I try different things at different times. The police can never figure me out. I've always been ten steps ahead of them!"

"Did you use the shotgun in the house?"

"Sure did. I went downstairs after the stocking job and found the guy and his other daughter watching Cosby on TV. You ever watch Bill Cosby?"

"I've seen him."

"Funny, huh?"

"He can be funny, sure. What did you do downstairs when you found them watching television?"

"I tied them both on the couch and then used big sofa pillows to muffle the sawed-off. A barrel for each one. It really wasn't noisy at all. Got some blood and stuff on my shirt, but the noise was no problem."

"How'd you feel then . . . after eliminating the whole family?"

"Felt great. All charged up. I mean, doing four in one night. It was special."

"Sexually, how did it affect you?"

"Sexually?"

"Were you aroused? You used the word 'excited' earlier."

"I don't like to talk about sex. It's personal."

"You told me you'd answer any question I asked you with no bullshit."

"Okay, all right . . . sure, I had a hard-on if that's what you want to know. The second daughter did it. But I beat off before leaving the house and that took care of it."

"Have you ever had intercourse with any of your victims? After killing them?"

"Jesus, no! I don't fuck corpses if that's what you mean."

"It's not uncommon."

"It is with me. That's not my trip."

"Are you bi-sexual?"

"Look," he said, "let's skip all this sex shit, okay. I'm a normal guy when it comes to gash. I screw *women*. Period. Can we get off this?"

"Fine. Uh . . . have you ever collected body parts? Like, souvenirs of your kills?"

"This is sick."

"You didn't answer the question."

"The answer is—shit, no, I don't collect body parts. And I don't stuff people either. Didn't that guy in the *Psycho* movie stuff people?"

"I don't think so. I think it was birds. But he kept his mother's corpse in the basement. In a rocking chair. What about *your* mother? Were you close to her?"

"Let's keep my parents out of this. I'll answer any question about myself, but I'm not going to get into anything about my folks."

"All right, then," I said. "Tell me about the most bizarre killing you've ever done. The weirdest one."

"That guard's giving us the eye. Maybe we'd better save it for the next visit."

"I guess we better."

"Time's up," said the guard. "Look, it's none of my business, mister, but I gotta wonder just why you'd want to waste your time talkin' with 'The Butcher.' Even his own family stays away from him."

"I have my reasons."

"Yeah, I guess you do," said the guard.

"I'm ready now," I said.

And he led me back to my cell.

"The Partnership" was dramatized on television as part of the Darkroom series which was produced by Universal. It was also selected, in England, for Great Tales of Terror. The story's main locale is a boarded-up funhouse in the Midwest. As a boy, I loved to go stumbling through the narrow wooden corridors of the big funhouse at Fairyland Park in Kansas City, and I have never forgotten the shivery joys of feeling trapped in the seemingly-endless dark.

Such memories led me to write "The Partnership." I think you'll like Tad Miller. He's a nice, quiet, easygoing fellow, always fun to talk with. Yes, just about everyone likes Tad. But his partner . . . well now, he's not so popular.

As you'll see for yourself.

THE PARTNERSHIP

(Written: July 1979)

Me and Ed, we're in business together. Which is what I want to tell you about eventually because I think you folks will find it interesting. But this is also about the stranger with the beard. And he comes first.

You like ghost stories? Bet you do! Everybody does. But this isn't one of those. Not a ghost in it. Still, it's a little spooky, I'd guess. I mean, to some it will be. Strange—that's a good word for it.

Strange.

Anyhow, Ed and me, we got ourselves a real nice partnership going. For one thing, we trust each other, and that's the basis you build on. No trust, no partnership. Learned that long ago. My Irish grandaddy, bless him, came over from County Cork. Bought into a saloon in Virginia City with a partner who "stole him blind." That's how he always put it: "That man stole me blind!"

Now, with Gramps long gone, I'm as old as he was when I was a tad. That's how I got my first name. Ralph's the legal one, but I've always been Tad since Gramps called me that. Tad Miller. Simple name for a simple man.

I grew up in Nevada, but we moved to Chicago when I was still a boy—but you don't really want to know all about how I got here to this little town stuck down in god-knows-where country. It's in Illinois, a good piece out from Chicago, and we're on the lake. That's what counts—not how I got here or what brought me.

I'm here. That's enough.

Name of this town's not important, so I won't give it out. If I did, some of you folks might come here one day, looking to say hello, and I wouldn't like that much since I'm not partial to meeting just anybody. No offense.

Ed's the same way. When he's ready to meet a stranger he'll go all out, but in between he's like me. Keeps to home.

Don't get me wrong. When a stranger comes to town, and I see he's lonely, I'll strike up a conversation as quick as the next fellow. I just don't *advertise*, if you know what I mean.

This town's on a spur highway into Chicago, and we get our share of hitchers. Road bums, sometimes. Others—like kids on the run from home, heading for life in the big city. Some on vacation. All kinds, drifting in for coffee and grub at Sally Anne's. They all end up at Sal's. Only eatery left in town, so she gets the business.

Real nice sort, too. You'd like her. Kind eyes. I always notice a person's eyes, first off. And hers are soft and liquid, like a deer's.

Me and Sally kid each other a lot, but we're both too old to have it mean anything. But she likes me. Most folks do. And that's nice. Person wants to know he's liked, even if he keeps mostly to home.

Well, before I tell you about the bearded stranger I met at Sal's last month you need to know some things about this town.

For instance, it's dying fast. Getting smaller every year. Most of the young ones are gone now. Us diehards are still hanging on. Me and Ed, we'll have to split up one of these days because this town's due to just wink out like a star in the sky. Bound to happen. Be a sad day for me. Ed, too. We're not that close, understand, but there's a lot between us. Still, like my mama used to say, nothing lasts forever.

Anyhow, the town's slowed down a hellish lot since I first moved here from Chicago after Mama and Pop died. Expressway gets most of the traffic. Puts us in the backwash. The *big* change came when Moffitt Paper closed their factory. Town lost its main source of revenue, and things slowed way down.

That's when I had to leave Happyland. It's what they call the amusement park on the lake. Closed now. Boarded up. Left to rust and rain.

I ran the Funhouse out at Happyland. For twenty years. Slept there on summer nights. Knew every turn and twist of the place, every creaking board and secret passage and blind tunnel in it. Still do, for that matter. Which is where the stranger comes in, but I'll get to that.

First, a little more about me and this town if you don't mind. (I'm in no hurry, are you?)

I got married here. Surprise, eh? Guess, on paper, I don't come across as the romantic type—even though Sally still kids me that way. But married I was, and to a good woman who never liked kids so we didn't have any. When she died I was left alone. No family, not even cousins. (I didn't know Ed then.)

Her heart gave out. One day, fine, the next she's gone. Hit me hard. Made me kind of wacky for a while. But I got over it. We get over things, or things get over us, take your choice. Nowadays I'm used to being on my own, and I do fine. Enjoy my privacy. Enjoy the woods and some fishing in the fall. Like I said, a simple man. I miss her bad some nights, just like I do Happyland. But they're both gone—and everything has to die. Nature's way. Accept it. Flow with the tide.

She's buried out at Lakeside. Strangers think it odd, us having our cemetery right there on the lake, smack next to Happyland. Graveyard and amusement park snug-a-bug together on the lake. Odd, they say. Or *used* to, when Happyland was still open. "Spooky" is what they called it, having them together that way. But I never saw a ghost in twenty years out there. Oh, once in a while some big rats would wander in and give the ladies a real scare in the dark. (I'd always refund when it happened.) They'd come from the burrows under the cemetery, the rats, that is. Big suckers. And scared of nothing. That's the way of a rat; he scares you, you don't scare him.

Anyhow, my good wife's buried out there, or was. Guess the rats have her by now, though that isn't very nice to think about, is it? They got mighty sharp teeth, can gnaw right through the side of a coffin unless you can afford a steel one. Me, I've never had one extra dime to rub against another! Spend what I earn. To the penny. But I pay my way. No debts for Tad Miller.

Better get on with telling you about the big stranger who passed through here last month . . .

I was at Sally's, kidding with her—and we didn't see him walk in. She was joshing me about a new ring I had on. Big shiny thing, and Sal said it looked like I was wearing a streetlight. I was joshing her back about her new hairdo, saying it looked like a hive of bees could make honey in there. That kind of stuff. Just kidding around, passing the time of day.

Next thing, the stranger is banging the counter and yelling for some service. Sal broke off quick and moved over there to ask him what he'd have.

"Coffee and your special," he growled. "The coffee now. And a small tomato juice."

She told him no tomato juice, just orange. That made him madder than before.

He was big and mean looking. Maybe a lumber man. Had one of those shoulder-hike rigs, which he'd taken off and put on the counter next to him. Man of about forty, I'd guess. Muscled arms and a wide back. Thick dark beard. But honest eyes. I noticed his eyes right off.

He wore one of those space-age wristwatches with

all kinds of dials and dates on it and little panels that light up. I'd never seen one like it before, and was plain curious, so I took the empty stool next to him. He gave me a scowl for doing that, because the rest of the counter was empty, and I guess he didn't want company.

"Hello, mister," I said. "My name's Tad Miller."

"So what's that to me?"

Hard-voiced. Not friendly at all.

"Want to apologize for all that jawing I was into when you came in. Customers come *first* in this place."

He grumbled "all right" while stirring his coffee, but he didn't look at me. Ignored me. Hoped I'd go away.

I leaned toward him. "Couldn't help but notice that timepiece you're wearing. Handsome thing. Never saw one quite like it."

He swung around slowly, holding up his left wrist. "Got it in Chi," he said. "You like it, eh?"

"Prettiest damn watch I ever did see."

He was warming up fast. Like a woman will do when you tell her how cute her kid is. Works every time.

"What are all those little dials and things?" I asked.

He worked back his sleeve so I could get a better look. "Tells you the time in ten parts of the world," he said. "Tells you the month of the year and the day of the week."

"Well, I'll be jinged!"

He twisted a doodad at the side of the watch. "Set this," he said proudly, "and it rings every hour on the hour."

By now Sally was spreading out his lunch special, and she couldn't resist getting into the conversation. "What's a thing like that cost?" she asked him.

Bad manners. I'd never have asked it that way, straight out. And he didn't like it. He scowled at her. "That's my business."

Watch could have been stolen, for all I knew. You just don't ask folks about how they get hold of a thing like that or how much they paid for it. But Sal was never one for laying back.

She huffed into the kitchen, all tight-faced.

He was eating in silence now. Sally's question had put him back into his sour mood. I felt bad about that.

"Look . . ." I said, "don't mind her. She don't see many new folks around here. Sticks her nose in too far, is all."

He grunted, kept eating. Really shoveling it in. It was beef stew. I knew Sally made good beef stew, so he was bound to be enjoying it. I tried him again.

"You just . . . passing through?"

"Yeah. Hitching. Can't hitch on the express so I'm on the spur. Not many cars, I'll tellya. Waited two hours for a ride this morning."

I nodded in sympathy. "Like you say, not many cars. But the fruit trucks go through this time of year. In the afternoons. One of those'll stop for you. Those truckers are good people. Just you give 'em a wave, they'll stop."

"Thanks for the tip," he said. "Usually, with trucks, I don't even try. Regulations about riders and all."

"Just give 'em a wave," I repeated.

There was some silence then. Him finishing Sally's stew, me sitting there sipping at my own lukewarm coffee. (I drink too much of the stuff, so I've learned to nurse a cup. Can't sleep nights if I don't.)

Then I said to him, "You ever go to amusement parks as a kid?"

He nodded. "Sure. Who hasn't? Every kid has."

"I ran the Funhouse in one," I told him. "Down by the lake just this side of town."

His face brightened. A smile creased it. His first of the day, I'd wager.

"Hell, I loved those frigging funhouses! Used to sneak into 'em when my allowance was all spent and I couldn't afford to buy a ticket. They had an air vent inside that blew the girls' skirts up. Used to hide in there and watch." He scrubbed at the side of his dark beard. "Haven't been in one since I was eleven—back in Omaha."

"Never made it to Nebraska, but I hear it's a nice state."

"Used to scare myself half to death in those places. Bumping around in the dark . . . Couldn't see a thing. Scary as hell!"

"Folks like to be scared," I said. "Guess it's part of human nature."

"Trick doors . . . blind tunnels leading nowhere . . . things that popped out at you!" He chuckled. "One place had a big gorilla with red eyes . . . I musta jumped ten feet when that ape popped outa the floor at me! Had gorilla nightmares for a month after that. Wouldn't go to bed unless Ma left the light on."

I've noticed one thing in the years with Happyland: people love to talk about funhouses. It's a subject everybody just plain likes to talk about—how scared they got as kids, lost in the dark tunnels, with things jumping at them. Funhouses are just that— *fun*.

"I miss running the place," I told him honestly. "Used to get a real kick out of scaring the folks. I'd work all the trick effects . . . and how they'd yell and scream! Especially the girls. Young girls love to scream."

He nodded agreement.

Suddenly I turned to him, grinning. "I got me an idea."

"What's that?" he said, pushing away his last empty plate. He put his hand on his stomach and belched.

"Why don't you and me go out there—to Happyland? I can take you through the Funhouse!"

He blinked at me, a little confused. "You mean—right now?"

"Sure. The park's closed, has been for years, but I can get in. Be no problem for me to show you through my Funhouse. Be proud to!"

The big man shook his head. "Well . . . I dunno. That stuff's for kids."

"Hell, *we're* kids, aren't we? Just wearing adult bodies. No man ever stops being a boy. Not inside. Not all the way." I grinned at him. "Want to have a go ? . . . give it a try?"

"Sounds a little crazy."

"Funhouse is for fun!" I said. "It's not even noon yet. You can take the tour with me, come out of the park and still grab a hitch with one of the truckers."

He slapped the countertop. "Why not? Why the hell not?"

I grinned at him. "Be fun for me, too. Haven't been out to Happyland for a longish while. Be like going home."

I owned a Ford pickup. Old, like I am. Got a missing taillight. Clutch is bad. Needs a ring job. Tires are mostly bald. And the paint's gone altogether. But it putters along. Gets me where I have to go.

Happyland's only ten minutes out from town. As I said, right on the lake, at the deep end. Lot of boats used to be on the lake, but it's quiet now. Just black water, and too cold to swim in most of the year. Deep and black and quiet.

I parked next to the gate and we slipped under the rusted chain fence. The park was sad to see, all deserted and boarded up and with old newspapers and empty beer cans and trash everywhere. Vines growing right into the boards. Holes in the ground. I told the stranger to watch where he walked.

"Break an ankle out here at night," I said.

"I'll bet."

We passed the Old Penny Arcade. All the machines were gone. It was like a dirty barn inside. No color or movement or sound in there now. Just a rat or two, maybe. Or a spider trapping flies.

Sad.

We walked on in the noon heat, past the Loop

and the Whip and the Merry-go-Round, with broken holes in the floor where all the painted horses had galloped.

"No gorillas today," I said as we approached the Funhouse. "Electricity's shut down, and they took all the trick stuff away to Chicago. But at least we can run the tunnels. They're still the same."

"This is crazy." said the bearded man. "I've gotta be nuts, doing a thing like this."

"Be proud of yourself!" I told him. "You're not afraid to let out the boy in you! Every man would like to, but most are chicken about it. You've got guts."

We stood outside, looking at the place. The big laughing fatman at the entrance was gone. I can still hear his booming *Ha-Ha-Ha-Ha* like it was yesterday. Twenty years of a laugh you don't forget.

The ticket booth was shaped like the jaws of a shark—but now most of the teeth were missing and the skin was peeling in big curling blisters along the sides. The broken glass in the booth had two boards nailed over it, like a pair of crossed arms.

"How do we get in?" the stranger asked me.

"There's bound to be a loose board," I told him. "Let's take a look."

"Oke," he nodded with a grin. "Lead on."

I found the loose board, pulling some brush away

to clear it. Illinois is a green state; we get a lot of rain here, and things grow fast. The Funhouse was being choked by vines and creepers and high grass. It looked a thousand years old.

Sad.

The sky was clouding over. Late summer storm coming. They just pop up on you. It would be raining soon.

More rain, more growth. At this rate, in another fifty years, Happyland would be covered over—like those jungle temples in Mexico. No one could ever find it.

"Watch that nail near the top," I warned, as the stranger stooped to squeeze through with me. "Tear your shirt easy on a nail like that."

"Thanks."

"Got to watch out for my customers," I said.

Now we were inside. It was absolutely tar-pit black in the Funhouse. A jump from daylight to the dark side of the moon. And hot. Muggy hot inside.

"Can't see an inch in front of me," the stranger said.

"Don't worry, I'll walk you through. I've got a flash. It could use a new battery. Kind of dim, but we should be all right with it."

For emergencies, I always keep a flash in the Ford's glove compartment, with a couple of spare batteries. Never know when a tire might let go on you at night. But I keep forgetting to put in the new batteries when the old ones wear out. I guess nobody's perfect!

"Lot of cobwebs in here," I said, as we moved along. "Hope you don't mind spiders."

"I'm not in love with 'em," said the big man. "Not poisonous, are they?"

"No, no. Not these. Mostly little fellers. I'll clear the way for you." And I did that, using a rolled newspaper to sweep the tunnel as I moved through it.

"Where are we?" he asked. "I mean—what part of the Funhouse?"

"About midway through from where you start," I said. "But the fun part is ahead. You haven't missed anything."

"This is crazy," he repeated again, half to himself. Then: "Ouch!"

I stopped, flashed the dimming light back at him. He was down on one knee.

"Hurt yourself?"

"I'm okay. Just stumbled. A loose board."

"Lots of those in here," I admitted. "Not dangerous, though. Not the way I'm taking you."

As we moved down the narrow wooden tunnel there was a wet, sliding sound.

"What's that?" he asked.

"The lake," I told him. "This part of the tunnel is built over the shore. That's the sound the lake water makes, hitting the pilings. The wind's up. Storm's coming."

We kept walking—going down one tunnel, turning, entering another, twisting, turning, reversing in the wooden maze. Maze to him, not to me. It was my world.

The rain had started, pattering on the wooden roof—dripping down into the tunnels. And the end-of-summer heat had given way to a sudden chill.

"This is no fun," said the stranger. "It's not what I remembered. I don't like it."

"The fun's up ahead," I promised him.

"You keep saying that. Look, I think we'd better—"

Suddenly my flash went out.

"Hey!" he shouted. "What happened?"

"Battery finally died," I said. "Don't worry, I've got another in the pickup. Wait here and I'll get it."

"Not on your life," the stranger protested. "I'm not staying alone here in the pitch dark in this damned place."

"You *afraid* of the dark?" I asked him.

"No, dammit!"

"Then wait for me. I can't lead you back without a flash. Not through all the twists and turns. But I know the way. I can move fast. Won't be ten minutes."

"Well . . . I—"

"One thing, though. I want to warn you carefully about one thing. *Don't* try to move. Just stay right where you are, so I'll know where to find you. Some of the side tunnels are dangerous. Rotting boards. You could break a leg. The tunnels are tricky. You have to know which ones to stay out of."

"Don't worry, I'll stick right here like a bug on a wall."

"Ten minutes," I said.

And left him there in the tunnel.

Of course I didn't go back to the pickup for any batteries. Instead, I went to the control room at the end of B Tunnel.

The door was padlocked, but I had the key. Inside, feeling excited about the stranger, I let Ed know I was here. Which was easy. I'd rigged a low-voltage generator in the control room, and when I pulled down a wall switch a red light went on under the tunnels and Ed knew I was back with a stranger.

I'll bet he was excited, too. Hard to tell with Ed. But *I* sure was. My heart was pounding.

Fun in the Funhouse!

I didn't waste any time here. I'd done this many

times before, so it was routine now: unlock the door, go inside, throw the switch for Ed, then activate the trap.

Trapdoor.

Right under the bearded stranger's feet. Even if he moved up or down the tunnel for a few yards (some of the nervous ones did that) there was no problem because the whole section of flooring was geared to open and send whoever was inside the tunnel down onto the slide. And the slide ended on the sand at the lakefront.

Where Ed was.

He would come up out of the lake when he saw the light. It would shine on the black water and he would see it from where he lived down there in the deep end and he would come slithering up.

Ed wasn't much to look at. Kind of weird, really. His father was one of those really big rats that live in the burrows under the cemetery, and his mother was something from deep in the lake. Something big and ugly and leathery.

They'd made love—the rat and the lake thing— and Ed was the result. Their son. He doesn't really have a name, but I call him Ed the way Gramps called me Tad. It fits him somehow, makes him more appealing. More . . . human.

Ed and me, we get along fine as partners. I bring

him things to eat, and he saves the "goodies" for me. Like wallets, and cash and rings (that big one Sally was joshing me about came from one of Ed's meals) and whatever else the strangers have that I can use.

Ed is smart.

He seems to know that I need these things to keep going now that the factory's shut down and I've lost my job here and all. That's why the partnership works so well. We each get our share. After I take what I want (one time I got a fine pair of leather boots) he drags the body back into the lake.

Then he eats.

Lucky for me, one meal lasts Ed for almost a month. So I don't have to worry if no stranger shows up at Sally's for two, three, even four weeks. One always ambles along sooner or later. Like Mama always said, Everything comes to those that wait. Mama was a very patient woman. But she could be nasty. I can testify to that.

It gets bad in winter—for strangers, I mean— when the roads are closed, but that's when Ed sleeps anyhow, so things even out.

By the time I got back to the stranger's tunnel that afternoon it was really coming down. Rain, I mean. Dripping and sliding along the cold wood, and getting under my collar. Most uncomfortable. Somehow, rain always depresses me. Guess I'm too moody.

The stranger was down there with Ed where I expected him to be. Sometimes there's a little yelling and screaming, but nobody ever hears it, so that's no problem either. One fellow tried to use a knife on Ed, but Ed's skin is very tough and rubbery and doesn't cut easy. The stranger was just wasting his time, trying to use a knife on Ed.

I took a ladder down to the sand where the body was.

Ed was off by the water's edge, kind of breathing hard, when I got there. His jaw was dripping and his slanted black eyes glittered. Ed never blinked. He was watching me the way he always does, with his tail kind of moving, snakelike. He looked kind of twitchy, so I hurried. I don't think Ed likes the rain. Ed makes me nervous when it rains. He's not like himself. I never hang around the Funhouse when he's like that.

The bearded stranger was already dead, of course. Most of his head was gone, but Ed had been careful not to muss up his clothes—so it was no problem getting his wallet, rings, cash, coins . . .

When I climbed the ladder again Ed was already sliding toward the body.

Guess he was hungry.

* * *

Three and a half weeks later the stranger at the counter in Sally's was looking at my watch.

"I've never seen one like that," he said.

"Tells you the time in ten parts of the world," I said. "Tells you the month of the year and the day of the week. And it rings every hour on the hour."

The stranger was impressed.

After a while, I grinned, leaned toward him across the counter and said, "You ever go to amusement parks as a kid?"

In my sports-car racing days, I was lucky on the track (even winning a trophy!), but unlucky on the street. I had trouble with traffic cops. My bright red Le Mans Austin-Healey seemed to attract tickets the way an open watermelon attracts flies. Since I couldn't take out my mounting frustration on the cops, I decided to write this story as a form of catharsis. And it did the job; I felt much better after finishing it.

As an exercise in sheer style, I think "Violation" is one of my best pieces of fiction. Of course, if I didn't think so, it wouldn't be in this collection.

Oops! You just ran a red light. Watch out!
Violation!

VIOLATION

(Written: November 1971)

It is 2 A.M. and he waits. In the cool morning stillness of a side street, under the soft screen of trees, the rider waits quietly—at ease upon the wide leather seat of his cycle, gloved fingers resting idly on the bars, goggles up, eyes palely reflecting the leaf-filtered glow of the moon.

Helmeted. Uniformed. Waiting.

In the breathing dark, the cycle metal cools: the motor is silent, a power contained.

The faint stirrings of a still-sleeping city reach him at his vigil. But he is not concerned with these; he mentally dismisses them. He is concerned only with the broad river of smooth concrete facing him through the trees, and the great winking red eye suspended, icicle-like, above it.

He waits.

And tenses at the sound upon the river—an engine sound, mosquito-dim with distance, rising to a hum. A rushing sound under the stars.

The rider's hands contract like the claws of a bird. He rises slowly on the bucket seat, right foot poised near the starter. A coiled spring. Waiting.

Twin pencil-beams of light move toward him, toward the street on which he waits. Closer.

The hum builds in volume; the lights are very close now, flaring chalk-white along the concrete boulevard.

The rider's goggles are down and he is ready to move out, move onto the river. Another second, perhaps two . . .

But no. The vehicle slows, makes a full stop. A service truck with two men inside, laughing, joking. The rider listens to them, mouth set, eyes hard. The vehicle begins to move once more. The sound is eaten by the night. There is no violation.

Now . . . the relaxing, the easing back. The ebb tide of tension receding. Gone. The rider quiet again under the moon.

Waiting.

The red eye winking at the empty boulevard.

*   *   *

"How much farther, Dave?" asks the girl.

"Ten miles, maybe. Once we hit Westwood, it's a quick run to my place. Relax. You're nervous."

"We should have stayed on the gridway. Used the grid. I don't *like* these surface streets. A grid would have taken us in."

The man smiles, looping an arm around her.

"There's nothing to be afraid of as long as you're careful," he says. "I used to drive surface streets all the time when I was a boy. Lots of people did."

The girl swallows, touches her hair nervously. "But they don't anymore. People use the grids. I didn't know cars still *came* equipped for manual driving."

"They don't. I had this set up special by a mechanic I know. He does jobs like this for road buffs. It's still legal, driving your own car—it's just that most people have lost the habit."

The girl peers out the window into the silent street, shakes her head.

"It's . . . not natural. Look out there. Nobody! Not another car for miles. I feel as if we're trespassing."

The man is annoyed. "That's damn nonsense. I have friends who do this all the time. Just relax and enjoy it. And don't talk like an idiot."

"I want out," says the girl. "I'll take a walkway back to the grid."

"The hell you will," flares the man. "You're with *me* tonight. We're going to my place."

She resists, strikes at his face; the man grapples to subdue her. He does not see the blinking light. The car passes under it swiftly.

"Chrisdam!" snaps the man. "I went through that light! You made me miss the stop. I've broken one of the surface laws!" He says this humbly.

"What does that mean?" the girl asks. "What could happen?"

"Never mind. Nothing will happen. Never mind about what could happen."

The girl peers out into the darkness. "I want to leave this car."

"Just shut up," the man says, and keeps driving.

Something in the sound tells the rider that this one will not stop, that it will continue to move along the river of stone despite the blinking eye.

He smiles in the darkness, lips stretched back, silently. Poised there on the cycle, with the hum steady and rising on the river, he feels the power within him about to be released.

The car is almost upon the light, moving swiftly; there is no hint of slackened speed.   .

The rider watches intently. Man and a girl inside, struggling. Fighting with one another.

The car passes under the light.

Violation.

Now!

He spurs the cycle to metal life. The motor crackles, roars, explodes the black machine into motion, and the rider is away, rolling in muted thunder along the street. Around the corner, swaying onto the long, moon-painted river of the boulevard.

The rider feels the wind in his face, feels the throb and power-pulse of the metal thing he rides, feels the smooth concrete rushing backward under his wheels.

Ahead, the firefly glow of taillights.

And now his cycle cries out after them, a siren moan through the still spaces of the city. A voice which rises and falls in spirals of sound. His cycle-eyes, mounted left and right, are blinking crimson, red as blood in their wake.

The car will stop. The man will see him, hear him. The eyes and the voice will reach the violator.

And he will stop.

"Bitch!" the man says. "We've picked up a rider at that light."

"*You* picked him up, I didn't," says the girl. "It's your problem."

"But I've never been stopped on a surface street," the man says, a desperate note in his voice. "In all these years—never once!"

The girl glares at him. "Dave, you make me sick! Look at you—shaking, sweating. You're a damn poor excuse for a man!"

He does not react to her words. He speaks in a numbed monotone. "I can talk my way out. I know I can. He'll listen to me. I have my rights as a citizen of the city."

"He's catching up fast. You'd better pull over."

His eyes harden as he brakes the car. "I'll do the talking. All of it. You just keep quiet. I'll handle this."

The rider sees that the car is slowing, braking, pulling to the curb.

He cuts the siren voice, lets it die, glides the cycle in behind the car. Cuts the engine. Sits there for a long moment on the leather seat, pulling off his gloves. Slowly.

He sees the car door slide open. A man steps out, comes toward him. The rider swings a booted leg over the cycle and steps free, advancing to meet this law-breaker, fitting the gloves carefully into his black leather belt.

They face one another, the man smaller, paunchy, balding, face flushed. The rider's polite smile eases the man's tenseness.

"You in a hurry, sir?"

"Me? No, I'm not in a hurry. Not at all. It was just . . . I didn't see the light up there until . . . I was past it. The high trees and all. I swear to you. I didn't see it. I'd never knowingly break a surface law, Officer. You have my sworn word."

Nervous. Shaken and nervous, this man. The rider can feel the man's guilt, a physical force. He extends a hand.

"May I see your operator's license, please?"

The man fumbles in his coat. "I have it right here. It's all in order, up to date and all."

"Just let me see it, please."

The man continues to talk.

"Been driving for years, Officer, and this is my first violation. Perfect record up to now. I'm a responsible citizen. I obey the laws. After all, I'm not a fool."

The rider says nothing; he examines the man's license, taps it thoughtfully against his wrist. The rider's goggles are opaque. The man cannot see his eyes. He studies the face of the violator.

"The woman in the car . . . is she your wife?"

"No. No, sir. She's . . . a friend. Just a friend."

"Then why were you fighting? I saw the two of

you fighting inside the car when it passed the light. That isn't friendly, is it?"

The man attempts to smile. "Personal. We had a small personal disagreement. It's all over now, believe me."

The rider walks to the car, leans to peer in at the woman. She is pale, as nervous as the man.

"You having trouble?" the rider asks.

She hesitates, shakes her head mutely. The rider leaves her and returns to the man, who is resting a hand against the cycle.

"Don't touch that," says the rider coldly, and the man draws back his hand, mumbles an apology.

"I have no further use for this," says the rider, handing back the man's license. "You are guilty of a surface-street violation."

The man quakes; his hands tremble. "But it was not *deliberate*. I know the law. You're empowered to make exceptions if a violation is not deliberate. The full penalty is not invoked in such cases. You are allowed to—"

The rider cuts into the flow of words. "You forfeited your Citizen's Right of Exception when you allowed a primary emotion—anger, in this instance—to affect your control of a surface vehicle. Thus, my duty is clear and prescribed."

The man's eyes widen in shock as the rider brings

up a beltweapon. "You can't possibly—"

"Under authorization of Citystate Overpopulation Statute 4452663, I am hereby executing . . ."

The man begins to run.

". . . sentence."

He presses the trigger. Three long, probing blue jets of star-hot flame leap from the weapon in the rider's hand.

The man is gone.

The woman is gone.

The car is gone.

The street is empty and silent. A charred smell of distant suns lingers in the morning air.

The rider stands by his cycle, unmoving for a long moment. Then he carefully holsters the weapon, pulls on his leather gloves. He mounts the cycle and it pulses to life under his foot.

With the sky in motion above him, he is again upon the moon-flowing boulevard, gliding back towards the blinking red eye.

The rider reaches his station on the small, tree-shadowed side street and thinks, *How stupid they are! To be subject to indecision, to quarrels and erratic behavior—weak, all of them. Soft and weak.*

He smiles into the darkness.

The eye blinks over the river.

And now it is 4 A.M., now 6 and 8 and 10 and

1 P.M . . . the hours turning like wheels, the days spinning away.

And he waits. Through nights without sleep, days without food—a flawless metal enforcer at his vigil, sure of himself and of his duty.

Waiting.

Junkyards are filled with metal corpses. Automobiles, motorcycles, trucks, all crushed and mangled from bloody smashups. Grotesque reminders of our fragile mortality. God knows how many bleeding bodies have been removed from these piled masses of wreckage.

I had such road carnage in mind when I wrote "The Yard." It partakes of death and sudden disaster, mixed with a tinge of grim humor.

This story rated inclusion in The Best of Masques and New Masterpieces of Horror. It's meant to shock and surprise.

I believe it does both.

THE YARD

(Written: January 1986)

It was near the edge of town, just beyond the abandoned freight tracks. I used to pass it on the way to school in the mirror-bright Missouri mornings and again in the long-shadowed afternoons, coming home with my books held tight against my chest, not wanting to look at it.

The Yard.

It was always spooky to us kids, even by daylight. It was old, had been in Riverton for as long as anyone could remember. Took up a full city block. A sagging wood fence (had it *ever* been painted?) circled all the way around it. The boards were rotting, with big cracks between many of them where you could see all the smashed cars and trucks piled obscenely inside, body to body, in rusted embrace. There were burst-open engines with ruptured water hoses like spilled guts, and splayed truck beds, split and swollen by sun and rain, and daggered windshields filmed with dark-brown scum. ("It's from people's brains, where their heads hit the glass," said Billy-Joe Gibson, and no one doubted him.)

The wide black-metal gate at the front was closed and padlocked most always, but there were times at night, *always* at night, when it would creak open like a big iron mouth and old Mr. Latting would drive his battered exhaust-smoky tow truck inside, with its missing front fenders and dented hood, dragging the corpse of a car behind like a crushed metal insect.

We kids never knew exactly where he got the cars—but there were plenty of bad accidents on the Interstate, especially during the fall, when the fog would roll out from the Riverton woods and drape the highway in a breathing blanket of chalk white.

Out-of-towners who didn't know the area would come haul-assing along at eighty, then dive blind into that pocket of fog. You'd hear a squeal of brakes. Wheels locking. Then the explosion of rending metal and breaking glass as they hit the guardrail. Then a long silence. Later, sometimes a lot later, you'd hear the keening siren of Sheriff Joe Eggar's

Chevy as he drove out to the accident. Anyway, we kids figured that some of those wrecked cars ended up in the Yard.

At night, when you passed the Yard, there was this sickly green glow shining over the piled up metal corpses inside. The glow came from the big arclamp that Mr. Latting always kept lit. Come dusk, the big light would pop on and wouldn't go off till dawn.

When a new kid came to school in Riverton we knew he'd eventually get around to asking about the Yard. "You been inside?" he'd ask, and we'd say heck yes, plenty of times. But that was a lie. No kid I knew had ever been inside the Yard.

And we had a good reason. Mr. Latting kept a big gray dog in there. Don't know the breed. Some kind of mastiff. Ugly as sin on Sunday, that dog. Only had one good eye; the other was covered by a kind of veined membrane. Clawed in a fight maybe. The good eye was black as a chunk of polished coal. Under the dog's lumpy, short-haired skull its shoulders were thick with muscle, and its matted gray coat was oil-streaked and spotted with patches of mange. Tail was stubbed, bitten away.

That dog never barked at us, never made a sound; but if any of us got too near the Yard it would show its fanged yellow teeth, lips sucked back in silent

fury. And if one of us dared to touch the fence cir-
cling the Yard that dog would slam its bulk against
the wood, teeth snapping at us through a crack in
the boards.

Sometimes, in the fall, in the season of fog, just
at sunset, we'd see the gray dog drift like a ghost out
the gate of the Yard to enter the woods behind Sutter's store and disappear.

Once, on a dare, I followed him and saw him leave
the trees at the far edge of the woods and pad up
the slope leading to the Interstate. I saw him sitting
there, by the side of the highway, watching the cars
whiz by. He seemed to enjoy it.

When he swung his big head around to glare at
me I cut out fast, melting back into the woods. I was
shook. I didn't want that gray devil to start after me.
I remember I ran all the way home.

I once asked my father what he knew about Mr.
Latting. Said he didn't know anything about the
man. Just that he'd always owned the Yard. And the
dog. And the tow truck. And that he always wore a
long black coat with the frayed collar turned up,
even in summer. And always a big ragged hat on his
head, with a rat-eaten brim that fell over his thin,
pocked face and glittery eyes.

Mr. Latting never spoke. Nobody had ever heard
him talk. And since he didn't shop in town we

couldn't figure out where he got his food. He never seemed to sell anything, either. I mean, nobody ever went to the Yard to buy spare parts for their cars or trucks. So Mr. Latting qualified as our town eccentric. Every town has one. Harmless, I guess.

But scary just the same.

So that's how it was when I grew up in Riverton. (Always thought Riverton was a funny name for a place that didn't have a river within a hundred miles of it.) I was eighteen when I went away to college and started a new life. Majored in engineering. Just like my pop, but he never did anything with it. I was thirty, with my own business, when I finally came back. To bury my father.

Mom had divorced him ten years earlier. She'd remarried and was living in Seattle. Refused to come back for the funeral. My only sister was in California, with no money for the trip, and I had no brothers. So it was up to me.

The burial that fall, at Oakwood Cemetery, was bleak and depressing. Attendance was sparse—just a few of Pop's old cronies, near death themselves, and a scattering of my high school pals, as nervous and uncomfortable as I was. On hand just to pay their respects. Nothing in common between any of us, nothing left.

After it was over I determined to drive back to

Chicago that same night. Riverton held no nostalgic attraction for me. Get Pop buried, then get the hell out. That was my plan from the start.

Then, coming back from the cemetery, I passed the Yard.

I couldn't see anybody inside as I drove slowly past the padlocked gate. No sign of life or movement.

Of course, twelve long years had passed. Old Latting was surely dead by now, his dog with him. Who owned the place these days? Lousy piece of real estate, that's for damn sure.

A host of dark memories rushed back, crowding my mind. There'd always been something foul about the Yard—something *wrong* about it. And it hadn't changed. I shuddered, struck by a sudden chill in the air. Turned the car heater up another notch.

And headed for the Interstate.

Ten minutes later I saw the dog. Sitting at the wooded edge of the highway, on the gravel verge, at the same spot I'd followed it to so many years before. As my car approached it, the big gray animal raised its head and fixed its coal-chip eye on me as I passed.

The *same* dog. The same sightless, moon-fleshed eye on the right side of its lumped skull, the same mange-pocked matted fur, the same muscled shoulders and stubbed tail.

The same dog—or its ghost.

Suddenly I was into a swirl of opaque fog obscuring the highway. Moving much too fast. The apparition at the edge of the woods had shattered my concentration. My foot stabbed at the brake pedal. The wheels locked, lost their grip on the fog-damp road. The car began sliding toward the guardrail. A milk-white band of unyielding steel *loomed* at me. Into it. Head on.

A smashing explosion of metal to metal. The windshield splintering. The steering wheel hard into my chest. A snapping of bone. Sundered flesh. Blood. Pain. Darkness.

Silence.

Then—an awakening. Consciousness again. I blinked, focusing. My face was numb; I couldn't move my arms or legs. Pain lived like raw fire in my body. I then realized that the car was upside down, with the top folded around me like a metal shroud.

A wave of panic rippled over me. I was trapped, jack-knifed inside the overturned wreck. I fought down the panic, telling myself that things could have been worse. Much worse. I could have gone through the windshield (which had splintered but was still intact); the car could have caught fire; I could have broken my neck. At least I'd survived the accident. Someone would find me. Someone.

Then I heard the sound of the tow truck. I saw it through the windshield, through the spider-webbing of cracked glass, coming toward me in the fog—the *same* tow truck I'd seen as a boy, its front fenders missing, hood dented, its front bumper wired together . . . The rumble of its ancient, laboring engine was horribly familiar.

It stopped. A door creaked open and the driver climbed from the cab. He walked over to my car, squatting down to peer in at me.

Mr. Latting.

And he spoke. For the first time I heard his voice—like rusted metal. Like something from a tomb. "Looks like you went an' had yerself a smash." And he displayed a row of rotting teeth as he smiled. His eyes glittered at me under the wide brim of his ragged hat.

Words were not easy for me. "I . . . I'm . . . badly hurt. Need to . . . get a doctor." I had blood in my mouth. I groaned; pain was in me like sharp blades. All through my body.

"No need to fret," he told me. "We'll take care'a you." A dry chuckle. "Just you rest easy. Leave things to us."

I was very dizzy. It took effort just to breathe. My eyes lost focus; I fought to remain conscious. Heard the sound of chains being attached, felt the car lifted, felt a sense of movement, the broken beat of an engine . . . Then a fresh wave of pain rolled me into darkness.

I woke up in the Yard.

Couldn't be, I told myself. Not *here*. He wouldn't take me *here*. I need medical care. A hospital. I could be dying.

Dying!

The word struck me with the force of a dropped hammer. I was dying and he didn't care. He'd done nothing to help me; I was still trapped in this twisted hulk of metal. Where were the police? Mechanics with torches to cut me free? The ambulance?

I squinted my eyes. The pale green glow from the tall arclamp in the middle of the Yard threw twisting shadows across the high-piled wreckage.

I heard the gate being slammed shut and padlocked. I heard Latting's heavy boots, crunching gravel as he came toward me. The car was still upside down.

I attempted to angle my body around, to reach the handle of the driver's door. Maybe I could force it open. But a lightning streak of pain told me that body movement was impossible.

Then Latting's skeletal face was at the windshield, looking in at me through the splintered glass. A grin pulled at the skin of his mouth like a scar. "You all right in there?"

"God, no!" I gasped. "Need . . . a doctor. For Christ's sake . . . call . . . an ambulance."

He shook his head. "Got no phone to call one with here at the Yard," he said, in his rasping voice. "Besides that, you don't need no doctors, son. You got *us*."

"Us?"

"Sure. Me an' the dog." And the blunt, lumpy head of the foul gray animal appeared at the window next to Latting. His red tongue lolled wetly and his bright black unblinking eye was fixed on me.

"But . . . I'm bleeding!" I held up my right arm; it was pulsing with blood. "And I . . . I think I have . . . internal injuries."

"Oh, sure you got 'em," chuckled Latting. "You got *severe* internals." He leered at me. "Plus, your head's gashed. Looks like both yer legs is gone—an' your chest is all stove in. Lotta busted ribs in there." And he chuckled again.

"You crazy old fool!" I snapped. "I'll . . . I'll have the sheriff on you." I fought back the pain to rage at him. "You'll rot in jail for this!"

"Now don't go gettin' huffy," Latting said. "Sheriff ain't comin' in here. Nobody comes into the Yard.

You oughta know that by now. Nobody, that is, but ones like you."

"What do you mean . . . like me?"

"Dyin' ones," the old man rasped. "Ones with mosta their bones broke and the heart's blood flowin' out of 'em. Ones from the Interstate."

"You . . . you've done this before?"

"Sure. Lotsa times. How do you think we've kept goin' all these years, me an' the dog? It's what's up there on the Interstate keeps us alive . . . what's inside all them mashed-up cars, all them rolled-over trucks. We *need* what's inside." He ruffled the mangy fur at the dog's neck. "Don't we, boy?"

In response, the big animal skinned back its slimed red lips and showed its teeth—keeping its obsidian eye fixed on me.

"This here dog is kinda unusual," said Latting. "I mean, he seems to just know *who* to pick out to cast the Evil Eye. Special ones. Ones like you that nobody's gonna miss or raise a fuss over. Can't have folks pokin' around the Yard, askin' questions. The ones he picks, they're just into the fog and gone. I tow 'em here an' that's that."

Numbly, through a red haze of pain, I remembered the fierce *intensity* of that single dark eye from the edge of the highway as I passed. Hypnotizing me, causing me to lose control and smash into the guardrail. The Evil Eye.

"Well, time to quit jawin' with ya and get this here job done," said Latting. He stood up. "C'mon, dog." And he led the animal away from the car.

I drew in a shuddering breath, desperately telling myself that someone must have heard the crash and reported it, that the sheriff would arrive any moment now, that I'd be cut free, eased onto cool crisp linen sheets, my skin gently swabbed of blood, my wounds treated . . .

Hurry, damn you! I'm dying!

A sudden, shocking, immediate smash of sound. Again and again and again. The cracked curve of safety glass in front of me was being battered inward by a series of stunning blows from Latting's sledge as he swung it repeatedly at the windshield.

"These things are gettin' tougher every year," he scowled, continuing his assault. "Ah, now . . . here she goes!"

And the whole windshield suddenly gave way, collapsing into fragments, with jagged pieces falling on my head and shoulders, cutting my flesh.

"There, that's better, ain't it?" asked the old man with his puckered-scar grin. "He can get at ya now with no bother."

Get at me?

The dog. Of course he meant the dog. That stinking horror of an animal. I blinked blood from my eyes, trying to push myself back, away from the raw opening. But it was useless. The pain was incredible. I slumped weakly against the twisted metal of the incaved roof, refusing to believe what was happening to me.

The gray creature was coming, thrusting his wide shoulders through the opening.

The fetid breath of the hellbeast was in my nostrils; his gaping mouth fastened to my flesh, teeth gouging; his bristled fur was rank against my skin.

A hideous snuffling, sucking sound . . . as I felt him draining me! I was being . . . *emptied* . . . into him . . . into *his foul body* . . . all of me . . . *all* . . .

I felt the need to move. To leave the Yard. The air was cold, edged with the promise of frost. The sky was steel gray above me.

It was good to move again. To run. To leave the town and the woods behind me.

It was very quiet. I gloried in the strong scent of earth and concrete and metal which surrounded me. I was alive. And strong again. It was fine to be alive.

I waited. Occasionally a shape passed in front of me, moving rapidly. I ignored it. Another. And another. And then, finally, the *one*. Happiness rushed through me. Here was one who would provide my life and strength and the life and strength of my master.

I raised my head. He saw me then, the one in the truck. My eye fixed on his as he swept past me with a metallic rush of sound. And vanished into the fog.

I sat quietly, waiting for the crash.

When Karl Wagner selected "Ceremony" for inclusion in The Year's Best Horror Stories I was pleased but not surprised. I knew that this one was going to rate serious attention. As I've stated earlier, I consider myself a good judge of my own work, and this story had an offbeat quality, a sustained mood and depth that marked it as special.

It was inspired by a bus ride from Chicago to the World Fantasy Convention in Providence, Rhode Island. A 20-hour trip that seemed to last forever. Surreal and exhausting. But I really can't complain. Without that bus ride I would never have written the story you are about to read.

Welcome to Doour's Mill.

CEREMONY

(Written: December 1983

He hated riding cross-country in a bus almost as much as he hated *driving* cross-country, but the problem was he'd missed his rail connection getting into Chicago and just couldn't wait for the next train. He *had* to be in Providence by Thursday evening to meet the Sutter woman. So it was the bus or nothing.

Mrs. Sutter was leaving that same night for Europe, and when she returned she expected her husband to be dead. The contract had to be settled before she left and the advance paid him. He didn't ice rich, unfaithful husbands unless he was well paid for the job, half down, the other half after the hit. Funny part of this one, he would have done old

Sutter for *free*. Because of the total. He'd dispatched 13 people (would joke sometimes about "working as a dispatcher") since he'd gone into this business and he needed to break the total.

It wasn't that he was superstitious. Never had been. But, in plain, hard truth, that damned number 13 *was* unlucky for him. No question about it. He was 13 the time his father had split out for good, when they were living in that crummy, red-brick, coldwater flat in St. Louis. Not that he loved his old man. Not that bum. It was just that his father was usually able to keep his mother from beating the crap out of him. She beat him senseless twice that week, after the old man had split. Took it out on him. Way she took everything out on him. Always had. He was missing three teeth because of her. Good ole Mom.

That was the same week he ran off to Kansas City and got a job as a stacker in a paper-box factory after lying about his age. He'd looked a lot older than 13.

Then there was a double-13 on the license plate of that big, pink Lincoln convertible the blonde had driven when he'd hitched into Boulder City a few winters back. The blonde had been fun, sure, but she was coked out of her gourd when she flipped the car on a hairpin turn in the mountains and almost killed both of them. She thought it was funny, having a double-13 on her plates. Yeah, funny.

And, in Nam, there was a transport number, 13-something, painted on the tail of that lousy chopper that went down in the rice paddy. He'd been sent back to the States after that, with a Purple Heart, but the crash had killed his best buddy—the one real friend he'd ever trusted. He didn't trust people as a general rule. People screw you up when you trust them. But he'd trusted Eddie . . .

There had been a lot of 13s in his life, all tied into hard times, bad breaks, heavy losses. And now, by Christ, his *job* total was 13. Bad luck. But Mr. Sutter would make it fourteen and everything would be okay again. Life was fine, so long as he stayed away from the 13s.

"The bus will get you into Providence by late Thursday afternoon," the train clerk had assured him in Chicago. "But it's a long trip. Rather exhausting. We'd suggest a flight."

"I don't take planes," he told the clerk. He didn't tell him why.

It wasn't the chopper crash in Nam. Not that. It was the dream. About a commercial airliner, a big 747. Falling, with him strapped inside, staring out the window. Going down fast, people screaming, a jet engine on fire with the right wing burning. Paint cracking and peeling in the fierce heat, with the flames eating at a number on the trailing edge of the wing. A number ending in 13.

The *one* job he'd had trouble with, killing Wendl, that banker in Tucson, when a piss-ass schoolkid had seen him come out of Wendl's house after the job and called the cops, *that* one had been on the 13th. He originally planned it for the weekend, but when he found out Wendl's family was returning from their trip a day early, he was forced to make the hit. But never again. No more jobs on the 13th, no matter *how* much he got paid. He'd learned a lesson there, in Arizona. Cops had almost nailed him for sure.

So now he was on a bus in late October, heading for Providence, Rhode Island, ready to eliminate Mr. James T. Sutter at the personal request of his loving wife, Jennifer. He'd get the advance from Mrs. S. and spend a week in Providence, then ice the old fart before taking a train back to the Coast.

Bringing his job total to fourteen.

He grinned, closing his eyes . . .

. . . and woke with a jolt, feeling cold glass strike his forehead. He'd nodded off, lulled by the rocking motion of the bus, and his head had bumped the window. He straightened, coughing, and wiped a small trickle of saliva from his chin. That's how it was on a long bus ride, with those fat tires hypnotically thrumming the road, setting up a measured vibration in your body, making you drowsy. Your eyelids get heavy, slide down; your mouth gapes, and you doze. And wake. And blink. And doze again.

Time is meaningless. You don't know where you are, what town you're passing through. Don't care. Your back aches, and your feet are swollen inside your shoes. Your clothes itch, tight and sweaty around you. You smoke, but the cigarettes taste sour.

Hours of travel along strange highways, suspended in a surreal vacuum between night cities and day cities, looking blankly out at hills and rivers and passing traffic, chewing on stale Clark bars from paint-chipped vending machines in musty-smelling depots. Riding endlessly through country you'd never seen and never wanted to see.

It was early afternoon on Highway 95. Sun half down along a rolling horizon of green hills. They'd just crossed the state line from Connecticut. He'd seen the big sign with a girl's smiling face painted on it . . .

WELCOME TO RHODE ISLAND!
A Nice Place to Visit.
A NICER Place to Live.

He suddenly remembered a song he'd heard when he was very young. His old man had this classic recording of the Andrews Sisters—Patty, Laverne and somebody—singing energetically about "poor little Rhode Island, smallest of the forty-eight . . ." There had been only forty-eight states when the Andrews Sisters had made the record, and he remembered feeling sorry for the place. He'd been a little kid, shorter than most of his schoolmates, and he identified with smallness. One summer he'd found an abandoned pup, a real little guy, obviously the runt of the litter, and had taken it home. But his mother strangled it. She didn't like pets.

Poor little Rhode Island . . .

They were passing through farm country in the western part of the state. Lots of big rocks, with dirt-and-gravel roads branching off into fields (what were they growing?—he sure as hell didn't know) and with pale white Colonial farmhouses off in the distance. He spotted some apple orchards, and there were plenty of elms and oak trees along the road, all fire-colored. Like passing a circus. He wasn't much for scenery, but this was special—New England in October, putting on a class show for the customers.

How many hours had it been since they'd left Chicago? Twenty, at a guess. At least that long. It seemed like weeks, riding these endless gray highways.

The bus was nearly empty. Just him in the back section and an elderly couple up front. It had been crowded at first—but people kept getting off. More at each depot stop. Finally, it was just the three of them and the driver. Well, nobody in his right mind rode a bus for twenty hours. But it was almost over. Not long now into Providence.

He closed his eyes again, let the singing tires take him into sleep.

He woke to darkness. Thick black Rhode Island night outside the glass, an interior dark inside the bus. He'd been jarred awake by rough road under the wheels. Narrow and bumpy. Why had they left the main highway? Jesus! He'd been due into Providence before dark.

He got up numbly, bracing himself against the seat back, then walked forward unsteadily along the aisle past the elderly couple (godawful bony-looking people) until he reached the driver.

"Where are we?" he asked, squinting into the night. "Why aren't we on 95?"

The driver was a thin character, with a gaunt, stretched skin. He stared intently ahead at the narrow road, illuminated in floury-white patches by the probing lights. "Sorry, buddy, I had no choice."

"What's *that* mean? How late are we going to be getting into Providence?"

"Won't be there till morning," said the driver. "You'll have to spend tonight at the Mill. We'll be coming in soon. Maybe another ten minutes."

"The hell you say!" He leaned over to grip the driver's thin shoulder. "Turn this thing around and get us back on the main highway! I'm due in Providence tonight, and by God you'd better *get* me there!"

"No can do, buddy. Engine's fouled up. Overheating real bad. May be the carburetor, dunno. Only place to get 'er fixed is at Doour's Mill. They got a garage there. You ask me, lucky we made it this far. Gotta admit it sure beats being stuck someplace out on the road."

"Is there a phone at this garage?"

"Oh, sure. You can call from the Mill. No problem."

He started back toward the rear of the bus, thinking it's 13 again. *That's* why this job has gone sour. He checked his watch. Damn! Won't do any good to call Providence now. She's gone. Off to sunny Italy. Figured it for a chicken job; figured I didn't want the contract. She'll hire it out later, after she gets back.

Unlucky.

Okay, he told himself, ease down. You can score another contract in New York. Just have to put off going back to the Coast for a while. Plenty of action in New York. He had some good contacts there. He'd make it fourteen in New York. Just relax. What's done is done. Don't fight it.

"Happy Holiday!" said the couple, one after the other, both saying it to him as he passed them on the way to his seat.

He paused, gripping an upper handrail as the bus shuddered over a deep cut in the gravel road. "Uh, yeah . . . same to you."

When he reached his seat in the SMOKING PER-MITTED section, he slumped down heavily, got out his cigarettes. Dead pack. He tossed it away, dug out a fresh one. He lit a Salem, drew in smoke, sighed, settled back into the cushion.

He'd forgotten; tonight was Halloween! This was it, all right, October 31st. As a kid, it had been his favorite holiday.

He never got presents for Christmas, or for his birthday, and Easter was a drag. But Halloween was nothing but great—the *one* night in the year when people *gave* you things. Free candy . . . cake . . . ap-ples . . . doughnuts . . .

He smiled, remembering.

The bus lurched to a creaking stop. Doors hissed open.

They were at the garage, a weathered building with light seeping from its fogged windows. A dented Ford pickup was parked in front with the words HARLEY'S REPAIR SERVICE painted on the side.

"All out, folks! Doour's Mill."

He stepped down onto the gravel roadway. The driver was helping the elderly couple from the bus. They moved slowly, cautiously, their bones like breakable china. That's how you get if you stick around long enough, he thought.

The garage owner, Harley, began talking to the driver. Very tall, in baggy trousers and a torn denim work jacket. Then the driver came around to open the luggage door on the bus.

He reached in for his travel bag. Light, compact, good leather. Had it custom-made to fit his needs. With a hidden compartment for the short-barrel .357 Magnum. Sweet piece of equipment. He'd started with a Browning .380 automatic, but he'd never trusted it. The Mag he trusted. Always got the job done. Easy to carry, with a real kick to it.

"You wanna use the phone, one's right inside."

"No, it's too late now. Forget it. There a cafe around here?"

"Straight ahead. Two blocks up. If it's open."

"Thanks." He checked his watch. Nine-thirty. "What time do we leave in the morning?"

"Be here by six," said the driver. "She'll be ready to roll by then."

"Okay."

He passed the dim-lit garage. In the smoked gloom, standing next to a high-piled stack of discarded truck tires, a lean, unshaven mechanic in greased blood-dark overalls stared out at him.

He continued along the street. The gravel gave way to concrete, but the ground was still uneven. Tufted grass spiked up from wide cracks in the surface. The ancient Victorian houses along the street were in equal disrepair, their gabled bay windows cracked and shadowed. Porches sagged. Roofs hunched against the night. Doour's Mill had gone to seed, a time-worn New England relic of a town that seemed totally deserted.

It wasn't. A pair of teenagers, holding hands, came toward him, heads together, talking quietly. They looked underfed. The girl had no figure at all. "Happy Holiday," they said to him as they passed.

He didn't answer them. No point in it. Terrific town for a holiday.

He had no trouble finding the cafe. It was the only building along the main street with a neon sign.

MA'S PLACE. Reminded him of his mother. He didn't like that. When he got closer, he saw that the first two letters had burned out. It was ALMA'S PLACE. Several other letters in the sign were dying, slowly dimming, flickering and buzzing in the air above his head like trapped insects.

He opened the door, stepped inside.

He was the only customer.

The waitress behind the worn linoleum counter was obviously young, but she looked like an anorexic. Pasty skin. Long, bony face with watery brown eyes. She blinked at him. "Hi, mister."

He said hello, asked if they served hot food.

"Sure, till ten o'clock we do. I mean, no steaks or specials this late, but I can fix you some eggs."

"Okay, that'll do. Scrambled easy, with hash browns and wheat toast."

"Easy it is," she said, and walked back to the kitchen to fix his order.

He sat down on one of the counter stools, laid his travel bag over another, and glanced idly around. A few greenish-colored tables, some crooked wooden chairs, an old broken-faced jukebox in one corner. Dark, not working. Near the antique cash register somebody had tacked a paper plate to the wall. On it, scrawled in black crayon: HAPPY HOLLOWEEN!

He chuckled. They can't even spell Halloween in this godforsaken town.

The waitress ambled out of the kitchen with eggs and toast. "Sorry, no more hash browns," she said. "But I can give you some sliced tomatoes. As a substitute, no extra charge. Not too fresh, though."

"This'll be all right," he told her. "With coffee."

She nodded, pouring him a cup. "It's kinda strong. You use cream?"

"No."

"Well, it's kinda strong."

"It'll be fine," he said, spooning sugar into the cup.

"I hope the toast is okay. I tried not to burn it."

"It's fine," he said.

He began to eat. One thing you can order safely in a joint like this, he told himself, is eggs and toast. Hard to screw up eggs and toast. These were all right.

He sipped the coffee. Ugh! Bitter. Damn bitter. He spooned in more sugar. Helped some, but not much.

"I toldja it was strong," the girl said.

He didn't say anything.

"Guess you wonder, this being Alma's Place, who's Alma, huh?"

"Hadn't thought about it."

"Alma was my mother."

"*Was?*"

"She died. Little over a month ago. Just didn't last till the Holiday."

He looked up. "You mean—until Halloween?"

"Right. She just didn't last."

"Sorry."

"Well, we all gotta go sometime. Nobody lives forever, right? It's like the Indians used to say—about how when it's your time an' all."

He spread butter on his toast. It *was* burned. "Guess you don't get much business around here."

"Not much. Not anymore. Used to be the cotton mill was open. They named this town after it, Doour's Mill. Owned by Mr. Jonathan Doour."

"What happened to him?"

"He died and it closed down. All the mill folk moved away. We got only a real few left in the town now. Real few."

"Why do *you* stay?"

"I own the place is why." She shrugged, picking at a shred of loose skin on her lower lip. "Mama wanted me to keep it going. Besides"—and for the first time she smiled—"people gotta eat!"

"I didn't see any other lights along the street," he said. "Are you the only one open at night?"

"Mr. Exetor's drug store stays open. Half a block down." She pointed. "He's open to ten, like here."

"Good. I could use some cigarettes."

"He's a widowman, Mr. Exetor is. Wife passed on end of the summer. Just *wasted* away."

He finished eating, pushed his plate back.

"More coffee?"

"I'll pass. Too strong for me."

"Yeah, like I said, it's kinda strong." She looked at him with intense, shadowed dark eyes. "You're invited to the Ceremony."

"What?"

"You're invited. We have it each Holiday. On October 31st, each year. And you're invited."

"I don't go to church," he said. "But thanks anyhow." He got out his wallet. "How much do I owe you?"

"That'll be one seventy-five," she said.

"Here's two bucks. Keep the change."

"Thanks, mister." She rang up his order on the ancient cash register. "Ceremony's not in church. Fact is, we don't have a church here anymore. I mean, we *have* one, but it's boarded up. They broke all the windows."

"I see." He picked up his travel bag, moved to the door.

"Happy Holiday," said the girl.

"Same to you," he said, and walked out.

It was raining now. A thin misting foggy rain. The

street glistened like black leather under the pale light cast by the cafe's overhead neon.

He turned up the collar of his coat and walked to the drugstore. No sign outside, but the window said EXETOR'S, in chipped gilt. He walked in, and a tiny bell tinkled over the door.

Exetor was round-shouldered, cadaverous, with a bald head and long, big-knuckled hands. A thick vein pulsed, wormlike, in his mottled neck. Looked as if he'd be joining his wife soon. Well, in a town like this, it didn't matter much whether you were alive or dead. The old man had been fiddling with a box of pipe cleaners and now he put the box down. "Might I help you, sir?"

"Salem Hundreds. Two packs."

Exetor walked behind a dust-filmed tobacco counter and got the cigarettes. "You from the bus?"

"That's right."

"I saw it come in."

"Our driver had some engine trouble. We were due in Providence. Is there a hotel in town?"

"Certainly," said Exetor, accepting payment for the cigarettes and ringing up the sale. "The Blackthorn. Just down the way. Right at the intersection. You walk left. Big three-story building on the corner. Can't miss it."

"I sure never expected to be staying *here* tonight."

"No problem getting a room at the Blackthorn. Not many folks around anymore. Expect they'll be closing one of these days. Like me. Just not enough business to keep any of us going."

He nodded. "I can see that."

Exetor smiled thinly. "Sad. About this town, I mean. So much history here. Have you heard of Roger Williams?"

"Can't say I have."

"Strong-minded man, he was. They banned him from Massachusetts for religious nonconformity. But that didn't stop him. He established the first settlement in Providence, in 1636. Remarkable man." Exetor's voice drew more intense. "Jonathan Doour was related to Williams. Had an oil painting of him hanging on the wall of his office at the mill. So this town's part of history, you see. All of it, tied together—going back to 1636."

"Gives you something to hang on to, I guess." The old guy was a real bore. Who gives a damn about some religious nut from the 1600's? Maybe that's what the Ceremony was all about—honoring his memory or some such crap.

"Each year, more of us pass on," said Exetor. "Just don't make it to the Holiday."

"You people seem to think a lot of Halloween."

"Oh, yes, indeed we *do*." Exetor nodded, the neck

vein pulsing. "It's very important to us here at the Mill. We have our Ceremony at this time each year."

"So I've been told. I'm not much for ceremonies."

Exetor clucked his tongue against yellowed teeth. "It's the only day I really look forward to anymore," he said, his voice soft with regret. "My wife and I always attended together. I'll be alone this year."

"Oh, yes—I heard about your wife. That's tough." He edged toward the door. This old geeze planned to talk all night.

"It's extremely difficult, getting on without Ettie."

He was almost to the door when a wall sign caught his eye.

HAPPY ALL HOLLOW'S EVE

Again, misspelled. Should be All *Hallows*. Didn't anybody ever go to school in this burg?

He reached the door, opened it. The bell tinkled.

"You are invited to the Ceremony," said Exetor.

"No thanks." He started out—and heard Exetor say: "Attendance is not voluntary."

He left the drugstore. Now what the hell did *that* mean? He looked back through the cracked plate-glass window at the old guy. Exetor was standing there, staring out at him, not moving.

Weirdo. Him *and* that chick at the cafe. Both of them, weirdos.

It was still raining. He shifted the weight of his travel bag from right to left hand and began to walk in the direction of the Blackthorn. He was feeling kind of lousy. Stomach upset. Headache. Maybe it was the long bus ride and his missing the Sutter contract. He'd be fine once he'd moved up his total to fourteen.

Right now, he just needed a good night's sacktime. He checked his watch. Getting toward ten. Exetor and the cafe girl would be closing up, probably heading for their Ceremony. Fine. Just so they were quiet about it. No loud music or dancing. He grinned, thinking what old Exetor would look like hopping around the floor. Exetor, the Dancing Skeleton!

He heard something behind him—the low-purring sound of a car's motor in the misting rain.

Cop's car. Sheriff. And with a deputy in the seat next to him. The car glided slowly alongside, stopped. Jeeze, he hated cops. *All* cops.

"Evening," said the sheriff.

"Evening," he said.

The lawman was gaunt and sharp-featured. So was his deputy. And both solemn. No smiles. But then, cops don't smile much.

"Just inta town, are you?"

They damn well *knew* he was—but they liked playing their cop games.

"I came in earlier with the bus. They're fixing it. We had a breakdown."

"Uh huh," said the sheriff. "Harley, over to the garage, he told me about the trouble."

A pause—as they stared at him from the car's shadowed interior. The motor throbbed softly, like a beating heart in the wet darkness.

Finally, the sheriff asked: "You staying at the hotel?"

"I plan to. Guess they've got plenty of room."

The sheriff chuckled wetly, a bubbling sound. "That they have, mister." Another pause. Then: "Mind if we look over your suitcase?"

He stiffened. The Mag .357! But unless they tore the travel bag to pieces, they wouldn't find it.

The sheriff remained behind the wheel as his deputy got out, knelt in the wet street to open the bag.

"Gonna ruin your pants, Al," said the sheriff.

"They'll dry," said the deputy, sifting through the contents, patting down shirts, fingering coats.

He tried to look normal, but he was sweating. The hidden gun compartment was just under the deputy's right hand. If he . . .

"Thanks, mister," said the deputy, snapping the

bag closed. "Never can tell what folks'll carry."

"Guess not."

The deputy got back in the car, leaned out from the rolled-down window. His voice was reedy. "Happy Holiday," he said.

And the car rolled forward, gradually losing definition in the misting darkness.

The hotel was no surprise. Meaning it looked crappy. Sagging. Falling apart. Paint-blistered. Wood missing from the upper porch steps.

Well, it's like my sweet mother used to say, beggars can't be choosers.

He walked up the steps, avoiding the broken areas, and entered the lobby through a loose-hinged, leaded-glass door. The lobby was bare, dusty, deserted.

A clerk dozed behind the wall counter. Another skinny character. Middle-aged scarecrow in a rumpled suit. His nose was long, thin, almost transparent.

"I'll need a room."

The clerk's head jerked up like a stringed puppet. He blinked, reached for a pair of thick-lensed glasses, put them on. Pale blue eyes swam behind the lenses. "Cost you five dollars."

"I think I can handle that."

"Sign here. Name and address." The clerk pushed a card across the grimed counter.

He signed it, using a phony name and address. Never tell anybody the truth about yourself. He'd learned that in Kansas City. And a lot of other places.

He gave the clerk a five-dollar bill. And got a key.

"Guess I'm not the first here tonight," he said.

"Don't get you, mister."

"There was an elderly couple on the bus with me, coming in. They must have registered earlier."

"Nope." The clerk shook his head. "You're our first in 'bout a week. Nobody else tonight."

Strange. Where would they *go*?

"Yours is on three. Use the elevator. Stairs are rotted out. Sidney will take you up. If he's sleepin', just give him a poke. Room 3-H."

He nodded, moved across the wide, vacant lobby with his travel bag to the elevator. Its metal-pleated door was open. Inside, draped over a high wood stool like a discarded bundle of dirty clothes, was a stick-thin old man. His patchy hair was streaked gray-white over his long skull.

"You got a customer, Pop."

The deep-socket eyes opened slowly. He stared at the stranger out of large milky pupils. "What floor?"

"The top. Three."

He stepped into the cage and felt it give perceptibly under his weight. "This thing safe?"

"Weren't, I wouldn't be in it," said the old man.

The pitted grill-door slid closed and the old man pushed down a corroded wall lever. His wrist was ropy, spotted with sores. The ancient cage creaked rustily into upward motion.

The old man's odor was strong, almost fetid. "Staying the night, are you?"

"I'm not here for the floor show."

He was getting sick of dealing with these weirdos. Nothing to gain by continuing to answer their stupid questions. He *was* amused by the fact that a sleazy hotel like this actually employed an elevator operator. No wonder the old croak slept on the job; nothing the hell *else* to do.

"We were the first state to declare independence from the Mother Country. You know that?"

He grunted.

"May the 4th, 1776, it was. We declared *two* months ahead of all the other colonies! Little Rhody was first, yes sir. First to declare."

"Were you *there*, Pop?"

The old man chuckled like dry leaves scraping. "Not hardly. But I've been around a spell. Seen things happen. Seen a lotta people die. But I made it again this year. Made it to the Holiday."

Another Halloween freak.

They reached the top, and the black door folded back into itself like an iron spider.

He stepped out. The cage rattled downward as he walked toward 3-H. The hall reeked of mold and decay. Rug was damp, lumped. Ceiling was peeling away in thick, hanging folds, like strips of dead meat. He could hear the steady drip-drip-drip of rain coming in through holes in the roof. Jeez, what a pit!

He reached the hallway's end. The door on 3-H startled him. It was a lot fancier than the others, ornamented in an intricately carved rose design. The knob was scrolled brass. He keyed the door open and swore softly. They'd given him the bridal suite! Well, why not? Nobody was about to pick the Blackthorn in Doour's Mill for a honeymoon!

It wasn't a suite, actually. Just one big chamber, with a bathroom off to the side. The bed, centered in the room, was enormous. Talk about your antiques! The tall gilt headboard was decorated with plaster angels. The gold paint had dimmed, and most of the angels had cracked wings, but he had to admit that the effect was still damned impressive.

A big faded-pink dresser loomed against one wall. Two black iron chairs, seedy but elegant, stood beside a huge cut-velvet couch fitted with rose-carved brass studs. A large mirror dominated the wall above them, framed in faded gold.

He walked over to it, looked at himself. Needed a shave. Coat and shirt wrinkled, damp from the rain. Looked like his old man. A bum.

The bathroom was full of badly chipped tile and rusted brass fittings. But at least there was a shower. He hadn't counted on one. Real bonus in a fleapit like this.

He opened his bag, took out the travel clock, set it for five-thirty. That would give him plenty of time to get dressed and down to the garage by six, when the bus was ready to leave. He'd be glad to shake this freak town. Gave him the creeps. After Doour's Mill, New York would be Paris in the spring!

Damn! No inside chain lock. Just the regular knob lock. Well, that was okay. He always slept with the .357 under his pillow. Best protection in the world.

He had expected that the hot shower would make him feel better, but it hadn't. He still felt lousy, really kind of hung over. Dog tired. And sickish. Had to be the food at Alma's. Those eggs were probably half-spoiled. And that rat-piss coffee—that stuff would kill Frankenstein!

He slid his loaded Magnum under the pillow and

put on a pair of white silk pajamas. The bed was great. Deep and soft, not at all lumpy or damp. And the sheets were crisp, freshly ironed. Not so bad after all.

It wasn't much past ten. He'd get a full night's rest. God, but he was beat. He stretched out on the big mattress, closed his eyes—and was instantly asleep.

He awoke slowly. Not to the clock alarm. To a low murmur of voices. Here. *In* the room with him.

"It's wearing off." Man's voice. Old.

"He's coming round." Woman's. Also old.

His eyes opened. He blinked, trying to get a clear focus on the dim figures in the room. The only light came from the bathroom and the door was partially shut. Things were murky.

There were several of them, surrounding the bed in a rustling circle.

"Welcome to the Ceremony," said the bus driver.

It was him, all right, and no mistake. Before he could fully register the shock of this, another voice said: "Happy Holiday!"

Focus. On the source of this second voice. It was Harley, the garage owner. His greasy mechanic stood next to him.

Now, rapidly, he ran his gaze over all of them:

the elderly couple from the bus . . . Exetor . . . Alma's daughter . . . the lobby clerk . . . the old elevator man . . . the two skinny teenagers . . . Even the sheriff and his bony-faced deputy were here. Everybody he'd seen in the whole damn town—all here, around his bed, smiling down at him. And all of them thin, gaunt, wasted-looking.

He counted. There must be . . . Oh, Christ, yes, there were 13 of them!

A long iced wave of absolute fear engulfed him, and he closed his eyes to shut out the horrific ring of skulled faces.

"As I pointed out earlier this evening," said Exetor, "your attendance at the Ceremony was not voluntary. It was *required*."

"Yes, indeed," agreed the hotel clerk, peering down at him with swimming fish eyes. "You're our Guest of Honor."

He tried to speak but could not; the words were choked bile in his throat.

"Can't give our Ceremony without a Guest of Honor," said the elevator man.

The elderly couple were holding hands. The woman spoke slowly, distinctly. "Henry and I weren't at all sure we'd last till the Hollow Day. Not at *all* sure."

"Each year at this time we gather to be replenished," said Exetor, "thanks to our Guest of Honor. Believe me, sir, we *appreciate* what you are giving us."

"I can have my baby now!" said the teenaged girl excitedly. The boy put his arm around her narrow waist. He kissed her gently on the cheek. Beside them, the garage owner's eyes shone with pride.

"Ain't many new babies born to Mill folk anymore," he said. "We cherish our young, we surely do. Laurie here—she'll have the strength to bear, thanks to you."

"That's right," the bus driver said. "I tell ya, buddy, we're *deeply* grateful!"

"I'm sure sorry that coffee I served you was so darn bitter," said Alma's daughter. "But the stuff I had to use in it tastes plain *awful*. Still, it's very restful. Keeps you from hurting when we're getting you ready."

He was fully awake now, and anger flushed through him. Under his pillow. The loaded .357 Magnum. He'd blow them away, every damned freakish one of them!

But he couldn't reach the gun. He suddenly became aware that his wrists were strapped to the sides of the bed, as were his ankles. And there was another wide leather strap across his chest, holding him down.

And . . . oh, God . . . there were the snakes!

Thirteen of them!

No, not snakes, they were . . . some kind of rubbery tubes. Coiling out from his body into the figures surrounding him, a tube for each of them, attached to his flesh and ending in *their* flesh—like obscene umbilical cords.

Jesus—they were *feeder* tubes!

"Ettie so wanted to be here," said Exetor sadly. "It would have meant more months of life for her. But she just couldn't last to the Ceremony."

The sheriff patted the old man's arm in sympathy. "Ettie was a mighty fine woman."

He strained desperately against the straps, but they held firm.

"No use pushin' like that," said the mechanic in the rotted dark coveralls. "You ain't goin' nowhere. Sheriff Morland fixed them straps personal. They're good and tight."

He felt himself weakening now. Moment by moment, his strength was being bled away—into them. As he grew weaker, they grew stronger. Their eyes were brighter; their cheeks began to acquire a glow.

The waitress tipped back her head, closed her eyes. "Ummmm, sure feels *good!*"

"Nothing will be wasted, I assure you," Exetor said. "We use *everything*. Even the marrow."

"Bone marrow's good for the teeth," said the teen-aged boy. "And we need healthy teeth for our baby."

"Tell us your name and we'll call it after you," said the teenaged girl. "As a gesture, you might say."

"He won't tell," said the hotel clerk. "Gene Johnson was on the card, but I bet you ten dollars that name's a fake." He blinked downward. "*Will* you tell us your real name, mister?"

He gasped out the words: "You . . . can . . . all . . . go . . . to hell!"

They looked at one another. The bony deputy shook his head. "Well now, we sure hope the good Lord don't see fit to send us down *there*. We're all decent folk, here at the Mill. Always have been."

The figures in the rustling circle nodded agreement.

Things were dimming in the room. He blinked, feeling weak as a newborn cat. The anger was gone. The fear was gone. He was tired. Very, very tired. It was like being on the bus again, with the thrumming wheels making him drowsy. His eyelids were heavy. He wanted to close them. Did.

Darkness now.

And rest.

No more worry.

No more pain.

Everything was fine.

In researching the career of Dashiell Hammett for a biography, I was informed that he had once written a "Möbius strip" story, a tale that turned back endlessly into itself. I failed to locate Hammett's story, but the idea continued to fascinate me. I challenged myself to write one of my own.

The idea for "Coincidence" was based on a night I spent in a Manhattan hotel during a publishing trip to New York. The man in the next room kept moaning, "I've killed . . . I've killed . . . I've killed." Over and over again. I was spooked, and this story was the result.

It begins—but it never ends.

COINCIDENCE

(Written: January 1972)

When Harry Dobson's wife suggested they spend their last night together (before Harry's trip) in a New York hotel he agreed. It was to be a kind of instant second honeymoon, and Harry savored the drive down from Westport with his wife cuddled close to him. It reminded him of the early days, before the house and kids had aged them both. The kids were grown and gone, but the house in Westport, with its high upkeep and higher taxes, dragged at Harry like a weight. He enjoyed the overnight stay in a New York hotel, enjoyed the sexual passion he was still able to inspire in Margaret.

What Harry Dobson *didn't* enjoy was having his wife bump him awake with a naked hip at 6 A.M.

"What's wrong?" he wanted to know.

"It's the man in the next room," whispered Margaret, pressing close to him in the double bed. "He's been moaning. He woke me up."

"So he's probably sick, maybe drunk. Who cares?"

"It's what he's moaning that spooks me," said Margaret. "I want you to listen. I think he's some kind of maniac."

"Okay, okay," Harry grunted. And he listened to the agonized words which filtered through the thin walls of the hotel room.

"I've killed," moaned the man. "I've killed. I've killed."

"He keeps repeating that over and over," Margaret whispered. "I think you'd better do something."

"Do what?" asked Harry, propping himself against the pillow to light a cigarette. "Maybe he's just having a bad dream."

"But he keeps saying it over and over. It really spooks me. We could be next door to a murderer."

"So what do you suggest?"

She blinked at him, absently stroking her left breast. "Call the manager. Have someone investigate."

Harry sighed, kicked off the blankets and padded barefoot to the house phone on the dresser. He picked up the receiver, waited for the switchboard to acknowledge.

"This is Harry Dobson in room 203. There's a character next door who's moaning about having killed somebody. He's been keeping us awake. Yeah . . . he's in 202. Right next door."

Harry listened, holding the phone, slowly stubbing out his cigarette on the glass top of the dresser.

"What's happening?" asked Harry's wife.

"They're checking to see who's in 202."

"He's stopped moaning," she said.

"No, no," said Harry into the receiver. "*I'm* in 203. Okay, forget it, just forget it."

He slammed down the phone.

"What's wrong?"

"The stupid idiot on the desk has my name down for *both* rooms!"

"Couldn't it be a coincidence?" Margaret asked. "I mean, your name isn't *that* unusual. There must be several Harry Dobsons in New York."

"Not door-to-door in the same damn hotel," he said. "Anyhow, they claim they can't do anything about the guy and unless he gets violent in there to just ignore him." He shook his head. "That's New York for you."

"I think we'd better leave," said Margaret. She got up and walked to the bathroom.

Harry blew out his breath in disgust, got his pants off the chair and began dressing. He was scheduled to fly back to L.A. this morning anyhow, so he'd get to the airport a little early. He could have breakfast there.

He and his wife left the hotel room.

In the elevator she told him she'd write him at least once a week while he was gone. He was sweet, she told him, and if it hadn't been for the maniac in 202 their night together would have been beautiful.

"Sure," said Harry Dobson.

They said goodbye in the lobby. Then Harry checked out, giving the desk clerk hell for mixing up the room numbers.

"I represent a major firm," he told the clerk. "I'm an important man, dammit! What if someone wanted to reach me? My messages might have gone to a nut in 202. Do you understand me?"

The desk clerk said he was very sorry.

Harry walked out to a cab. Gray rain drizzled down from a soot-colored sky and a chill November wind blew the rain against Harry's face.

"Kennedy airport," he said to the driver. But before he climbed into the taxi he paused. *He's watching you. That bastard in 202 is watching you.* Harry shaded his eyes against the rain and peered upward at the second-floor street window of room 202.

A tall man was at the open window, ignoring the

blowing rain, glaring down at him. The man's face was dark with anger.

Harry stared, unblinking. *Jesus! He even looks like me. Like an older version of me. No wonder the clerk mixed us up. Well, to hell with him!*

By the time his jet soared away from New York, Harry Dobson put the man from 202 firmly out of his thoughts. Harry was concerned with the report he'd be making to the sales manager back in California. He was working out some statistics on a board in his lap when he happened to notice the passenger in the window seat directly across the aisle.

What—it's him! Can't be. Left him back in New York.

The passenger had been reading a magazine; now he raised his head and swung his eyes slowly toward Harry Dobson. Cold hatred flowed from those eyes.

The tourist section was only half filled and Harry had no trouble getting another seat several rows back. Damned if he'd sit there and let this creep give him the evil eye. Maybe Margaret was right; maybe the guy *was* some kind of maniac.

At Los Angeles International Harry was the first passenger to disembark. Inside the airport building he arranged for a porter to collect his flight baggage.

Then he waited for it in a cab near the door. Harry didn't want to risk running into the weirdo at the baggage pickup.

So far so good. The guy was nowhere in sight.

His baggage arrived and Harry tipped the porter and gave the taxi driver an address in West Los Angeles. As the car rolled on to the freeway Harry relaxed. Apparently the creep had made no attempt to follow him. It was over.

Harry paid the driver, carried his bags into the rented apartment, took a bottle from his briefcase and poured himself a drink. He felt fine now. He checked the window just to be certain the guy hadn't followed him. The street below was empty.

Harry unpacked, took his suits to the closet, opened the sliding door—and fell back, gasping.

The man was *there*, inside the closet! He stood in the darkness, smiling like a fiend. Then he dived at Harry's throat, hands closing on his wind-pipe. Harry kicked free, tumbled over a chair, twisting away from his attacker.

That's when the man pulled the knife from his belt.

Harry scrambled around the bed, putting space between himself and his attacker. No good trying for the door; the man would have him if he tried that.

"Who—are you?" gasped Harry. "What—what do you want from me?"

"I want to kill you," said the man, smiling. "That's all you need to know."

Keeping himself between Harry and the door, he began slashing with the knife—ripping the blade into mattress, chairs, curtains, clothing—as Harry watched in numb terror.

But when the man pulled Margaret's photo from Harry's briefcase, and drove the knife through it, a red rage replaced the fear in Harry Dobson; the bastard was human, after all. Harry was ten years younger, stronger.

The man was half turned toward the bed when Harry struck him with a heavy table lamp. The man fell backward, stunned, dropping the knife.

"You crazy sonuvabitch!" Harry shouted, snapping up the knife and driving it into the man's back. Once. Twice. Three times. The man grunted, then did not move. Harry stood over him for a long, long moment—but he did not move again.

Who is he? Who the hell is he? Harry could find no identification on the body. He thought of calling the police but decided that was too risky. There were no witnesses. The apartment had not been burglarized nor were there signs of a forced entry. Bastard must have had a key. To the police it would appear that Harry Dobson had coldly murdered this man.

Insane! I don't even know him. Which is exactly why you must get rid of the body. Once he's gone there'll be no way to link you to his death.

That night Harry cleaned up the apartment, placed the blanket-wrapped corpse in the trunk of his car and drove out along the ocean, past Malibu, to a deserted stretch of beach—where he dumped the weighted body into the water.

He was a madman. Simply because you complained about him at the hotel he followed you to the West Coast and tried to kill you. You have no reason to feel guilt. Forget all this. Live your life and forget him.

Harry Dobson tried to do that. When his wife called him he didn't mention what had happened. And when his business trip ended he returned to New York, and resumed his life.

A decade passed. Each time the face of the dead man from 202 loomed in his mind Harry Dobson shut down the vision. Finally he could look back upon the entire incident as a kind of bizarre dream. He felt neither guilt or fear.

Then, almost ten years to the month, Harry found himself at the same hotel in New York. He was in town on his annual business trip and, this particular visit, had decided to stay at this hotel to prove that the ghost of the man he'd killed was truly exorcised.

In fact, to close the circle, he asked the clerk for the old room, 203.

"Sorry, sir, but that room is occupied. However, I can give you the one right next door to it, room 202. Will that be satisfactory?"

Irony. The dead man's room. All right, Harry said, that would be satisfactory.

Room 202 contained a double bed, white glass-topped dresser, circular table and chair, a standing brass lamp in the corner . . . He remembered the furniture! But that was because it was the same, exactly the same, as 203. The rooms on this floor were no doubt identically furnished. The odd thing was that the decor hadn't been changed in ten years.

Harry took a fresh bottle of Scotch from his suitcase and poured a solid drink for himself. The Scotch eased him, reduced his tension. It was late, near midnight, and after several more belts of Scotch he was ready for sleep, amused at the drama of the situation, no longer tense at the prospect of sleeping in a room once occupied by a man he had stabbed to death.

Near morning, Harry began to mumble in his sleep. He was having a bad dream, a nightmare about being convicted of murder. The attorney was hammering at him on the witness stand and Harry had broken under the verbal assault. "I've killed," he admitted. "I've killed. I've killed." Over and over. "Killed . . . killed . . . killed . . ."

He finally awoke, sweating, wide-eyed. *Wow, what a hellish dream! It's this room. That's what triggered it, allowed it to take control of my subconscious. But I'm all right now. I'm fine. The dream's over.*

He became aware of voices in 203 filtering through the thin wall of the room. A woman's voice, whispery but sharp, and upset. "I think you'd better do something."

"Do what?" asked a man's voice, muffled but distinct. "Maybe he's just having a bad dream."

"But he keeps saying it over and over. It really spooks me. We could be next door to a murderer."

"So what do you suggest?"

"Call the manager. Have someone investigate."

Harry heard the springs squeak as the man climbed out of bed. He heard him pick up the phone and say, "This is Harry Dobson in room 203. There's a character next door who's moaning about having killed somebody . . ."

Harry didn't want to hear any more. He walked into the bathroom and vomited into the bowl, remaining on his knees until he heard the door finally slam in 203.

Then, shaking, he walked back into his room and called the desk. "Who—who's registered in 203?"

"Uh . . . that's Mr. Dobson, sir. But he's checking out."

"All right," said Harry evenly. And he put down the phone. He walked over to the street window, threw it open. Gray rain, whipped by a chill wind, blew in upon him, stinging his face.

A man came out of the hotel, hailed a cab. Just before he got into the taxi he turned to look up at Harry, shading his eyes against the wet. Younger. A face like his, but ten years younger. *The murdering bastard!* Harry glared down at him.

And when the man was gone, and he had called the airport to confirm his flight back to Los Angeles, Harry Dobson took the knife out of his suitcase and held it in his hand for a long, long moment.

Knowing, beyond any doubt, that he would eventually die by it.

They're gone now. Those special advance "sneak previews" (always spelled PREVUE on the marquee) at the local downtown movie theater. The film's title was never revealed. You'd purchase your ticket with a delicious feeling of anticipation. On this night you were one of the privileged few who were allowed to see a major film prior to its release.

After the screening, you were asked to fill out a review card in the lobby. Was the film too long? What were the best and worst scenes? What did you like most about the picture? What least? Then, based on these audience response cards, the film would be edited back at the studio, maybe cut or perhaps expanded, before being given its general release at a later date. Your opinions had helped to shape its final form.

No more. The sneak preview is a thing of the past, along with the neighborhood theater itself, now shuttered and dark in thousands of towns across North America, a victim of the devouring multiplex.

In this story, I recreated one of these lost sneak previews. With a twist.

A very lethal twist.

MAJOR PREVUE HERE TONITE

(Written: December 1987)

The trees were burning.

That's how they appeared to ex-Californian Hubbard Rockwell—blazing around him in furnace reds and shades of dazzling orange and flickered sunbursts of yellow. A gusting wind aided the illusion, releasing flurries of brittle, flame-colored leaves that blew like sparks of fire across the black asphalt in front of Rockwell's moving car.

Connecticut in the fall. Everything Hub Rockwell had hoped it would be: an endless lariat of red-barn roads, looping through loam-rich October woods, broken by clear-running creeks, dipping into quiet valleys with small towns curled like sleeping cats in the cool shadows of easy-rolling hills.

No wonder so many businesspeople commuted each day to their jobs in the roaring steel-and-concrete maelstrom of New York. It was worth the effort. As he built his sales career, he'd be able to afford a home here in Connecticut. It was certainly a goal worth working toward.

Hub was ending his second month on the job and considered himself lucky to have found a downtown bachelor apartment complete with cockroaches (no escaping them in the Big Apple), wall cracks, and a puce-green plaster-bulged ceiling that threatened to collapse on his head. By California standards (he'd grown up in Riverside), the rent was outrageous, but he had expected that. At least the job held solid promise.

These relaxed weekend drives, when he could be alone and free, were balm to his city-stressed soul; they provided Hub Rockwell with an alternate reality. The shrouding gray cinder smoke of New York gave way to the clear blue sky of Connecticut. He valued these unhurried trips as personal therapy, a way to keep sane after five days in the crazed sprawl of Manhattan.

Milly would love it out here in these woods, he told himself. Millicent Therese Kelly, a Fresno girl, just out of college, ambitious and strong-minded, with an Irish temper that had flared up once too often to sustain their fragile relationship. After they'd lived together, tempestuously, for a year, she had finally split away from him on a tide of bitter accusations. Some of which were true. He *had* been seeing another woman on occasion, but it wasn't anything serious. Not to him, at least. Milly thought otherwise. Too bad; they might have had a life together. Their relationship was the closest he'd come to marriage in his twenty-five years.

Once she had talked of touring New England in the fall "to see all the trees burning." Her phrase— and he thought about her words now as he drove through these flame-bright, wind-tossed woods. He missed her. Maybe he'd give her a call when he got back to New York on Monday, just to establish contact again. Perhaps a bit of what they'd shared could be salvaged. Friendship in place of passion? No, probably not, since Milly was at her best in bed. Phoning her was a lousy idea. Wouldn't accomplish anything.

He'd met a girl at work (Sandra) who reminded him of Milly. Same sensual mouth and heated blue eyes. Something might ignite between them. Hub smiled. The fires of October . . .

* * *

He had a thick steak and some good wine at the Brookville Inn; then he took a post-dinner stroll along the quiet sidewalk, looking for the theater. There was always a local movie house along the main street in these small Connecticut towns—but, one by one, the theaters had gone under in the competitive wake of television and home video.

The Roxy in Brookville was no exception. It had obviously been out of business for some while now, with a hand-lettered sign in the dusty box office reading:

> Sorry, We're Closed. Thank You
> For Past Patronage.

Hub looked at a faded lobby card behind cracked glass, advertising the last film shown here: Julie Andrews, at the top of a tall green hill, arms raised, her mouth wide in joyous song. From *The Sound of Music*. But there was no longer any music inside the Roxy—just dust and silence. Sad, thought Hubbard Rockwell. That was the word for it. Each closed theater seemed to drain life from the heart of the towns. He always felt angry, standing in front of these boarded-over relics of yesterday. A damn shame, really.

He walked back to his parked car, turning up the

collar of his coat. It was getting chilly. The wind had risen as the afternoon lengthened, and the sky was bulked and swollen with storm clouds. Looked like rain for sure.

He'd had fine clear weather since Friday night when he'd left New York; it was Sunday now, and time to be heading back to the city. At least the rain hadn't spoiled his weekend.

Rainstorms always managed to depress him. As if the skies were weeping. Milly thought rain was romantic—but then women are like that. They build romance into everything.

It was almost dark as Hub unlocked the door of his metallic-silver Mazda. The rain was suddenly here; as he eased behind the wheel it made flat, spatting sounds on the windshield and roof. Well, in a couple of hours he'd be safe and dry in his apartment, ready to launch a fresh assault on his job tomorrow.

That's what you have to do in sales—mount aggressive campaigns. Push, push, push. And Hub Rockwell knew how to push. Which had become a problem in his relationship with Milly. She accused him of amorality, but you can't afford to worry about morals in business. Not if you expect to reach the top. And he had total confidence in himself. In the next five years Hub fully expected to be vice president of sales, and in ten years he'd be running the firm. *And* have his house in Connecticut. Just a matter of pushing to the edge of the envelope.

The storm turned into a bitch. The wind kept getting stronger as he drove the black strip of highway, unwinding in front of his low beams like the shining back of a snake.

Rain volleyed the windows, and he felt the wind thumping the side of his Mazda with hard-knuckled blows. He had to keep adjusting the wheel to compensate for these sudden gusts. His windshield wipers struggled to clear the swimming glass, forcing him to cut his speed to a crawl. Too dangerous, going any faster. Hell, at this rate, he'd be driving half the night to reach New York!

Then, as he breasted a low-sloping hill, he saw the lights.

Hub squinted, pressing his face closer to the windshield. Through the blowing curtain of rain he could make out a distant, flickering glow ahead of him at the bottom of the hill. A town. It didn't make sense. He'd studied the latest map for this area, and the next town was a good twenty miles farther.

The rain was abruptly sliced off as he entered a long covered wooden bridge spanning a swirl of muddy water. As he bumped across, his tires banged dull echoes from the weathered boards.

The town lay just beyond the bridge, with a sign identifying it as: EDGEFIELD. He'd never heard of it. Must be no more than a village.

The storm resumed its assault as Hub eased the Mazda down the main street. The sidewalks were deserted; no surprise on such a hellish night. All the shops were closed and lightless; the glow that had beckoned him emanated from the far end of the street. Neons. Tubes of raw color blinking red, yellow, and blue through the down-slash of rain.

A theater! A local movie house, by God! Hub could make out the name as he drove closer: Styx. And on its marquee, in bold black letters:

MAJOR PREVUE HERE TONITE

Why would any studio wish to preview their film out here on a rainy Sunday night in the dead-smack middle of nowhere? Somebody's head was going to roll in the publicity department. Stupid. Pointless.

Yet here it was.

Hub stopped his car in the loading zone directly facing the box office. There was a small parking lot next to the theater. The lot was empty. And no other cars were parked along the street. Then who was *inside* the place?

He could make out a ticket seller perched on a

stool behind the fogged glass of the box office. A little bald-headed man with a pale face, just sitting there staring out into the rain. He didn't seem to notice the silver Mazda parked at the curb.

Inside his car, with the engine pulsing and the wipers tick-tacking steadily, Hub Rockwell grinned to himself. Why not? Why not buy a ticket and get inside out of this damn rain? Maybe in another couple of hours the storm would die and he'd have a clear run into New York. The latest radio report had indicated an upcoming break in the weather. Besides, he was always complaining about these local movie houses being closed down and here was one going full-blast, wide open for business. And showing a brand-new film in the bargain. Then don't just sit here gawking, he told himself. Support the natives. Keep movie theaters alive in America. Get your ass in there!

He got out of the Mazda, locking it. A plastic trash barrel bumped his leg, then rolled on across the lot, propelled by the wind. Hunched against the cold rain, Hub walked rapidly to the theater.

A large gray tom was crouched under the sheltering edge of the marquee—a rag-tail stray with smoky yellow eyes. Ears flattened along its skull, the animal opened a fanged mouth to hiss at Rockwell as he came around the corner of the brick building.

A feral odor drifted up from the gray cat. Hub kicked at the animal, but it dodged away, still hissing. He'd never liked cats and couldn't understand people who did. The Chinese had the right idea: Cook 'em for soup!

Rockwell was impressed by the theater's Art Deco facade. The lobby was shining black and silver under the blaze of lights. Two female water nymphs, painted in gold leaf, embraced at each side of the box office, creating a mildly erotic effect.

Now the thin-faced little man inside the booth was looking through the glass at Rockwell with flat, impassive eyes. Well, at least I've caught the fellow's attention thought Hub, with a trace of annoyance. He should be grateful to see me. On a foul night like this he's lucky anybody stops here. Lucky to have a job. A miracle the place is still open in a town this small. Maybe teenagers come here. Somewhere to go on a date.

Hub glanced at his wristwatch. It was almost 9:00 p.m. Which meant the film had probably started.

"What's the title of this picture?" he asked, getting out his wallet.

"We don't give the title. Not for our sneak previews." The little man's voice was as flat as his eyes. "But you're right on time. It hasn't started yet."

"Good," said Rockwell, pushing a new five-dollar

bill across the box office counter. Along with his change, he got back a small red pasteboard, pretorn. Meaning the Baldie was cashier *and* ticket taker. It figured, given the low profit margin of a place like this.

"I'm sure you'll enjoy the show," said the little man, and his bloodless lips curved into a faint smile.

Hub entered the inside lobby. Again he was impressed. A wine-dark rug cushioned his steps, and the walls were ornately decorated in a scrolled silver-and-gold motif. Sea nymphs capered with long-necked swans across the ceiling.

The candy counter was surfaced in beveled mirror glass and outlined in blinking red neon. It seemed amply supplied with a variety of sweets, ice cream, and soft drinks. An old-fashioned popcorn machine was working busily behind the counter, fresh corn bubbling from a silver urn and spilling against the steamed glass.

But no one was there to sell anything.

Hub thought about getting a Coke and a Snickers bar, but he knew he'd have to tap on the door of the booth to get the ticket seller out to the candy counter, and he wasn't that hungry.

Also, there was something unsettling about the little man. Hub experienced a distinct sense of unease when he thought of listening to that flat voice again. Ridiculous, actually. An overreaction——but there nonetheless.

Rockwell parted a fold of hanging velvet, pushed open an inner door, and entered the main auditorium. He paused at the head of the aisle. The screen was curtained and the overhead lights were on. Hub had a clear view of the seats, row on row, two hundred or more. They were empty. All empty. He was alone here.

No wonder these hick theaters were closing. Weekend night with a brand-new film to be screened and nobody shows up. One ticket sold. To Hubbard Rockwell. What a lousy place to hold a sneak preview!

Should he leave, go back to his car, forget the whole thing? An outside rumble of thunder reminded him of the storm. Dumb to go back out there. No, he'd stay for the movie. A private showing, just for ol' Hub.

Now that he looked it over, the auditorium was even grander than the lobby——with ornate, intricately carved ceiling decorations and superbly executed wall paintings of vast flowered gardens. Angelic forms floated through the gardens, their outspread wings reflected in painted pools of shimmering purple. The wall scenes were designed to soothe and pacify: soft yellows, gentle greens, muted earth browns.

All wasted, thought Hub. Wasted on a town that didn't give a damn about Art Deco or unique craftsmanship. No doubt about it, the era of the local movie palace had definitely ended.

Rockwell walked to a row of seats halfway down the aisle, entered the row, and moved to the exact center seat. And sat down.

The instant he was settled the house lights dimmed and the spangled velvet curtain drew back with a creaking rustle to reveal the wide white screen.

A strident blast of music swelled from high wall speakers. The screen darkened to black. Night black. Sky black. Now the sound of a heavily gusting wind filled the auditorium and rain slivered down; thunder cracked and rumbled.

A car, silver like the rain, breasted a hill, wipers working vigorously against the storm. The car paused there, then began a slow descent, headlights probing the rainy darkness.

Hub shifted in his seat, wondering when the credits were going to roll. But the action continued without them. Not so unusual. Many current films begin with a dramatic prologue, establishing a mood prior to the picture's title. Hub settled against the thickly cushioned seat and watched the silver car bump its way across a covered wooden bridge, a twin to the one just outside of town. Not many of these old antiques left in Connecticut. By daylight, on a clear and sunny afternoon, they exerted a nostalgic charm. By night, during a storm, they seemed squat and ugly, almost *dangerous* to cross.

The car paused again on the other side of the bridge. From the driver's point of view, the screen revealed the single main street of a small town, with a rain-hazed glow of lights at the far end.

The car rolled slowly forward, past tight-closed shops and dark storefronts, stopping again at the end of the street. Near the lights. *Neon* lights.

Hub drew in a sharp breath when the camera panned up to the bright-lit marquee of a movie theater, to black display letters spelling out: MAJOR PREVUE HERE TONITE.

He was now rigid in his seat, hands gripping the armrests. What was happening? The onscreen theater looked *exactly* like this one. Was he watching some kind of documentary filmed in this town during another stormy night?

The film continued. Hub watched in cold shock as the driver parked his car in the lot (*precisely where I parked mine!*) and walked toward the front of the building. The man had his coat collar up, and Hub couldn't see his face. A gray tomcat hissed at the stranger as he approached the box office.

Hub felt beading sweat on his flesh; he was chilled. The muscles along his cheeks were ridged with tension. His eyes were locked to the screen.

Now the camera observed the man from behind as he talked to the ticket seller. Hub knew what the dialogue would be, what they would say to one another. He anticipated every word of it.

"What's the title of this picture?"

"We don't give the title. Not for our sneak previews. But you're right on time. It hasn't started yet."

"Good," whispered Hubbard Rockwell numbly in the darkness.

"Good," said the stranger onscreen.

"I'm sure you'll enjoy the show."

And the man walked inside.

Of course Hub knew who the stranger was. Rockwell watched Rockwell enter the main auditorium (*this auditorium!*) and select a seat halfway down the aisle (*this seat!*).

But how had it been done? Obviously, he had been filmed from the moment his car topped the hill into Edgefield. Cameras had tracked him as he drove into town. But how could this footage have been processed and screened? How was it possible for him to be sitting here *watching* it all?

Now the situation became truly insane as Hub realized that the film being unreeled on the screen of the theater within the picture was the *same* film he was watching!

But the action changed. Hub saw the man in the film suddenly leap from his seat and run for the lobby. When he reached the exit door it was locked. He banged a fist against it, jerking at the inside release bar. The camera swung to the rear box office door which was flung open—and Hub saw the pale, bald little man emerge to race like a spider across the lobby. In a horrific, fluid thrust, the little man plunged a long-bladed kitchen knife into the stranger.

The victim stumbled back, clutching at the knife handle, which protruded obscenely from his chest. Then he toppled to the rug.

The little man turned away from the body. He looked directly into the camera and smiled. "I'm free," he said.

And disappeared.

The screen went black.

The house lights were full on when Hub Rockwell, in shocked panic, bolted from his seat and ran up the aisle into the lobby.

Everything was changed. Grotesquely changed. The walls were scabrous, damp with mold. A single raw bulb near the ceiling cast twisting shadows. The water nymphs were headless, gilt paint flaking from their cracked-plaster flesh. The candy counter was draped in a gray lacework of cobwebs. A red-eyed rat scuttled, chittering, between Rockwell's feet, and the sour smell of wet cats befouled the air.

The dust-filmed glass exit door leading to the night street was nailed shut, boarded with heavy planking—as Hub pushed frantically at the rusted release bar. He tried to smash his fist through the glass. To no avail.

He was clawing at the splintered boards with bleeding fingers when the rear door of the box office abruptly popped open and the little man swept out, eyes wild, a glittering kitchen knife in his right hand. He closed swiftly on Rockwell—who let out a small choked gasping sound as the little man drove the blade deeply into Rockwell's chest.

With both hands clutching at the handle of the knife, Hub sprawled onto the faded, time-rotted lobby rug, lying on his back, his breath bubbling in his throat, his eyes dimming rapidly. And just before total, utter darkness possessed him, he heard the ticket seller deliver the final line of dialogue: "I'm free."

And the little man was gone.

Fade to black.

Outside, the rain is over. The thunder is silent. A full moon slides out from massed clouds to bathe the Styx in a wash of pale yellow. The building is in sorry disrepair. Its neons are dark, crusted with soot, and its grimed lobby is trash filled, smelling sharply of decay. A dead rat, partially decomposed, lies in front of the boarded-over box office amid fragments of broken glass. Several of the curled black display letters have fallen from the theater's cracked marquee. The night silence is almost palpable.

A storm-racked night exactly one year later.

A building in Edgefield, Connecticut, pulses into glowing life.

A car motors slowly through the rain along the main street. Stops before the neon dazzle of light. The Styx. With its marquee brightly announcing: MAJOR PREVUE HERE TONITE.

A ticket seller waits inside the gleaming Art Deco box office. The driver parks, gets out of his car, locks it. Walks up to the box office. Asks if he's too late for the preview. No, he's right on time.

Buys a ticket. Goes inside. Takes a seat halfway down the aisle. No one else is in the theater.

The house lights dim and the film begins.

In the box office, Hubbard Rockwell waits, staring into the rainy darkness, his ghost-white fingers convulsively gripping the handle of a long-bladed kitchen knife.

His bloodless lips curve into a faint smile.

It's time for the exchange.

He will soon be free.

"Dead Call" has proved to be one of my most successful efforts in terms of mass exposure. Chosen for six anthologies (including 100 Great Fantasy Stories), reprinted overseas, and dramatized on radio, it became part of a traveling theatrical presentation and was read aloud from stages around the nation.

I wrote it for Kirby McCauley's groundbreaking anthology, Frights, and the story's enthusiastic reception heartened me. I had been dabbling in the genre of dark fantasy, but now it became an area I wanted to explore more fully.

"Dead Call" marks an important turning point in my career.

DEAD CALL

(Written: December 1974)

Len had been dead for a month when the phone rang.

Midnight. Cold in the house and me dragged up from sleep to answer the call. Helen gone for the weekend. Me, alone in the house. And the phone ringing.

"Hello."

"Hello, Frank."

"Who is this?"

"You know *me*. It's Len . . . ole Len Stiles."

Cold. Deep and intense. The receiver dead-cold matter in my hand.

"Len Stiles died four weeks ago."

"Four weeks, three days, two hours and twenty-seven minutes ago—to be exact."

"I want to know who you are."

A chuckle. The same dry chuckle I'd heard so many times.

"C'mon, ole buddy—after twenty years. Hell, you *know* me."

"This is a damned poor joke!"

"No joke, Frank. You're there, alive. And I'm here, dead. And you know something, ole buddy . . . I'm really glad I did it."

"Did . . . what?"

"Killed myself. Because . . . death is just what I hoped it would be. Beautiful . . . gray . . . quiet . . . no pressures."

"Len Stiles' death was an accident . . . a concrete freeway barrier . . . His car—"

"I *aimed* my car for that barrier," the phone-voice told me. "Pedal to the floor. Doing over ninety when I hit . . . No accident, Frank." The voice cold . . . cold. "I *wanted* to be dead. And no regrets."

I tried to laugh, make light of this—matching his chuckle with my own. "Dead men don't use telephones."

"I'm not really using the phone, not in a physical sense. It's just that I chose to contact you this way.

You might say it's a matter of 'psychic electricity'. As a detached spirit I'm able to align my cosmic vibrations to match the vibrations of this power line. Simple, really."

"Sure. A snap. Nothing to it."

"Naturally, you're skeptical. I expected you to be. But . . . listen carefully to me, Frank."

And I listened—with the phone gripped in my hand in that cold night house—as the voice told me things that *only* Len could know . . . intimate details of shared experiences extending back through two decades. And when he'd finished I was certain of one thing:

He *was* Len Stiles.

"But, how . . . I still don't . . ."

"Think of this phone as a 'medium'—a line of force through which I can bridge the gap between us." The dry chuckle again. "Hell, you gotta admit it beats holding hands around a table in the dark— yet the principle is the same."

I'd been standing by my desk, transfixed by the voice. Now I moved behind the desk, sat down, trying to absorb this dark miracle. My muscles were wire-taut, my fingers cramped about the black receiver. I dragged in a slow breath, the night dampness of the room pressing at me.

"All right . . . I don't . . . believe in ghosts, don't . . . pretend to understand any of this, but . . . I'll accept it. I *must* accept it."

"I'm glad, Frank—because it's important that we talk." A long moment of hesitation. Then the voice, lower now, softer. "I know how lousy things have been, ole buddy."

"What do you mean?"

"I just know how things are going for you. And . . . I want to help. As your friend, I want you to know that I understand."

"Well . . . I'm really not . . ."

"You've been feeling bad, haven't you? Kind of 'down', right?"

"Yeah . . . a little, I guess."

"And I don't blame you. You've got reasons. Lots of reasons. For one . . . there's your money problem."

"I'm expecting a raise. Shendorf promised me one—within the next few weeks."

"You won't get it, Frank. I *know*. He's lying to you. Right now, at this moment, he's looking for a man to replace you at the company. Shendorf's planning to fire you."

"He never liked me . . . We never got along from the day I walked into that office."

"And your wife . . . all the arguments you've been

having with her lately . . . It's a pattern, Frank. Your marriage is all over. Helen's going to ask you for a divorce. She's in love with another man."

"*Who*, dammit? What's his name?"

"You don't know him. Wouldn't change things if you did. There's nothing you can do about it now. Helen just . . . doesn't love you any more. These things happen to people."

"We've been . . . drifting apart for the last year— but I didn't know why. I had no idea that she . . ."

"And then there's Janice. She's back on it, Frank. Only it's worse now. A lot worse."

I knew what he meant—and the coldness raked along my body. Jan was nineteen, my oldest daughter—and she'd been into drugs for the past three years. But she'd promised to quit.

"What do you know about Janice? Tell me!"

"She's into the heavy stuff, Frank. She's hooked bad. It's too late for her."

"What the hell are you saying?"

"I'm saying she's lost to you . . . She's rejected you, and there's no reaching her. She *hates* you . . . blames you for everything."

"I won't *accept* that kind of blame! I did my best for her."

"It wasn't enough, Frank. We both know that. You'll never see her again."

The blackness was welling within me, a choking wave through my body.

"Listen to me, old buddy. Things are going to get worse, not better. I know. I went through my own kind of hell when I was alive."

"I'll . . . start over . . . leave the city—go East, work with my brother in New York."

"Your brother doesn't *want* you in his life. You'd be an intruder . . . an alien. He never writes you, does he?"

"No, but that doesn't mean—"

"Not even a card last Christmas. No letters or calls. He doesn't want you with him, Frank, believe me."

And then he began to tell me other things . . . He began to talk about middle age and how it was too late now to make any kind of new beginning . . . He spoke of disease . . . loneliness . . . of rejection and despair. And the blackness was complete.

"There's only one real solution to things, Frank— just *one*. That gun you keep in your desk upstairs. Use it, Frank. Use the gun."

"I couldn't do that."

"But why not? What other choice have you got? The solution is there. Go upstairs and use the gun. I'll be waiting for you afterward. You won't be alone. It'll be like the old days . . . we'll be together . . .

Death is beautiful, Frank. I *know*. Life is ugly, but death is beautiful . . . Use the gun, Frank . . . the gun . . . use the gun . . . the gun . . . the gun . . ."

I've been dead for a month now, and Len was right. It's fine here. No pressures. No worries. Gray and quiet and beautiful.

I know how lousy things have been for you. And they're *not* going to improve.

Isn't that your phone ringing?

Better answer it.

It's important that we talk.

We all need someone to love. That's a basic human requirement—to share intimate companionship in this vast world of ours. Many people search throughout their lives and never find that special someone. Others (and I gratefully include myself) are much more successful; they find a mate to love and cherish who loves them in return.

Julie, the young girl in my story, has found the wrong someone, but she isn't smart enough to know it. Her "boyfren" is bad news. What he does seems all right to her (but it may bother a lot of readers).

As a character of mine, I'm partial to Julie. I'd like to think that she'll find happiness with her new companion, but her future is not bright.

In fact, it's very dark indeed.

BOYFREN

(Written: February 1992)

X~~XX~~

deare PA, I am writinng this to you so that
when you get here and I am gone away ~~XXX~~
X you will know ~~X~~why. I am useing this old
typewriting machine picking out the letters
with my finger because if I wrote by hand you
couldn't read any of the words clear. I cant
write any good as you know by hand. when
you left Ma and i to go to Kansas City to work
you said youd be back when you had some
money so I dont know when but ~~is~~ ill be gone
for sure so youll need this to know why.

Ma is dead but you already know that ~~xxxxe~~
since the telephonne call when she hd the cold

that turned to newmonia and the docter told you on the phone. i thought youd be back for her burying but i guess you didnt have the ~~mone~~ money so thats OK.

After Ma died I have been alone here in the woods but I get down to the ~~tw/~~ town store to mr. summers and buy food when i need it. Where did i get the money ~~wyy~~ you are asking so i8l tell you—from my Boyfren . . . Ha. Thats a long story.

first you know that I was a virgen when you left ~~BKXXBBBB~~ being only 14 and all but im not anymore. not ~~X~~ virgen. i am a full womman now for sure at 15.

it was my Boyfren   that made me not a virgen anymore. you want to know what he looks like i bet so i8ll ~~jell~~ you hes kind of wierd looking. i have never seen a boy look like him before like hes from Outer space or another kind of what they call a dimension but i dont know if this is so or if hes just wierd looking.

My ~~KKYXXXBBB~~ Boyfrens name is Pepper. i call him that and he says he doesnt care
what
~~when~~ i call him and its from my old Teddy bear i called Pepper when i was a little girl

remember??? so now hes Pepper which is a fun name

Ok what does he look like if hes so wierd looking ??? first of all hes about 6 and ½ feet tall with kind of furry skin—not like a kittykat or a mole or anything but furry. and hes got funny eyes real shiny. now dont get me wrong Pa he didnt come out of the sky in some flying fhing like in the Movies and hes not REALLY from some other world or anything. i dont mean that so dont get all upset over Pepper

his teeth are sharp at the ends but ive only seen him eat just one time and ill get to that later on. as you know we have this celler under our house where we grow things and Pepper just was there one day in the celler like he was one of the root things that grow there. There he was when i went down and i said hi im Julie and he smiled at me. youre real pretty he said.

he was cute kind of and real different so i smiled back to him and he went up stairs. I asked if he was ungry and he said no i only eat in CYCLES. thats how you spell it after i asked him how to. most boys are hungry all the time but not Pepper. where are you from i asked and he said i wouldnt know if he told me so we talked about the woods and about the folks in town. he wanted to know how many young ~~fw~~ girlsthere were in town like me—virgens. somehow he knew i was one. i said that Jenny Aker was one too and she was a year younger than me and Louann Sutter was ~~notxhxer~~ another and maybe there was more but i didnt know for sure.

he said would I like not to be a virgen anymore and i said sureit would be OK not being one. so we made love on the bed and it was kind of messy at first but the next day it was better and then i really got to like it alot. PPepper made me feel all hot and funny so hes a good Boyfren all right.

that was 10 monthes ago and he made love to Jenny Aker ~~nd~~ nd Louann Sutter for sure that i know about and maybe to others if they were virgens. he said he only lilked virgens. at first i got jealouse but he would come around the place and ~~weedxxxxtxxxexxxxxxe~~ and i knew he loved me from the way he acted
~~xxxx.~~ but he never put his thing into me anymore he just did other things to make me feel good so i had a baby a little girl i named Julie after me because i coudlnt think of a better name

~~XXX WX XX-XXXX XXXXX XX XXX XXX~~ Pepper came
by one morning when ~~XXXwXXX-XXtXX XXXXXXE~~
Julie was two weeks old and ate her up. he
said that was what he ate—babies from virgens and that he did it in 9 monthe CYCLES.
thats wierd isnt it ??? he told me that 9 monthes from now that Judy Aker would have a
baby and then hed go and eat that one too and
then eat the one from Louann when she had
it.

Pepper said it was all a matter of TIMING
to make sure he had at least one new one—
baby—to eat every 9 monthes. he wouldnt put
his thing back in me because i wanst a virgen
anymore but we did ~~didn~~ other sex things but
not that. Pepper said he only pregnated virgens and that they were like a rotten apple
afterwards which made me mad. i yelled at
him that i was no rotten apple but he just
smiled and kissed me down there and it was
all OK.

well Pa im coming to the end of this letter
to you and if you get back home out t here to
the woods house and find me gone i8ll be with
my Boyfren. i know i can make him love only
me if i ~~got~~ go where he goes with him all the
time and i dont care if hes ~~didn~~ wierd or not hes

my only tu true and loveing Boyfren.

so goodbye Pa i hope i see you agains some time in the future. i am real happy to be in love and to have such a ▮boy as Pepper.

i dont even miss Julie since i never ▮▮▮▮ really got to know her before Pepper ate her up so im very luck y to have a true and loveing Boyfren.

youre daughter Julie

PEACEABLE KINGDOM

JACK KETCHUM

When it comes to chilling the blood, fraying the nerves, or quickening the pulse, no writer comes close to Jack Ketchum. He's able to grab readers from the first sentence, pulling them inescapably into his story, compelling them to turn the pages as fast as they can, refusing to release them until they have reached the shattering conclusion.

This landmark collection gathers more than thirty of Jack Ketchum's most thrilling stories. "Gone" and "The Box" were honored with the prestigious Bram Stoker Award. Whether you are already familiar with Ketchum's unique brand of suspense or are experiencing it for the first time, here is a book no afficionado of fear can do without.